SHAKING ⌐ ⌐⌐⌐ ⌐
WITH ELVIS

Check Out Any Time You Like at the Grand Euthanasia Hotel

by

Paul Carroll

This edition published in 2024 by DreamEngine Media Ltd.

978-1-915212-17-7

Email: publishing@dreamengine.co.uk

Website: DreamEngine.co.uk

Social Media: @DreamEngineuk

For May

O, that this too too solid flesh would melt,
Thaw, and resolve itself into a dew!

Hamlet, Act 1, Scene 2

Chapter One

May you live long and die happy. It's an innocent enough valediction but the words cut Geraldine to the quick. Head down, she simply nods at the jovial official as her passport is returned and dashes straight to the gate. Within minutes they are boarding, and she finds herself squeezing past passengers who have used the rear instead of the front steps as she locates her seat in the middle of the plane. Noticing her struggle against the onrush, a kindly young man offers to place her bright red wheelie in the overhead locker for her. She bought it brand new last week, which was silly really as she had a perfectly good one at home with plenty of use in it still.

No sooner does she seat herself and start to buckle her belt, than she's aware of a smartly dressed young woman trying to catch her attention. A member of the cabin crew. 'Are you sure you want to sit by the emergency door?' comes the enquiry. Geraldine jumps involuntarily as she realises she is next to the exit. 'I'm sure your man here wouldn't mind swapping. He's got a better build for it, if that's all right with you,' she adds. Geraldine and the young man who's just helped her with her bag proceed to execute a clumsy exchange of seats within the confined space.

As the aeroplane taxies prior to take-off, he turns to her. 'Are you sure you don't mind giving up the window? For the views, like?' She is struck by his politeness, unlike a good many of the youths she's taught over her long career. She shakes her head, and continues to stare at her lap. Thinking her a nervous flier he returns to peering through the plexiglass as the aircraft strains to hit its take-off speed. It's a beautiful spring morning and, as the Boeing 737-800 gains height, she glimpses, over his shoulder, Malahide Marina off to the port side, its waters glistening in the bright sunshine. Her heart tightens at the sight. Her last view of Ireland, and it has to be Malahide, where she lived with Kieran all those years ago. Is he, she wonders, down there at this very moment? Still with that poor gullible girl he ran off with? How old would she be now? There were plenty of eyebrows raised at that for sure, she being only sixteen at the time. A scandal, and all he was bothered about was not being charged with having underage sex with a pupil. His relief at being let off the hook due to insufficient evidence sickened her at the time – and for a long time afterwards. The selfish bastard had entertained no thought for Geraldine, his wife of twenty years, or the shame and the humiliation he put her through. It was all *me, me, me.* She'd regretted the loss of her marriage at first – being tossed aside would be more accurate – but that was two decades ago when she'd just turned fifty. Would she have been any better off if she and Kieran had remained together? He'd be over seventy now as well. They could be making this trip together, for a city break, like other retired couples on the plane. It was hard to imagine. No – she'd been well shot of him. He'd probably be fat and bald by now, and boring to boot. He was boring then as well, she recalled, until his midlife crisis intervened and lit the blue touch paper. A pathetic cliché, a soap

2

opera she'd been cast in against her will. The girl, if she was still with him, would probably have gone to seed by now and be giving him hell every day over how he'd ruined her life. Yes, that would be about as much as he deserved. She pulls herself together – no, don't think of him, not now, not ever. What was the point?

As the golden strands of the east coast give way to the Irish Sea, she can see the cabin crew already pushing the catering trolley in their direction. Sixteen rows to go – they'd be landing before it got to them. Not that she wants anything, she has no appetite at all. Maybe nobody else does either, because in double quick time the same cabin attendant who spoke to her earlier is alongside. Any refreshments? She signals no. Your man asks for a Guinness, and yet another clumsy exchange takes place as the sale is transacted and the credit card, beverage and receipt are passed along the row. He'll have to get a move on – the captain has just announced their descent. He cracks the ring pull and watches in dismay as the drink erupts into his lap. Geraldine calmly reaches into her handbag and hands him a wad of tissues. The fizzing fountain stirs a memory. Is he aware that the round, plastic widget floating in the can is filled with nitrogen that is released into the beer on opening to form the distinctive creamy head? The perfect surge of nitrogen and carbon dioxide bubbles as the beer is poured. She'd used that example in chemistry lessons in the past – it always got the students' attention (well, the boys' interest at least, which was always the harder battle). She suppresses a smirk – whether he knows it or not, he'll be more careful next time.

Rudimentary cleaning up operations completed, he offers a sheepish face of apology and takes a long pull on the remnants of the stout. He raises the can in salute, 'Shaken not stirred,' he ventures. His little funny. She relaxes and for the first time that day a brief smile creases her lips. Encouraged, he makes further small talk. 'Visiting family?' he enquires. She shakes her head. 'Flying visit though,' he says, pointing towards the overhead locker. 'My Ma insists on the full 20-kilogram allowance even for a weekend away, and still can't fit everything in. My Da calls her suitcase the TARDIS because she thinks it must be bigger on the inside than it looks.' Geraldine lets out a little laugh. Time and relative dimension in space. She cited Doctor Who's time machine in her physics lessons too. Well, all that was in the past now, she's not needed any lesson plans – engaging or otherwise – since retirement. All that learning and knowledge rendered surplus to requirements. Just like her.

The captain announces five minutes to landing, and as the plane banks she spies the rolling hills of Cheshire looming into view as they approach Manchester Airport. It seems like they've only been airborne a few minutes. The hardest journey she's ever had to make, and it's gone in a flash. There must be a scientific explanation for that, too, only she can't think of one at this very second.

'When are you heading back?' asks her new acquaintance as he carries her case down the passenger stairs.

'A good question,' she says. 'The twelfth of never, I think.'

Now it's his turn to smile as he deposits the wheelie on the tarmac for her. 'Ah well, may the road rise up to meet you,' he bids her, before striding off towards the terminal. He could be off to meet a lover, or visiting a family member. Maybe he's here because of work, or to attend a football match or a concert. The possibilities of youth are endless, the opportunities limitless. You only really get to recognise that once it's too late, she reflects. Not for the first time lately.

Within a short space of time, she finds herself shuffling through the green channel and into the main terminal concourse. It doesn't take her long to spot a sombre-looking man in a dark blue suit holding up a sign bearing her name: Doherty. She raises her hand. Only one more leg of the journey to go.

Nerves are already fraying as Dawn's bag is loaded into the boot of the car. They could at least have got here on time – this isn't exactly a trip to the seaside. She can sense they've been arguing – nothing new there. When Kimberley married Ben, it had taken all of Dawn's powers of restraint to bite her tongue regarding her new son-in-law (well, bite her tongue as far as addressing her daughter on the subject, as she'd not held back on sharing her doubts with Mark). Her husband, bless him, said give him a chance, don't upset Kimberley, it's her choice and nothing to do with us. He joshed Dawn that you couldn't really judge a person on how close together their eyes happened to be, or how noisily they slurped their tea. On the odd family outing Mark would excuse Ben's outbursts of road rage as being down to tiredness or having issues at work, not realising, as she did, that he was simply irritated at having them in his car. Well, she'd been right all along – she *knew*. Even Mark would have to agree with her these days if he was still alive. And here she was once more, with Kimberley and Ben, him driving again. She should have ordered a taxi.

Ben sits ramrod straight in the driving seat, transmitting impatience as Kimberley fusses: *Have you got your bag, have you locked the door, turned the alarm on?* – the same questions Dawn would ask Mark in the days they *would* go to the seaside, in the days before Ben, when Kimberley's only concern was whether her bucket and spade were loaded into the Honda Accord.

No sooner is Dawn's travel bag (the Louis Vuitton Kimberley bought for her, although they both know it's a fake) aboard, then Ben is revving, anxious to be away. She doesn't even have time to look back at the house where she has spent the last forty years of her life. The semi-detached where, as newlyweds, a drunken Mark carried her over the threshold and nearly dropped her. The home they conveyed the two-week-old Kimberley to from hospital following a difficult birth, cautiously manoeuvring the carrycot as if it was a vial of nitro-glycerine. The last resting place from where the hearse bore Mark's coffin eight years ago. A quick reverse and a sharp left out of the cul-de-sac and all those memories are lost in the rear-view mirror, like none of it ever happened.

Dawn moves aside the smelly dog blanket shedding hairs on the back seat to make herself more comfortable. She can see Kimberley in the front giving Ben a steely death stare, willing him to behave himself – *be nice.* Ben glances over his shoulder: 'Motorway or the scenic route? There's not much in it – I looked it up on the satnav.' Oh, she gets a choice – that's a first (and a last, probably, as well). The sun is shining, the sky is blue, so she opts for the scenic route. What's the hurry, really?

Dawn can tell Kimberley is on edge – she always is with him, like a cat on a hot tin roof. 'Do you want a coffee, Mum?' she asks, rummaging in her Co-op Bag for Life for the flask. Dawn shakes her head. She doesn't want to have to ask Ben to stop anywhere en route if she needs to go.

Kimberley brightens, 'Do you remember that game we used to play in the car? I-Spy?' She laughs at the memory. 'Dad always used to cheat and make me cry.' The recollection sparks a thought in Dawn's mind: *I spy, with my little eye, something beginning with B. Ben, bully, or bastard – take your pick.* She offers a faint *hmmm* in response. In the uncomfortable silence that follows Ben switches on the car radio, instantly summoning Freddie Mercury into their presence with an ear-splitting account of how another one is biting the dust. Kimberley hisses at Ben and reaches across furiously to snap it off, causing him to swerve. Dawn is buffeted from right to left in the back seat, and thinks again about how much a taxi would have cost. Kimberley was insistent on taking her today, as if it were her responsibility, her duty. They've had all the conversations they need on this, but after that flare-up with Ben over the radio Dawn spots the tears welling up in her daughter's eyes once again. Here it comes. Kimberley swivels in her seat to look her mother squarely in the face and puts the same sorrowful question to her: 'Are you sure you're sure?'

Before Dawn can draw breath to deal with this entreaty, Ben slams on the brakes, bringing the car to a sudden halt as an errant sheep casually crosses the A635 with nary a thought to the Green Cross Code. 'Jesus Christ,' Ben rants. 'I told you we should have gone on the bloody motorway.'

Kimberley recovers the contents of her handbag from the passenger footwell and tersely enquires of her partner: 'How much further?' Fifteen minutes. Dawn is reminded of the old playground conundrum – what would you do if the world was going to end in fifteen minutes? No, it was five minutes, not fifteen – that was something else. Five minutes? Call your nearest and dearest, to say goodbye. Well, they were sat in front of her, so that would be a waste. It would be a waste if they weren't sat in front of her. Pray, maybe? She'd given that up a long time ago, but maybe as an insurance? Make love. ('Twice'.

As she recalled one wag saying.) It struck her that by the time you'd actually decided what to do, the five minutes would be up. Maybe that was the point of the question in the first place, to distract you, to deflect you from worrying over the imminent doom. She smiles. Boil an egg. That's what she'd do. Assuming, of course, that the water was already boiling.

The journey resumes without conversation, and soon they're dropping down from Saddleworth Moor to a landscape of old mills and giant sheds. Beyond, to the west, the high rises of Manchester punch the horizon, but they're not going that far. The road sign reveals they're almost there. The end of the line: Stalybridge. Dawn once had a sandwich and a coffee in the Victorian Buffet Bar at the railway station here, when Mark suggested they call in on a trip to Manchester. According to Mark, it was famous and, judging by the number of trainspotters hogging the tables that afternoon, he had a point. He also told her that the buffet bar had been used in the famous British film, *Brief Encounter*, sometime after the war, but when he mentioned it to the woman behind the counter, she tartly corrected him that was Carnforth Station, not Stalybridge. How Dawn had pulled his leg about that. They don't get to see the station today though, as the GPS is now telling them to turn left in half a mile before they enter the actual town. A high red brick wall soon appears on the right, with a line of tall mature poplars standing to attention behind it. As the indicator blinks and the car decelerates, she looks up to see a gatehouse and a huge sign reading Welcome to Charon House. They've arrived. Dawn feels her insides involuntarily tighten and knot.

Chapter Two

Inside Charon House, Doctor Callan Clay takes a seat in the breakout area of his palatial office – he wants to go for a casual vibe today – and inhales deeply to slow his heart rate, a technique he learned from his famous uncle. Thanks to his clean-living lifestyle – and his vanity – he's in good shape for a fifty-five-year-old. Buffed from a rigorous daily gym regime, tall, angular, smartly suited and well-manicured, he cuts an imposing figure. No sign of having any work done – one hundred per cent natural. He's been referred to as 'handsome', 'dashing' and even 'Prince Charming' by the media, proving that his PR team are worth the money he invests in them. At any rate, he doesn't look like he'll be calling on the services of his own company for a few decades yet. He buzzes his PA and thirty seconds later the reporter from The Nation is ushered into his presence. Doctor Clay – *call me Callan* – isn't a man outwardly given to nerves or lack of confidence; the entrepreneur's entrepreneur knows exactly what's expected of him in this showpiece profile on Go Gently. Admittedly, Lawrence Pestel, the secretary of state for wellbeing, has had a big hand in setting up this interview, but it's not as if they're working to different agendas. One hand washing the other, as Lawrence likes to call it. The right honourable friend has also made sure that a particularly 'onside' journalist will do the honours today: 'a cake walk, Callan, a cake walk.'

No sooner are they seated, pleasantries exchanged, the view admired and coffee served, Doctor Clay immediately forgets the journalist's name. No matter – press on. Certainly, the succeeding questions are lobbed up in gentle fashion, one after the other, rather reminding Callan of the automatic baseball pitching machines they had back home in his youth (although they'd never have set it at this slow a rate).

Mr Nation opens on the anniversary of the passing of the assisted dying bill – coincidentally the highwater mark (to date) in the career of the secretary of state for wellbeing. *How have attitudes changed, if at all, in the intervening period?*

A good start for Callan. 'I think what surprises many people these days is how long it took this country to come into the 21st century on this issue. There is nothing worthy about protracted dying, nothing noble in being subjected to prolonged pain and suffering in your final days. For too long, society was in thrall to centuries-old taboos that needed to be broken and, thanks to visionaries like Lawrence Pestel, people are finally able to make decisions about their own lives, without fear of the law, without interference from a nanny state. And that's entirely right.'

Ah – but what did Callan have to say to those who argued the bill would be the start of a slippery slope, that the criteria for qualifying for an assisted death would be watered down bit by bit once introduced?

Doctor Clay shakes his head slowly to express his sadness, or perhaps his astonishment, that anybody could hold such a view. 'Scaremongering, pure and simple. Self-appointed, sanctimonious do-gooders determining how an individual should or shouldn't live their lives. On whose authority? Their own. On what scientific basis? None.' His Tennessee twang is undiminished from his years in England. More 'Southern gentleman' these days, although, as he reminds everybody, he dragged himself up from nothing to be the man he is today. He's not yet finished on this subject. 'The positive news is, once that long overdue line was crossed five years ago, we've been able to widen choice for the individual – befitting a modern society. Thankfully, nobody listens to the voices of doom anymore – their arguments have been totally discredited and stuffed back down their throats.'

The journalist appears to nod in agreement. Next. *You established Go Gently in the immediate aftermath of the bill. What challenges did you face as you set about meeting demand?*

'That's a very good question. I can remember it as if it was yesterday. As you'd expect, in the beginning, we pretty much modelled Go Gently on other markets in the world where assisted dying had been on the statute books for years – like Switzerland, The Netherlands, Belgium, progressive US states like California and Colorado. I don't mind admitting business was challenging to start with. We had a sizeable education job on our hands – the law's one thing, but it was all so new our first major task was to put people at ease and reassure them. Before the bill, let's be blunt, things were bloody inhumane. Palliative care was the equivalent of medieval torture, stretching out the agony for as long as possible before release. And nobody gave a thought to the distraught relatives who had to witness their loved ones being treated like laboratory animals, kept alive in the interests of, what, outdated societal values or religion? Think back just ten or twenty years to the stories you used to see – poor patient sets off for Switzerland because he or she can't get the sort of care they need at home. Criminalising their personal choice. Well, all that takes some correcting in a cultural sense. I think, looking back, end of life was all a bit sombre – *too* medical, *too* clinical. Changing that mindset was the biggest test.'

The automatic pitching machine cranks up another floater. *And how did you go about that?*

Callan beams – he's getting into his stride now. 'In simple terms, we shifted the paradigm. That is to say, we recognised we were in a consumer market and our primary job was to offer choice and value for money at the same time as making our clients feel *good* about their decisions. Why does it all have to be so bloody dismal? Which is why, if you look at Go Gently now, we're light years away from where we were at the start. We thought: if we can give people the ending they need, why can't we give them the ending they want? In a nutshell, we knew we had to get away from the Switzerland model, if I can call it that. You know, everybody asking "Are you sure?" every two minutes, more legal paperwork than an international treaty, and the quasi-hospital environment. That's when we determined to evolve our offering and put the client – note, "client", not "patient" – in charge. We became all about the experience as opposed to providing a corporeal waste disposal service.'

So that's when you came up with the Go Gently Gallery?

'Exactly. We did tons of research and initially came up with four different packages that could be tailored to clients' preferences and pockets. We're reviewing, adapting and adding new offers all the time. Our best seller remains the traditional Requiem, with candles, harpist, incense for that churchy feel – that's popular because it's also our entry-level package. Then we introduced the Last Supper experience where the client shares their last meal with twelve special invitees – that's going well –

and the Hollywood, where guests gather *en famille* to view photos and videos on the big screen one final time. Last Dance is also popular – a sort of mash up between *Strictly* and Abba.'

'*You've also got a rock 'n' roll one too, I believe?*'

'Oh yes. The Room 658. That's particularly popular with our male clients. It's a perfect example of creating a market: go out in a blaze of glory with booze, recreational narcotics and as many hookers as you want in a tour hotel suite setting. Sex and drugs and rock 'n' roll, the perfect macho fantasy.' On grounds of confidentiality, Callan omits to mention that the inspiration for this package arose when he was approached privately by a household name rock star of many decades standing. Diagnosed with prostate cancer and with months to live, he was concerned that a mundane end, succumbing to a common illness, would tarnish his hellraiser reputation. What he really wanted was a rock 'n' roll exit that would cement his legacy and occupy the front pages for days. Go Gently duly obliged, on the QT of course. The recollection reminds Callan to underline the delicacy of his company's services. 'The important thing to remember is we refashion and reframe the final chapter on a bespoke basis to meet exact needs. No stigma, no guilt, just... I suppose you could call it wish fulfilment.'

The journalist has carefully read the Go Gently website as part of his interview prep: *And there's also, I believe, a market in bespoke packages too, for those with extra-special wishes?*

'Absolutely. The only limit is your imagination is what I say, so we now have a dedicated creative team to help clients shape their perfect dream farewell. It's so obvious when you think about it. People reach an age where they've worked hard all their lives, have a degree of disposable income, and total freedom to express themselves in a personal and individual way. And what better way to exercise that, before it's all too late? Our function is to make those desires a reality. However small the germ of an idea a client comes to us with, we will make it happen. As Shakespeare said, "Nothing in his life became him, like the leaving it." We've had some very unusual requests, but nothing that's stumped us yet.'

Mr Nation is full of admiration: *You make it all sound very attractive, I must say. The ultimate lifestyle choice.*

'Good! That's my job, after all. There's no doubt about it, the market is expanding all the time. But the last thing I will tolerate at Go Gently is complacency. We work hard on our customer care and communications, co-operate closely with government, and constantly look to innovate. We're *empathetic,* is the word.'

A serious sounding question is now required to offset any idea of cosiness. *So how many people are opting for assisted dying now they have the opportunity, and what is the growth trend?*

'Actually, I should say we don't really encourage the term "assisted dying" at Go Gently. I know it's the language of the bill but, to me, it's cold and legalistic, more suited to a veterinary surgery. We prefer "final journey". As for the figures, the government is due to publish its annual update shortly. For commercial reasons I can't go into our own figures too deeply, but I can tell you the trend is up, well up, year-on-year. Final journey facilitation is one of the biggest growth sectors in the economy and it shouldn't be forgotten that the change in the law has created all manner of spin-offs elsewhere. There's job creation for one, not to mention the massive reduction in pressure on healthcare. The removal of decision-making in these matters has given doctors a major boost too, eliminating arguments over the interpretation of the Hippocratic oath and, may I say, what many observers saw as a "God-complex" among certain practitioners. Another fascinating feature is the spike the country has seen in relation to inward tourism, with more and more individuals flying in from all over the world to take advantage, not just of our laws, but of our world-beating services.' Callan knows Lawrence will be purring over his muesli when he gets to that paragraph.

Time for the personal question. *As an American, you've now made your home in this country. What's been the main attraction for you?*

'My good lady wife for a start,' quips Callan. A good idea to mention her – won't do any harm – but this is a question he feels truly passionate about. 'I started my business career in the States at a time when prospects appeared unlimited. But now, seriously, the USA is finished. We had the opportunity to make America great again, but a conspiracy of lefties, liberals and loonies stabbed us in the back. It's very sad. Here, on the other hand, we have a government that has successfully wrestled the country back from the snowflakes whose mission in life was to run the country down. And in so doing, this intrepid nation has become *the* success story of the 21st century, a beacon of free enterprise. I, for one, am proud to make my own modest contribution to the spirit of progress found on this island.'

Very on-message for the readership thinks the journalist, his editor will be pleased. *So, finally, what's next for Go Gently and Callan Clay?*

This is the question, anticipated of course, Callan has given most thought to ahead of today's meeting. How far should he go? As happy as he is to do the interview, the timing isn't ideal. The biggest news announcement in Go Gently's history is imminent, but he can't reveal it prematurely. Yet the newspaper

SHAKING HANDS WITH ELVIS

will quite rightly question, when Callan finally does go live, why he didn't give them a heads-up today. Lawrence, of course, laughed at his concerns, saying the media will run whatever they are given, so stop worrying over what they think: 'It's what we think that counts.' All the same, Callan is absolutely bursting with his planned announcement. Could he tease it, just a little?

'The areas of most concern to me are cost and accessibility. Affordability in other words. Many of the solutions I've just outlined meet the needs of a certain category of client, with a certain level of affluence shall we say, but remain out of reach for citizens whose lack of financial flexibility denies them a breadth of choice. And costs are rising all the time. Let me give you an example. One of the first things that happened when the bill was passed five years ago was an overnight increase in the price of barbiturates. The average price now is tenfold what it was five years ago, and that's a cost we obviously have to pass on. But my mantra is, where there is a problem, if you can't go through it, go round it. That's why I'm working on an exciting new development, a step change that will have far reaching benefits for all. I can't go into too much detail here, but I can probably summarise it by saying my aim is to bring the entry price for the final journey within the grasp of a much wider community. My next goal is to democratise the end of life.'

Chapter Three

Geraldine stares in awe at the opulence of her new surroundings. This place should be on *Grand Designs*. From the outside, the building looks like a well-appointed 18th century country house: a vast rectangular red brick block, grey slate roof, rows of uniform windows and a statement colonnaded portico, bordered with a frieze of lollipop trees like in a nursery painting (except a child would have added smoke pouring from the numerous chimneys). Inside, however, the contrast couldn't be more marked. It's like touching down at a health spa on the moon. A gigantic atrium, necessitating the removal of at least three floors, has been carved out of the interior to accommodate a real live oak tree that stretches up to the lofty ceiling. How on earth did they get that in here? (Geraldine immediately wonders if they ever have a problem with squirrels? Do the cleaners get paid double in autumn when it sheds its leaves?) Encircling the bole of the oak is a 360-degree reception counter, fifty feet in diameter, manned by pink-suited attendants. Natural light pours into the open space, which is odd, as the original roof remains undisturbed. The source appears to be a huge sun-like disc suspended from the far wall.

Her driver registers her astonishment: 'It take one's breath away, doesn't it? The light is directed to the parabola from an intricate arrangement of mirrors, reflecting the phases of the sun and moon in real time. Doctor Clay commissioned it himself. He calls it "Eternity".' Geraldine considers this information for a moment – it's not a title she'd have gone for herself.

Barely sixty seconds after entering the front door she is passed over to check-in by her escort. Here she is greeted with a smile so dazzling she fears its owner may have accidently strayed into Eternity's reflective pathway. 'Welcome to Charon House, Miss Doherty.' No introduction required. 'And you're booked in for one of our VIP packages, I believe?' They're very efficient, thinks Geraldine as she nods in confirmation. From beneath the counter Miss Pink produces a tan leather document case with Geraldine's name embossed in gold lettering across the front. 'Here is your welcome pack, Miss Doherty, with the itinerary for your stay. Everything you need to know is in there, and we recommend that you read it before this evening's induction when any queries you may have can be addressed.' Geraldine ruminates whether the folders are recyclable. 'You'll also find this week's programme of activities in the pack. You're welcome to sign up for whatever takes your fancy.' Geraldine has rarely been treated with such deference – she has a faint recollection of a Club Med holiday she once took in the South of France. 'And we've reserved Poppy for your stay. It has beautiful views over the formal garden – I hope you'll approve.' The receptionist hands over a slim key card. 'Your room key is preloaded with your biometric data to allow access to public areas, and your credit card details for any purchases made during your stay.' Geraldine just wants to get to her room now – she's tired, and there is such a thing as too much information. As if she intuits this, Pink conveys an almost imperceptible signal to the other side of the atrium and a young man, his complexion the colour of his olive tunic, materialises at Geraldine's side. 'Adil will accompany you to your room, and make sure you're comfortable.' Adil inclines his torso forward in a discreet bow and picks up her wheelie. 'Unless there's anything else I can help you with today?'

Poppy turns out to be on the third floor, accessed by a tubular glass and steel elevator commanding a bird's-eye view over the atrium – any conservation orders relating to the property obviously covered the exterior only. As they ascend, Adil smiles ingratiatingly but offers no conversation. From the lift she follows him down a long corridor where a concealed lighting system casts constantly changing colours – like being inside a giant kaleidoscope. Once they reach Poppy, Adil points out various fittings, pronouncing *aircon, safe, screen, minibar* and *iron* in less than native English. He cocks his head to invite any further questions and, there being none, retreats slowly towards the door, leaving, like the Cheshire Cat, an impression of his eager-to-please smile in his wake. Geraldine walks over to the window and takes in the manicured splendour of the landscaped gardens below. A sudden involuntary shiver rattles her frame, as if somebody has just walked over her grave.

In Charon House's carefully-stacked arrivals schedule, as soon as Geraldine has cleared reception the next figure swings through the front door, rather like a Black Forest weather house. Dawn Birtwistle and her daughter tentatively step over the threshold as if they're expecting rain. There's no sign of Ben, who's decided to remain in the car park to check his vehicle for any ovine-inflicted damage. Dawn's welcome differs from that of the earlier arrival in that a small private room off the main atrium has been earmarked for her check-in. This is because the

Pink designated to welcome her has noted the code 'OAU' on her computer screen. In Charon House 'OAU' stands for 'over-anxious usher', a warning from the pre-screening procedure that a highly-strung, fussy, and unrelenting companion is accompanying the client. Such individuals, almost always family, tend to raise stress and disquiet levels in their charges, the very opposite of what's required. Experience has proved that greetings in these cases are better dealt with in private and by the most emollient of Pinks. (One eagle-eyed chaperone, spotting the 'OAU' on the screen and asking what it stood for, was told by a quick-witted Pink that it meant 'Offer Accommodation Upgrade' and her mother had just qualified for a superior room.)

'Welcome to Charon House, Mrs Birtwistle. And you're booked in for the Reunite, is that right?' Kimberley answers in the affirmative on her mother's behalf.

As soon as Kimberley spots the laminated ring-bound welcome pack Pink is about to proffer, she reaches over, plucks it from her hands and starts to leaf through the contents. 'There's an awful lot of information to absorb in here,' she declares.

Dawn's downcast look spurs Pink on: 'Oh, please don't worry about that. I know it looks a lot, but there's a full induction session tonight where we go through everything in detail. We know arrival can be fraught, which is why we recommend a good rest following check-in. There's plenty of time built in for questions.'

'Yes,' Kimberley replies, 'I get that, and I don't want to appear awkward, but I think it would really help to spend a few minutes on this before I get Mum settled in properly.'

Pink doesn't miss a beat. 'Of course, not a problem. Perhaps Mum might like to recover her strength after her journey while I assist you with your questions? What do you think, Mum?'

Dawn seizes the cue. 'I would like to go to my room now, if that's all right.' Turning to her daughter. 'I can manage from here, love. You don't want to keep Ben waiting.'

Kimberley is torn. It feels wrong just leaving Mum here, but then she doesn't really want to wind up Ben any further by leaving him outside too long – the journey back will be strained enough as it is. 'Well, maybe I can just go up with Mum and see the room in that case?'

Pink rises from her seat, her endorsement of a sensible solution. 'I see that you're down for a mid-week visit in any case. That's perfect – if there's anything you or Mum are still unclear about, we can address it then.'

Before Kimberley can reply, the door opens and, as if by magic, Adil appears. You'd have thought he'd been outside listening through the keyhole. Pink slips the key card to him in a smooth palm off and, within seconds, Dawn and her daughter are following Adil and the 'just like the real thing' Louis Vuitton into the atrium. There's no need for the glass elevator this time because they head straight out of the rear ground-level doorway to where a line of electric buggies is parked. Adil boards his passengers and transports them all of one hundred yards to a network of low-rise chalets hidden in a hollow beyond the main building. They stop outside the one with a picture of a Forget-Me-Not on the door. Dawn wonders exactly how many other similar doors there are in this place – it's a lot bigger than she'd imagined.

Kimberley, possibly because she's been reminded of Ben, grows restless as Adil demonstrates the key features of the room, and cuts him off with an impatient, 'Fine, fine. All very straight forward. Thank you.' He looks rather crestfallen as he is forced to retreat. 'Well, I didn't think much to him,' says Kimberley as she closes the door. 'You'd think at these prices they'd get staff who could speak English.' She brightens as she takes in the room. 'Still, it's very nice, isn't it? Compact.' They've not even talked about the main house. 'What about that entrance hall, though? It was like a giant yoga studio with all that tinkly music and scents wafting about. I'll have to get the girls down.' She giggles slightly, before suddenly remembering why she's here. Refocus. 'Look, Mum, are you sure you're all right? I could stay tonight if you want me to? It's not too late.'

Dawn is inspecting the view from her window – *I-spy, with my little eye* – and appears to direct her reply to the compost heap below. 'No, love. I'm fine. You get off. You're back in a few days, so no need to worry. I'd just like some time to myself. You understand, don't you?'

Kimberley huffs slightly at her mother's selfishness, but doesn't put up a fight. She crosses the room to give Dawn a clumsy hug. 'Later, then?' You'll call if you need anything?'

As Dawn closes the door behind her, she heaves a sigh of relief. Alone at last.

Chapter Four

Adil strolls to the staff quarters situated in the furthest corner of the grounds and changes into his jeans and lightweight hoodie. A lot of the staff live in, but Adil, as a new boy, is still on probation. He recovers his mobile phone from the staff supervisor – employees, residents and visitors are strictly forbidden from carrying phones or any recording apparatus on site – and clocks off following his ten-hour shift. Sometimes he catches the bus to the railway station, but tonight he has time to spare and fancies a walk along the leafy lanes. It's a stunning sunlit evening, the birds are singing, and the fresh air will help him gather his thoughts for later. As he heads into town Adil marvels at the lush greenery of the English countryside, a sight that's never lost its wonder for him since his arrival from Syria. So much change, so much fear, in that period.

An hour and a quarter later he's standing outside a high rise in central Manchester and nervously pressing the buzzer. The intercom sparks into life, he announces himself, and the latch clicks open. As the lift ascends, Adil wonders, not for the first time, exactly what he's got himself into. Exiting the lift, he sees the door to the flat has been left ajar and he slips inside. Time to do some good in the world. Despite his apprehension, he is welcomed by the couple he first met – or rather, the couple who recruited him three months previously – Doctor Ruth and Doctor Andy.

Since making the perilous journey to these shores from his homeland a dozen years ago, Adil's status has changed more times than the rate of inflation. From asylum seeker to illegal immigrant, from refugee to undocumented and unauthorised migrant before settling on his current designation of licensed guest worker. At least, being a licensed guest worker provides Adil with the chance to work and remain in the country. It also makes these encounters even riskier for him, as his licence, which has to be endorsed by his employer, must be renewed by the department of organised labour every twelve months and any infringement whatsoever will result in instant deportation.

Adil has long learned to keep his head down – if he could choose a super power for himself it would be one of invisibility. Detention centres and pitiless interrogation tend to do that to you. He was considered 'fortunate' in some quarters as, having lost his parents in the family's channel crossing, he qualified as an 'unaccompanied child' the moment he beached in Kent. It certainly helped the ten-year-old foreigner compared to many, as by the time he was twelve he'd been allocated to foster parents in Bolton. It was a purely transactional decision for them, but no further harm was done and the arrangement at least got him through his school years and into his first job in a care home (due to the hardship and grief he'd experienced first-hand in his own short life, Adil's instinct to help and bring comfort to those in greater need than himself equipped him ideally for the role). The care home, or age-atoriums as they were dubbed by the department of wellbeing who ran them, housed occupants who had nowhere else to go and nobody left to look after them. It put him in mind of his own ten-year-old self and he was determined to make a difference to these elderly lives, no matter how small that difference. His smile, his patience and his willingness to undertake any duty going were perfect attributes for the task. In reality, the age-atoriums were little better than the detention centres he'd experienced as a child. Staffing levels were low, manned predominantly by licensed guest workers like himself, and food and heating were purposely pegged at subsistence levels as a deterrent. Patients were expected to maintain their own personal health insurance but, as many had never been able to afford such cover in the first place, had to rely on the volunteer medics who visited once a week. There was only one way out. Residents were not expected to stay long and, under the circumstances, most gratefully obliged. At least, for a few aged and ailing residents, Adil managed to project one last faint ray of sunshine into the dimming of their days. It repulsed Adil that a government could treat its own citizens so callously, but he knew not to share such a view publicly. To him, life was so precious, every soul he lost was a blow, another weight piled on the scale of heartache. Many of his fellow workers laughed at his sensitivity, teasing him he'd grow out of it, but he knew he never would. Doctors Ruth and Andy, two of the volunteer practitioners who visited the sick every week, noticed his sensitivity too, which is why, totally out of character for Adil, he now found himself working at Go Gently as an undercover mole for the anti-assisted dying pressure group, Sacrosanct.

Not having much experience of activism, Adil was alarmed at being approached and sounded out by the two doctors – could it be a trap set by the department of organised labour to catch him out? He'd heard about assisted dying, of course, but like a lot of things in this country he was in no position to question or challenge. All he wanted to do was to get on with cherishing, with conserving, life in his own small way, and to avoid matters that didn't concern him. But Doctors Ruth and Andy were persuasive – they'd seen and heard for themselves that he cared and valued life. He could help them. He wasn't in favour of assisted dying, was he? Of course he wasn't, so he'd be doing humanity a favour if he could just help them out for a while. All they wanted was a pair of eyes inside Charon House for a few months. They weren't asking for photos or recordings or anything *dangerous* – just somebody to report back on the set-up, comings and goings. Intelligence. They reassured Adil there was no risk to him – well, hardly any – and the timing was perfect as Go Gently was expanding and looking for qualified staff – especially licensed guest workers whose pay was set lower than the national rate by law. In the end, Adil was so convinced – or was it confused, intimidated and tractable? – he agreed. The doctors helped with his application, and within weeks, he was in – it was that easy. It was Ruth who came up with the idea of pretending he couldn't speak English very well, so he'd be ignored.

His sessions with Sacrosanct – this is the third so far – tend to consist of a chat more than anything. Andy takes notes as Ruth leads on the questioning. She starts today trying to establish how busy Go Gently is in order to estimate the number being euthanised. (Skilled as he is in the English language, 'euthanise' isn't a verb Adil was familiar with three months ago. He's certainly never heard it used in Charon House where such language is strictly off limits.)

'Would you say you've had more, or less, people coming through?'

Adil has been paying attention to the footfall. 'It's definitely been a bit quieter in the past couple of weeks since Easter, but apparently that's normal going into the summer months. I heard one of the receptionists saying peak season for them starts in October, with a lull before Christmas, then January and February are totally stacked out. They put the prices up then as well.'

'Any change to working practices, any sign of them doing anything different?'

'No. It's like I explained before. The average stay is five days, irrespective of what package the client is signed up for. They all go through the same preparation stages, no matter what final journey they've chosen.' Adil is now unconsciously using the same jargon as the Go Gently brochure. But he has made one discovery. 'Oh – one big change apparently is the induction programme. They do group sessions now, with up to twelve people in a group, but that was only introduced last year. Before that they used to keep the clients apart as much as possible, but once the numbers got so big they had to find a way to speed up the process.'

'A bloody conveyor belt,' Andy rails in disgust.

Ruth pulls a face. 'They're taking a risk there. One dissenting voice in a group can unsettle the others.'

'I suppose so,' says Adil, 'but it's odd – nobody ever seems to change their mind. They all go through with it, and seem to be happy about it.'

Andy jumps on this, too. 'Turkeys voting for Christmas. Because they've been brainwashed, Adil, that's why.'

'And because of what they've done with the consent rules,' says Ruth. 'Once you start the countdown, it's virtually irreversible.'

Ruth moves on to soliciting Adil's observations regarding the staff at Charon House. Over recent exchanges with Adil she's been establishing employee levels, their various roles and backgrounds, training programmes, general morale, how strictly guidelines are adhered to and so on. 'What about new starters? And leavers?'

'Well, I'm restricted to the public areas and guest accommodation mainly so there's a lot of staff I don't get to see, but it looks to me like there's a fairly high turnover – new faces all the time. Apparently, there wasn't much work in the town before Go Gently opened, but there's no shortage now.'

'A toss-up between working there and in an abattoir,' Andy bristles. 'Except in an abattoir you actually need to possess some skills.'

Ruth ignores him. 'Have you managed to talk to any of the medics at all? Doctors, anaesthetists?'

Andy cuts in again. 'Executioners, you mean?' It's not exactly helping the flow of the debrief.

Adil shakes his head. 'I've not seen any,' he says nervously, 'and even if I had I could hardly just walk up to them and strike up a conversation.' It's all very well for her to suggest these things, but she's not the one carrying the risk. There's no way he can do that.

'Well, what about visitors?' Ruth persists. 'Relatives, obviously, but who else?'

Adil isn't sure. 'I only come into contact with the relatives. The treatment wing is out of bounds to me, and has a different car park. It's very sad to see them, though.' Initially, Adil had expected visitors would be beyond themselves with grief, but his experience has proved to be quite different. What really shocks him now is how many give the impression they have more pressing business elsewhere or actually look relieved when they leave.

'Last chance to get their hands on the family silver,' says Andy caustically.

Eventually, Ruth signals the end of the cross-examination by asking Adil if he'd like another cup of tea. No, he doesn't, but he does have some questions of his own. He's been doing this for a few months now, and his mind is in a spin. He hates being at Charon House, witnessing what they do there, and is petrified of being caught. As far as he can work out, he doesn't appear to have added much in the way of information since his first debrief. Another thing that's peeved him is how the representatives of Sacrosanct never ask him how he's coping with the burden of the undertaking they've thrust upon his shoulders. Adil has been thrown into a *de facto* charnel house, witnessing a stream of humanity go in at one end, with dead meat emerging at the other. It's against everything he's ever believed in and yet he's expected to, what, just ignore it and take notes? These two doctors never ask him how he keeps his emotions in check as he helps passengers aboard the end of the line express (one-way tickets only). Wherever he's been in this country it's assumed he should do what he's told and be grateful. He had expected more from Ruth and Andy, but it's almost as if they, too, see him as some sort of lackey. All of this is making him ill. He needs to know. 'How much longer do I have to do this?'

Andy immediately becomes defensive at the nature of his query. 'You don't have to *do* anything, Adil, I thought we made that quite clear? You're helping the cause – surely that's worth a few more months?'

'The cause?' says Adil. 'You've not really explained to me yet how Sacrosanct is planning to use this information to change the law. I want to help, but I can't quite see how I am at the moment.'

Ruth stirs at the insinuation the cause isn't in possession of a clear strategy. 'We refuse to give up the struggle. Assisted dying is an abomination and has no place in a civilised society.' She rises from her chair as if addressing a rally instead of Adil. 'We intend to fight, to get the word out there, to enlist support until the law is reversed. Why, we've not even ruled out sabotage at this stage.'

Andy looks less convinced than his counterpart. 'Well, within reason, Adil. We can't protest publicly or we'd end up in jail, and the government has the media in its pocket so we can't expect much cut through there. So, yes, we've a long way to go, but you never know – you could be the one to turn up something that makes a difference. We can't give up now, can we?'

It sounds to Adil like he's the only one taking a risk. 'What does everybody else in Sacrosanct think?'

The two doctors hesitate, waiting for the other to answer. Eventually, Andy responds. 'The thing is, Adil, Sacrosanct is just me and Ruth for now. And you. We've got to be careful about being exposed, or making our move too soon. We're at the intelligence gathering stage at present, but it will come. No campaign worth fighting was ever won overnight, was it?'

Adil looks from one doctor to the other. He knows a bit about failed revolutions, which is why he's in this country in the first place.

Ruth can see their undercover operative is feeling the pressure. 'Look, Adil, you're right. You've done a brilliant job so far and the intel is invaluable, but I fully understand how you'd want an end-date to all of this,' she smiles. 'So, let's set one last, specific task for you, and then we'll get you out. How does that sound?'

The suspicious expression on Adil's face betrays the self-evident question: *Exactly what specific task do you have in mind?*

Even Andy appears unsure as to what Ruth is referring to, and even more stupefied when she passes the ball to him with, 'Andy, do you want to brief Adil on this?' His blank look causes her to prompt him before Adil becomes too alarmed. 'The barbiturates, Andy. The barbs.'

'Oh, yes,' nods Andy, as he catches her drift. Not that he'd realised until now this was a specific mission, or to be Adil's last. 'Well, the thing is, a friend of mine who works in one of the large pharma companies let slip to me they've just lost their contract from Go Gently.' He hesitates, unsure of how this entails a brief for the young Syrian. 'So...'

'So the point is,' interjects Ruth, 'the order is for barbiturates, which they use by the barrowload, and it's not like they've found a cheaper supplier given there's a cartel in force, so what we want to know is why the change? The one thing Go Gently relies on is a steady supply of barbs, so something doesn't stack up.'

'Exactly,' adds Andy. 'What's going on?'

Caught between having no clue as to how to find out, and the prospect of an end to his tour of duty, Adil lets out an exasperated sigh in response.

Chapter Five

'Do you mind if I sit here?' Dawn asks as the induction session is due to begin. Geraldine, already gripping her Go Gently note pad and Biro in anticipation of capturing the key points, shifts her handbag to create space. Dawn slides in alongside and immediately spots her tablemate's stationery, causing her to look around to see if the other attendees are similarly equipped. 'Are we supposed to take notes? I've not brought a pen.' Geraldine automatically tears off a few pages from her pad and passes them to Dawn together with her spare ballpoint. 'What's this meeting for again?' whispers Dawn, who hasn't quite got round to reading her welcome pack yet. She's just been collected from her room by an olive tunic and didn't want to appear as if she wasn't up with the programme. 'Oh, it's Dawn, by the way.'

Geraldine manages to introduce herself just before the room is called to attention by a young woman dressed in a smart black blazer, matching skirt and crisp white blouse. 'Welcome, everybody, on behalf of Go Gently. Today's induction is designed to familiarise you with the various aspects of your stay and, of course, to answer any queries you may have.' Geraldine glances at Dawn and nods. *That.*

The PowerPoint fires up and the first slide is introduced, a list of bullet points outlining the areas the meeting is to address:

- Your decision
- Consent
- Legals
- Preparation
- Visits
- Leisure
- What happens next
- The Go Gently Guarantee
- Q and A

An hour later, as the twelve guests shuffle out in silence, Dawn points down the corridor and makes a cupping action to Geraldine. 'Coffee?' One thing she's learned in the induction is that the world's largest coffeehouse chain, Ground Swell, has a concession in the relaxation area off main reception. 'I'm dying for some caffeine.' Geraldine suppresses a smile and follows her.

Ground Swell is empty when they enter, so they try the vending machine in the corner. 'Ooh, look, it's free,' Dawn cries triumphantly. 'What a stroke of luck.'

Once served with their lattes, Dawn, who hasn't taken a single note in the induction, opens with, 'What did you make of that?'

Geraldine shrugs, 'It went over a lot of old ground, but I suppose they have to.'

Dawn, to whom much of the information was new, takes a sip of her drink before continuing. 'My daughter arranged most of this,' she giggles. 'I probably should have been paying more attention.'

Geraldine raises her eyebrows. She's researched the hell out of it. Who wouldn't? But it's not her place to probe. 'I suppose the main thing is that first point they raised: your decision.'

'Oh, you're Irish,' says Dawn. 'I can always place an accent. I worked in call centres for years, used to love working out where people came from.' She smiles. 'Do you know, it's nice to talk to someone in the same position. I've been avoiding the subject for months, but now it's happening, I feel, I don't know, free somehow.'

Geraldine is intrigued. Free? She's not spoken to anybody except Go Gently about her decision, and she's been as wound up as a ship's clock since making it. 'You sound very at ease with your decision, Dawn. That must be a great help. Do you mind me asking what brought you to… making your mind up?'

'How long have you got, Geraldine?' quips Dawn. 'I suppose we all reach that moment in life when we ask "what's the point?" Well, I reached mine, so here I am.'

Geraldine is taken aback at Dawn's nonchalance in the face of what's to come. She herself has wrestled with her decision for months. 'I admire your strength, Dawn,' is all she can muster.

'I wouldn't call it strength, Geraldine – I'd call it the opposite if I'm being honest. I just….' She falters.

Geraldine holds up her hands in apology. 'I'm sorry. I wasn't prying. Obviously, it's a very private decision.'

Dawn is momentarily silenced. She's surprised at how familiar she is being with a woman she's only just met, but then she's always been one for talking. Is it nerves? Partly, but more a need to articulate what's been going through her mind, an impulse to share. They say it's easier to open up to a stranger than a loved one or a friend, and it's true. She feels unjudged by this new acquaintance, somebody who's in the same boat as her (not like the Go Gently people who, she's noticed, are a bit overkeen on the sales spiel). This exchange feels comforting in an odd way. 'You're not prying, Geraldine. No, what I mean is, well, everything snowballed, and then you're faced with decisions, aren't you? It wasn't a question of me being strong. I looked at the cards I'd been dealt and thought, the game's up.' Geraldine doesn't know what to say. She can equate to a lot of what Dawn has just said, but wonders what specific cards she is holding compared to hers. The ultimate game of poker, but it's not her place to call. But there's no need because Dawn is about to turn her hand over. 'I might as well tell you. It's not going to make any difference now, is it?' She looks around to make sure nobody else is listening, but as the coffee house is empty except for the two to them, she needn't worry. 'Cancer.'

'Oh, I'm so, so sorry,' says Geraldine, as if it was her fault in the first place. 'Is there no hope?'

'It's more a case of there being no insurance,' Dawn snorts. She slaps her hand over her mouth like a naughty schoolgirl. She's not entirely sure where this is all coming from, but no point in holding back now. May as well go for full-disclosure. 'Well, that was the start, but I really put it down to what I call Black Monday. My husband died eight years ago, just after I'd given up at the call centre. We had retirement all mapped out and then "Goodnight, Vienna"! I do have a married daughter, but they have their own lives to lead, don't they? You don't want to be a nuisance. Anyway, Black Monday: I get diagnosed with ovarian cancer, my cat Milo gets run over and killed, and Kimberley, my daughter, tells me she's lost her job. All in one day. If you didn't laugh, you'd cry.'

Geraldine can't quite see the funny side. 'That's terrible, really awful. And there is nothing they can do medically?'

'I don't want them to.'

'Really?'

Dawn stares into her coffee cup. She's not spoken to anyone about this besides Kimberley and even then, her explanation was guarded to spare her daughter's feelings. But deep down she knows it's vital to give vent to her innermost thoughts before the end. She was accustomed to talking to complete strangers at work and this fellow traveller has somehow freed her inhibitions. 'The surgeon said they could operate, but as I didn't have insurance cover for cancer, I would have had to sell the house. My husband, Mark, died of MRSA when he had a routine hip operation – he had it done in a private clinic the last month he was working so it was covered on his company's scheme. Of course, there was no compensation; it was an "adverse outcome" according to them. So, did I fancy going through all of that, with no guarantee of it being successful, and being left penniless? No.'

Geraldine has read about the dismantlement of public health provision in this country and her heart heaves. If Dawn lived elsewhere, like Ireland for example, she'd receive the care that might save her. 'You poor thing,' is the best she can come up with.

'But it wasn't only that. To tell the truth, I was lonely. I felt cut off from everything I'd ever enjoyed in life. I missed Mark, obviously, but also work. I used to love my job, not just my colleagues, but the hundreds of different people I spoke to every week. I was a real gasbag – a natural they said. It's hard to replace all that when it just suddenly stops. You start off with good intentions when you retire, but it melts away so quickly. Going out, calling friends – you gradually withdraw and find yourself in a remote world with only a cat for company, where birthday and Christmas cards become the main point of contact. And even that list gets shorter year-on-year.'

Again, Geraldine is struck by some common threads in Dawn's words. But there is a major difference to her situation. 'But you still have your daughter?'

'Ah, Kimberley. Yes. And her pig of a husband,' Dawn sniggers, her guard well and truly dropped. 'The thing is, do I want to be a burden to her? I could live for years, especially if I had the cancer treatment and it worked, but what sort of life would it be for me, and what type of life would it be for her if she had to look after me?'

This is not a concept of family life Geraldine is familiar with. 'Surely, she'd be there for you?'

'Well, she might, but it would just cause too much trouble. I stopped going round there years ago – he made it very clear he didn't want me visiting. The first Christmas after Mark died was enough, him huffing and puffing and banging around. I felt like an intruder. He's a nasty piece of work, but he's Kimberley's husband so I can't say anything. I just stay away – it's easier.'

'But you still see Kimberley?'

'She calls round, but it's mainly telephone calls. I've a grand-daughter, Ava, too, so she's got her hands full. I understand.'

Geraldine isn't clear if she does. 'But what has she said about your decision? To be here?'

'She keeps asking me if I'm sure. But I am. I'm old, I'm knackered, the air has come out of my tyres. There's bugger all to live for and I ask myself is this life worth hanging on to at all costs? No is the answer – I'm finished. And this way, I'm in control and I can leave something to my daughter and grand-daughter without putting them through years of stress and worry about me, without being an inconvenience to them.'

Geraldine shifts uneasily. Her situation is quite different – or is it? 'It must be very hard for you both.'

'Yes and no. But when it's your time, it's your time. Kimberley has been quite helpful since I told her anyway.'

'She has?'

'When I admitted what I had in mind, she did some research, and discovered this new government scheme, Clean Bill. Basically, they buy your house and all your assets from you with a guaranteed no-quibble valuation, with an extra ten per cent on top *and* a discount for Go Gently. It saves money and makes money, so at least I can leave Kimberley a nice nest egg.'

The stunned look on Geraldine's face causes Dawn to elaborate further. 'Oh, it's not like that. Really. She's just being practical, and you can't argue it's not a good deal. No, the decision is all mine. Come Friday, I'm done.' At this, Geraldine's hand jerks involuntarily, threatening to spill her coffee, and Dawn realises she is being a tad too open with her new acquaintance. She changes course. 'But it's lovely here, isn't it? Like a five-star hotel or a cruise ship. Very handy for where I live. Have you come far?'

Placing her coffee securely on the table, Geraldine replies. 'From Ireland, earlier today.'

The penny drops with Dawn. 'Oh, right. You can't do this over there, can you? At least it's only a short flight. I suppose our government gets accused over all sorts of things, but at least this law has solved a lot of problems for a lot of people.' Dawn is naturally curious as to Geraldine's story, but her call-centre training kicks in and she remembers it's best to leave space for people to volunteer information. She returns to the general rather than the specific. 'My room's out the back, in one of those chalets. Where are you?'

Geraldine, too, is pondering this exchange. Is this candour and devil-may-care attitude of Dawn's some sort of stiff upper lip thing? Into the valley of death and all that? Or, like her, is Dawn simply trying to convince herself that she's made the right decision? Geraldine has run over the arguments a thousand times, weighing the pros and the cons, but in her case it's been an entirely insular debate. Then again, although Dawn has a daughter, the reasons for her presence here at Charon House don't appear to be much different to her own: what is there left to live for? No, that's not true. Dawn has cancer, and she doesn't. Dawn has a family she's giving up, and she doesn't. Dawn doesn't want to be a nuisance or a burden to anybody, but nobody will miss Geraldine when she's gone. 'Upstairs, at the front, on the top floor. It's got really nice views,' she replies.

'Very posh,' chortles Dawn, and they both break into laughter. 'I tell you what, Geraldine, I've got my eye on a massage and a facial tomorrow. Why don't we go together? It would be fun. You only live once, after all.'

Chapter Six

Lawrence Pestel is genuinely excited as his ministerial car sweeps towards the rear entrance of Charon House. For a man who has achieved so much for his country such animation is rare, and he is careful to keep it concealed from his aides. His rise from junior backbencher to secretary of state for wellbeing has been spectacular, but to him these are merely stepping stones on his way to Number Ten. To get there he needs to plot his course with yet more ground-breaking initiatives to shape and reform society, to smash another pane in the Overton window. Today promises to see the opening of the next chapter in the remarkable Lawrence Pestel story.

This early morning meeting isn't listed in his diary, and security is tight. Callan Clay himself meets him on the steps and they exchange a manly fist bump before heading inside. They pass through three keypad protected doors before entering what looks like a huge operating theatre. Bright overhead lights are focused on a large, sheet-covered object in the centre of the room. Four or five technicians in red scrubs scurry about making last minute adjustments on their keypads; the sense of anticipation is high.

Callan Clay seats Lawrence in the single chair positioned opposite the looming, spotlit shape, and stands to make his presentation. As there are only two of them it's all a bit formal, but the entrepreneur is determined to do justice to the moment. He and Lawrence have been discussing Project Doorway for months, but now it's arrived, it's important not to rush things.

'As you know,' opens Callan, 'the dissolution of a state-aided health service has saved the exchequer billions of pounds, which has been further augmented through considerably higher tax contributions from private health insurance and medical services companies. The legalisation of assisted dying pioneered by the government – by you, Lawrence – has been an enormous success, providing a humane, and convenient, end of life choice for many who in the past would have simply hung on, in pain and misery, and at great cost to the state.' Lawrence nods in recognition of these accomplishments. 'The Go Gently concept is ever-evolving and many lessons have been learned. First, cost controls. Our primary method of despatch remains barbiturates but, as the market has grown, we have seen big pharma exploit the situation by increasing its prices out of all proportion, significantly eroding our margins. Secondly, these same pharma costs have prevented us from widening the market on a price-led basis. The minimum cost we can charge for our services is constantly under threat, meaning we have been unable to create a price point that would significantly expand take-up.' Lawrence knows all this already, but is enjoying the framing of the pitch. He'll be able to use a lot of this himself in time. 'So, the challenge we set ourselves, with your guidance, was to find an alternative, cheaper, method of despatch. Quick, clean, painless, and capable of increased daily throughput.' Lawrence nods enthusiastically. 'One that will bring the final journey within the grasp – and the pocket – of a far higher percentage of the population.' He stops, as if waiting for a drumroll. 'At last, following months of exhaustive research, we are ready.' Another pause, this time even longer. 'Lawrence, prepare to meet the Peregrine Pod.' At this, with a dramatic flourish, Callan sweeps back the cover from the hidden object to reveal a gleaming capsule constructed of glass and aluminium. The supersized, coffin-shaped vessel is tilted at a forty-five-degree angle to present a clear view of its lush heliotrope-coloured interior.

Lawrence, like a little kid in Santa's grotto, jumps to his feet to take a closer look. 'Oh, I say, it's beautiful,' he purrs. 'Like the cockpit of a jet fighter. How does it work?'

Callan beams as he prepares to talk the minister through the myriad design features of his new invention. 'In a word, Lawrence, "hypoxiation". The subject enters the pod and the cabin is sealed. Once they are comfortable, and at the agreed countdown time, nitrogen gas is released, filling the chamber and displacing all the air. This causes a dramatic change in the subject's blood-oxygen level creating a dreamy – trippy – state, very pleasant, followed, very quickly, by unconsciousness. Full asphyxiation occurs within a minute. That's it – simplicity itself.'

Lawrence runs his hand along the sleek contours of the silver machine. 'Where does the gas come from?'

'Let me show you,' says Callan, warming to the task. He flicks a sunken catch in the belly of the pod and a door in the fuselage swings open to reveal a dark blue canister. He slides it from its housing. 'Liquid nitrogen. Colourless, odourless, non-reactive. Instant conversion to gas on release. Requires no refrigeration. Inexpensive.' He hands the canister to Lawrence to inspect.

Lawrence cradles it as if he's just been handed a gold nugget which, in a way, he has. 'And all you have to do is change the nitrogen canister each time?'

'Exactly. But the real kicker is we can buy twenty-five of these for the average price of a single barbiturate protocol kit.'

'Incredible,' says Lawrence as he mentally works out the potential net yield. 'I'm dumping my pharma shares when I get home.'

'And look at this,' says Callan, pointing to the console situated in the front of the pod. 'A state-of-the-art experiential panel, which can be preloaded with the client's favourite music, photos, movie clips. Or they can pick from pre-prepared templates, like outer space, dramatic sunset, birds and flowers – you know the sort of thing. They can even select from various scents and aromas. Plus, it's two-way glass, so while the technician can view inside, the inside of the cover becomes a giant video screen for the subject. They're fully immersed.'

'This is most impressive, Callan. Breakthrough technology.'

Callan doesn't need to be told, he knows it is, but it's still good to hear, especially from the secretary of state's lips. 'Ah, but it gets even better. Because it's so simple, you don't need a qualified medic to operate the process. Think of the cost savings there, as well.'

The abacus in Lawrence's head clicks a few more beads. 'Good point. I can make sure there's no trouble over that.'

'I've had another idea too,' says Callan. 'This system is fully portable, so consider this. We'll not only offer one-day, low-cost send-offs at our locations, we can also launch a fully mobile service where we go to the customer's house. A two-man job, in and out in an hour, up to five a day.'

Lawrence's eyes widen. 'Love it. I might even be able to push that through as a government assisted-programme, make it tax deductible too. Do you know, every person over the age of seventy costs the state in excess of £20,000 a year. This pod alone could save us...' he counts on his fingers... 'assuming a third increase in take-up... wow, a further £3 billion. A year.' He pauses. 'And that's just the first year, because you can multiply that by every year these people stick around,' he adds excitedly.

'A nice increase in business for our funerals offer too,' says Callan, who invited Lawrence's wife, Isabella, to become a director and major shareholder when he set it up following Go Gently's inception. (Vertical integration, he called it, whereas Isabella always joked it was more a case of horizontal integration.)

As Lawrence circumnavigates the pod, taking in its beauteous potential, a further thought occurs to him. 'And patents – we're good to go?'

Callan nods. 'All sorted. We'll be able to export this around the world once it's up and running, open franchise operations. We'll have them beating a path to our door.'

'Or you'll have a bid from pharma to buy you out of the market. Now that would be fun.'

'Can't wait,' says Callan gleefully. 'Oh, and I've taken the expedient step of acquiring a liquid nitrogen firm to ensure continuity of supply – make sure we don't get held to ransom like we did over barbs.'

The minister, not for the first time, is impressed at Callan's thoroughness. 'Can I get in?' he asks, pointing at the pod. 'Try it out?'

'Of course you can.' He gestures to one of the techs to bring over a small pair of stepladders and they help him into the capsule.

'It's not loaded, is it?' Lawrence jokes as he stretches out to his full length within the cosy cocoon.

Callan laughs. 'No. Firing blanks today. Don't want to waste gas anyway.' He reaches into the console. 'Any requests?'

'Have you got "My Way"?' shoots back the politician. 'I always liked that one.' He closes his eyes and crosses his arms across his chest in repose. An image of the Number Ten front door, zooming ever closer, imprints itself on his mind.

Ten minutes later, they repair to Callan's office.

'Friday,' says the minister.

'What, this Friday? Isn't that a bit too soon?'

Lawrence shakes his head. 'No, it's ready to be unveiled and I'm free.' Not only that, it's the party's annual spring conference in Blackpool next week and he intends to upstage the lot of them. (Inspired by an article he's read in The Nation that very morning he is considering the theme of 'Shifting the Paradigm' for his keynote speech and nothing will help shift it as much as this. He is aware relatively few people understand what paradigm means, but in his opinion that's half the beauty.)

Callan grimaces. He'd not been thinking of launching quite this early. But if the minister wants… 'Well, yes, it's possible.'

There is a delicate subject to be touched on, but Lawrence doesn't really do delicacy, so ploughs on. 'I see this as a joint launch. I know it's your pod, Cal, but when you think about it, the main directive and encouragement for its use is coming from my department and, well, it's been developed in conjunction with me personally. Government and enterprise working hand in hand and all that.'

Callan has been here before, flattened under the wheels of Lawrence Pestel's chariot, but is savvy enough to recognise he'll get more out of the partnership by continuing as stooge to the secretary of state's straight man role. 'Yes, absolutely.'

'Good. I'll get the media team on it right away, and they'll do the prep, speeches and so on. And a Q and A. Things like how you came up with the idea in the first place.'

The mention of what inspired the Peregrine instantly transports Callan back to the hog farm he grew up on in Tennessee. It was a hard life. One of his jobs was to collect the hog manure so it could be turned into liquid nitrogen fertiliser, which in turn was used on the soybean crop. In the pigsty one day, he accidentally ingested too many fumes. At first, he felt light-headed, before becoming euphoric, with all his preacher uncle's sermons playing in his head at the same time. After that, he couldn't remember anything at all until the reviving shock of a bucket of cold water hit him in the face and he came to in the yard. Daddy said he could have died if they'd not pulled him out in time. He snaps himself back to the present. He certainly won't be mentioning that. 'Sure thing.'

'Now, optics. It's all about the optics. Have you got two of these things?' Callan nods. 'Right – the photo is me and you, side by side, each in a pod. Space age. Peas in a pod. Blasting off. You like it?'

I must be going up in the world, thinks Callan, if I'm getting joint billing this time. 'That would work,' he ventures.

'Now, an obvious question, but have you tried it out on an actual person? We're bound to get asked.'

Callan shifts slightly. Despite the freedoms the country allows, and its championing of entrepreneurial progress, certain sensitivities remain from earlier, nanny-state days. Of course, he has done a couple of dry-runs with some, well, not quite volunteers, but Alzheimer's patients who wouldn't know the difference. It worked like a dream and he was doing them a favour if you think about it. He can certainly vouch for the pod's efficacy, but he'll have to find another way of demonstrating that point. He clears his throat to essay an illustrative answer. 'The lethal aspects of liquid nitrogen have been the subject of intense scientific research over the years. In the past, due to the incorrect handling of liquid nitrogen, a surprisingly high number of accidental deaths were recorded annually, mainly in agricultural settings. More tellingly, back in the days when assisted dying was outlawed, the use of liquid nitrogen as a means of suicide was particularly championed by underground deathing groups. It was crude, but highly effective. Fortunately, we have evolved from that sorry state of affairs and, based on the considerable data we have amassed, together with extensive clinical modelling, this state-of-the-art technology is now triple-A rated for function and the end result it is designed to deliver – quick and painless, every single time.'

Lawrence, who is not so green as cabbage looking, claps his hands in pretend applause. 'Very good,' he smirks. 'And now, I've got something for you, Callan.' It's his turn to wait for the imaginary drum roll to play out. 'Peregrine Phase Two.'

If events move fast in politics, nothing moves quite as rapidly as Lawrence Pestel. Callan has been focused on Project Doorway for months, developing the design, technology and rollout strategy. Now, at the very moment of realisation, it seems Lawrence is already wanting to up the ante somehow. Should he be surprised that the secretary of state is hankering to hang more baubles on an already heavily decorated Christmas tree? Perhaps it would have been more of a shock if Lawrence had simply agreed to go ahead with Plan A. 'Oh, really?' says Callan, weakly. Realising that doesn't sound sufficiently enthusiastic, he quickly adds, 'Sounds intriguing.'

Lawrence rises from his chair, as if to receive an ovation from rapturous conference attendees. 'Having seen this, Callan, it strikes me that Peregrine can be applied to more than one societal problem. Sadly, despite our numerous advances, the nation still faces many challenges. However, you'll be pleased to know I've just come up with the solution to one knotty issue cabinet has been wrestling with for some time.' He looks like he might combust with self-congratulation. 'And I think, as far as demonstrating the Peregrine works safely on a real-life subject, that's not going to be an issue for much longer.'

Chapter Seven

D awn wanders over to the main building in search of breakfast. It's only just struck her there isn't a telephone in her room, just an intercom to reception, so she has no means of contacting Geraldine to make arrangements for the spa. Her own mobile was 'stored' on checking in, as Go Gently deems they are potentially 'upsetting' for residents.

She heads for Ground Swell, only to find it deserted of clientele. 'Quiet today,' she says to the girl behind the counter as she orders a latte and a croissant.

The barista, who has noted Dawn's wristband, gives her a quizzical look as she coldly replies: 'Most people have breakfast in their rooms. I'll bring it over.' She turns her back to the single customer and, constantly casting glances over her shoulder, attends to preparing the coffee.

Dawn occupies the same seat as the previous evening and takes in her surroundings. There's nothing to read – you think they'd have newspapers in here or something – and begins to feel slightly adrift. She should have arranged to rendezvous with Geraldine. That would have been the easiest thing to have done. It was silly of her, but how was she to know?

When the barista – after a considerable delay – places her coffee and pastry on the table, Dawn tries to engage her. 'Must be boring for you if it's like this all the time.'

The girl, mindful her job description actively discourages dialogue with customers – service with a sulk is the mandatory stipulation, general chitchat inevitably leading to questions being asked that are way above the server's pay grade – replies curtly. 'We'll get busier later. With visitors.' She takes off before Dawn can follow up.

Well, thinks Dawn, she'll not be winning employee of the month any time soon. So, visitors are the cafeteria's main customers? Well, she and Geraldine were in here last night and nobody said anything then. She nibbles at her croissant, wondering what to do next. Go to reception and ask to get connected to Geraldine's room? Find the spa and see if she turns up? She's got until two o'clock before her scheduled 'Blessings' session. (There, with the aid of a therapist, she is to compile a list of the high points in her life. The interchange has been allocated a sixty-minute slot, which tickles Dawn as she wonders what they're going to do with the three quarters of an hour left over.) She drums her fingers on the table. Just as she's about to make a move, a figure appears at the doorway and peers in. Geraldine. Dawn waves enthusiastically and beckons her over.

'Great minds, eh?' says Dawn. 'There was no way of getting in touch, but here we are.'

Geraldine nods. She'd been aware the previous evening that no hard and fast arrangement to meet had been made, but hadn't said anything. It was, after all, the sort of conversation you have with a casual holiday acquaintance, 'Let's meet up back home', or what you'd write on a Christmas card to somebody you'd not seen for a decade: 'Next year – definitely!' It was small talk, a form of politeness where both parties understood it was socially acceptable to dissemble. So why was she here? The truth is Dawn had moved her last night with her openness and total lack of edge. Life had dealt Dawn a pretty shitty hand, but she remained, well, Geraldine couldn't quite work it out. Stoical? Accepting? Practical? Cheery? She'd been fascinated. She, too, felt she'd had the best of her life, that there was no point in soldiering on, but there the similarities ended. There was an enormous chasm between Dawn's circumstances and her own. As for meeting up, Geraldine had read the entire welcome pack and knew there was no easy direct contact between residents – or with anybody outside for that matter. She had noted that room service was encouraged and the coffeehouse was primarily a facility for visitors to enjoy. Yet, having taken breakfast in her room this morning, all she could think about was Dawn. Would her new acquaintance remember having suggested going to the spa? Where might she bump into her? More than anything, Geraldine realised she wanted to see her again, so set off to the obvious spot. She was right. 'Another coffee?' she asks.

'Only if Godzilla's up to it,' Dawn suggests, indicating the barista. Confused, Geraldine places the order. This time there is no offer to bring the drinks over – they are eventually alerted to their availability by a cry of 'Gaberdine'. Dawn dives into her second latte, and wipes the foam moustache from her upper lip. 'I have to say,' she cackles, 'that girl might have a face like a bulldog chewing a wasp, but she knows how to make a decent coffee – not like that machine stuff last night.'

Geraldine sniffs at her cup before taking a delicate sip. 'Hmmm, lovely,' she concedes. 'Do you think it's the milk? Oat, or Soya, or something exotic like that?'

'You can be the one to ask her,' Dawn suggests. 'She puts the fear of God in me.'

Geraldine shakes her head and smiles – maybe another time.

'Are we going exploring, then?' asks Dawn when they're settled. 'The spa? And the gardens look nice too.'

Geraldine's plans had focused on further intense periods of introspection over the course of the next few days. Her worldly affairs were all in order and there were no goodbyes she needed to make – the only person she needed to make peace with was herself. So why was she succumbing to Dawn's siren's call, enticing her away with diversions and entertainments? She didn't know. Dawn had explained to her why she was here at Charon House, but Geraldine hadn't reciprocated. Last night, as she tossed and turned, she felt she at least owed Dawn an explanation, a rationale, for her decision. She imagined it might do her good to share.

Before she can reply to Dawn's question, they are distracted by the arrival of two newcomers, both smartly dressed and wearing visitor badges on their lapels. The woman is visibly irked, griping under her breath, while the man looks deeply unhappy and harassed. He goes to the counter to order drinks as she sits at the table next to the window; the temperature of the room suddenly seems to drop a few degrees. Her stony face suggests whatever argument they are having is yet to reach its conclusion. When he joins her again the intense conversation continues, in that curious way where they think, because they're whispering, nobody can hear them. Dawn, non-too-subtly, puts their conversation on hold as she takes in the action playing out over Geraldine's shoulder. This, by way of running commentary, she communicates to her new friend with a succession of contorted facial expressions. Soon they're both tuned into the urgent and hushed exchange playing out a few feet away.

'It's what he wanted?' bristles the woman. 'I'll try to remember that if I ever have to make the same choice for you.'

The man rolls his eyes. 'How many more times?' he pleads. 'You know what he said. "If I ever become doolally, no messing. Straight to Switzerland with me." He couldn't have been clearer.'

She throws her head back in scorn. 'Well, he'd be really pleased to know Stalybridge is the new Switzerland. I haven't seen any St Bernards yet.'

'It's a metaphor, that's all. You know perfectly well what he meant.'

'Yes, I do. It's the sort of thing people say when they're well, when they don't really understand the implications. An easy enough line to trot out when you think you'll never have to go through with it.'

While the exchange has Dawn and Geraldine's undivided attention the sullen barista carries on polishing the Gaggia – she's overheard all this before.

The man buries his face in his hands. 'Whatever I do, it's the wrong decision. How do you think it makes *me* feel? How do you think it's going to make me feel every single day for the rest of my life?'

At this she softens, and places her hand on his. 'I know, Simon, I know. But Jeffrey shouldn't have placed his life in your hands like this. I'm sure he didn't mean to, either. "Going to Switzerland" – Stalybridge – is just something people come out with. You don't have to follow it to the letter.'

This well-intended advice seems to cause him even more upset. 'And what's the alternative, then? Let him suffer for years, not recognising anybody, lost in a world of confusion and fear, incapable of wiping his own arse? It's all very well to say don't honour his wishes, Vicki, but do you want to condemn him to *that*?'

'No, but it's less final than being here. He's not been poorly that long; you don't really know for sure what direction his illness will take. He could be helped.'

Simon shakes his head in sorrow. 'You've seen how quickly he's deteriorated in just six months. What will he be like in another six months? Then you'll be saying we should have acted sooner.'

Vicki is not having it. 'I don't even think he's that bad. Sometimes he's quite lucid. It's too soon to be doing this. I'm not sure we should be doing it at all if I'm being honest.'

It's a circular argument, and it spins around to Simon again. 'The doctor was unequivocal – there's only one direction this is going. Dad made his wishes clear to me and I agreed to fulfil them if it ever came to this. That's what I'm doing, and it makes me feel like a murderer.'

Silence descends on the room. They've nothing left to say. Dawn and Geraldine exchange glances. They have nothing to say either. Spas and gardens are forgotten as their thoughts plunge down familiar rabbit holes once more.

Jeffrey Heath is distracted. *Where's Rosemary? Is she making tea? I never say no to a cuppa. Hello, who's this? Never seen him before. Foreign chap. Did I let him in? You have to be careful with these dark-skinned types – you never know what they're up to. He could be a doctor. A lot of these doctors are. Not that I'd let one loose on me, no way. I've got my eye on you, mister, oh yes, I have. What was it I was supposed to be doing again?*

Adil places the mug on the table in front of Jeffrey. 'Tea. Milk, no sugar,' he cheerily pronounces.

'Two sugars,' shouts Jeffrey. 'Two.'

Adil hurriedly grabs two sachets from the tray and stirs them into the cup. Jeffrey takes a sip and immediately spits the tea out on to the carpet. 'Ugh. Gnat's piss.'

Adil cared for dementia sufferers of varying degrees in the age-atorium, finding it a peculiarly rewarding duty. Grown men and women reverting to a dreamlike state, childish and full of wonder; incapable of articulating their thoughts – possibly not in possession of any thoughts. Sometimes innocent and playful, other times moody and ill-tempered. Occasionally violent. Totally dependent on others – on him – for food, comfort and distraction. Nobody could cure these hapless souls, but it was he, not some doctor or nurse, who was best able to ease their plight. It gladdened his heart to coax a smile, a memory, from minds as erasable as a blackboard. Of all the angst and self-recrimination he's experienced working at Charon House, looking after dementia sufferers is perhaps his most painful regret. While he rationalises that most of the clients here are making a personal choice, enacting their own free will, it's impossible to say that about unfortunates like Jeffrey who have sailed off the edge of their known worlds. All Adil can do is care for them all the more, even if it does make him feel like the reluctant shepherd boy driving his flock to the slaughterhouse.

Adil clears up the mess, and says never mind. He makes up a fresh cup, skips the sugar, and presents it anew. 'Look, Jeffrey. A nice cup of tea, just as you like it.'

The old man beams and takes a sip. 'Lovely,' he exclaims. 'I never say no to a cuppa.'

The other thing about dementia patients is that Adil feels free to talk to them normally, even if it is on a perfunctory level. There's no need to follow Doctor Ruth's advice and pretend he can't speak English with them – they're not going to ask him any questions or report him. He regularly finds himself conducting both sides of a conversation, like a ventriloquist, articulating thoughts that might be going through his charges' minds, words that would never be uttered without his assistance.

Jeffrey sits quietly now, letting his tea go cold. He wonders when Rosemary will be back, she's been gone ages. On that, at least, he's right, as she died six years ago following a stroke. He occupies his own place in time and space; the captain of a probe, the crew in suspended animation, en route to a distant star.

Adil wonders what kind of life he has left behind. Today, he is Jeffrey, who has taken his medicine and eaten all his food like a good boy. There is nothing to suggest that this defenceless, grey-haired gentleman in slippers and stained cardigan once bestrode the insurance company he worked for like a colossus, salesman of the year so often they joked about retiring the accolade. There are no clues that this loving husband and proud father once lit up whatever social or family event he attended; no trace of his wit, humour or bonhomie remaining on the surface. A man who loved life; a man whom life has ratted on in return.

What's even less obvious to Adil – and anybody else bothering to enquire – is how sudden and dramatic Jeffrey's decline has been. His first episode was a little over six months ago. Prior to that, Jeffrey's stock answer to the question 'How are you?' was: 'Can't complain. Nobody listens anyway.' Boom Boom. Retired, mid-seventies, widowed, he was doing all right. Well provided for (the salesman of the year awards had seen to that), still a member of the golf club, and down the pub every weekend to 'meet the lads' and watch the football (despite having numerous sports subscription channels at home). Always up for a chat with anyone who would chat back.

Healthwise, he had a few creaking joints, but who didn't when you've racked up miles on the clock? He'd been prescribed anti-depressants after Rosemary died, which he never came off so couldn't tell if they worked or not. They came with his private health insurance (he'd boast to Simon he was 'copper-bottomed' when it came to his cover – still on staff discount) and they seemed to help, so where was the harm? His stay and treatment at Charon House are being paid for by the same gilt-edge insurance plan. (Jeffrey retired the same year the mis-selling laws were scrapped, and would often joke at how he'd got his timing completely wrong.)

A year ago, anybody coming across Jeffrey would consider him to be in reasonable nick for his age, comfortably off and with plenty going on in his life. But how quickly that came to change with his 'episode'.

Admittedly, he'd not been feeling himself the day it happened, following a bout of diarrhoea. He blamed the golf club catering. The pharmacist told him the best treatment was no treatment – just drink lots of water. Later, feeling brighter, he determined to stick to his normal Friday routine of a chippy tea. It was there, in the brightly-lit, black and white tiled Cod Father, his life suddenly became deep-fried. Standing at the counter he was overtaken by the oddest sensation, as if a light had been switched off, plunging him into a netherworld of confusion. He didn't know where he was, and fear ripped through every fibre of his being. A kindly couple noticed his distress and intervened. They asked his name, and where he lived, but this only caused Jeffrey to become more agitated as he realised he no longer had command over this information. Panicking, he tried to push his way out of the shop, only to find his legs collapsing from under him. The next he knew he was in hospital, on a drip, with Simon by his side. Jeffrey couldn't remember anything about the fish and chip shop, but knew who he was, and who Simon was. The doctors just look at each other and nod knowingly. Simon is taken to one side: *classic onset of dementia, prepare yourself for the decline that will surely follow.* Simon doesn't believe it – Dad seems OK to him and is quickly released from hospital. Then, later that week, when he calls to check up on his dad, Jeffrey freaks out – *I have no son. I know your game, you're trying to rob me. I'm calling the police; you see if I don't.* This sets the pattern for the next few months – one day up, good old Jeffrey, the next down, with hallucinations, repetitions, obsessions and delusions. Simon bears this grim turn of events heavily. Uppermost in his thinking is his filial duty regarding a pledge, made in better times, not to let his father suffer any more than necessary if he ever lost his faculties. A fatal compact, signed in familial blood. On his father's more lucid days he obliquely attempts to address the subject with him, desperately seeking a cancellation of the contract. 'Chuffing hell,' Jeffrey laughs, 'if I ever show any sign of going off my rocker, don't hang about! Straight to Stalybridge.' (A pro to the end, he'd kept up with the occasional modifications to his policy.)

What really set the cat among the pigeons was the incident at Simon's old primary school. Despite his son having left there forty years previously, Jeffrey decides to pick him up one afternoon after classes. It's the middle of February, but Jeffrey has got it into his head it's Halloween so, wearing the boilersuit he keeps for car maintenance and an old ski mask, he decides to surprise Simon and his friends with some trick or treating at going home time. As Simon pointed out afterwards, Dad looked nothing like Michael Myers and it's not like he was carrying a knife or anything, so the armed response to the 'security breach' was wholly over-the-top. Nevertheless, the incident had parents, the school and the neighbourhood demanding action.

On checking his dad's insurance policy Simon discovers the cover for an assisted exit – he was one of the first to sign up for it when it was legalised. Conflicted and tortured, Simon determines he has a duty to fulfil his father's wishes before things slip much further. It turns out to be more straight forward than expected. Simon has power of attorney, and his dad's insurance policy provides sufficient evidence of intent and consent under the new rules. All the insurance company is bothered about is pointing out it's the basic package Jeffrey is entitled to, and they quickly pass him on to their approved supplier, Go Gently. They might as well be fitting him in for a short back and sides: 'Is next week all right?' Jeffrey thinks he's going on holiday, which in a way, he is. Simon, full of self-reproach, remains stoically determined to honour his father's wishes while his wife, Vicki, is distraught. It's been only six months since Jeffrey called in for a large haddock and mushy peas at The Cod Father.

Adil knows none of this, and this level of detail is largely missing from Jeffrey's admission notes as it's not considered material. What Adil does recognise is a man in need. In need of care, in need of kindness. He can provide that. And he will.

Chapter Eight

Wayne 'Woody' Woodham is escorted from his cell to a cacophony of catcalls and whistles from inmates who consider themselves less fortunate than Prisoner A1801MB. *Lucky sod. Who've you bribed? Gimme your spice. You'll be back.* Except Woody has determined he will never be coming back to this place. The warder marches him down the gantry, through a series of remote-controlled secure doors and into the admin block. The journey takes a fair bit of time yet no words are exchanged between con and turnkey as they walk. Rather, the screw keeps shaking his head in disbelief at how this jailbird has managed to find a way to shorten his sentence. *Where's the justice?* The temperature thaws slightly as Woody reaches the governor's office and he is handed over to a panel of earnest, besuited men and women sitting around the conference table. The topic of their meeting is the prisoner himself, and all eyes immediately lock upon him.

The governor proceeds. 'A1801MB, you understand why you are here?' Woody nods. 'And you have volunteered for this programme fully cognisant of the outcome, and with your consent freely given?'

'I have,' replies the prisoner.

'Present today are representatives of the prison service, the government, and the welfare and wellbeing professionals who have been responsible for monitoring you over the past few weeks. Is there anything you'd like to say, A1801MB?'

Woody looks slowly round the table and lugubriously shakes his head. 'No. I'm all on board. It's my decision.'

The governor closes his file. 'Well, Woodham, on behalf of the team here at Strangeways, may I wish you all the very best on your onward journey. You are a true pioneer.' And with that, Woody – no longer Prisoner A1801MB – is escorted from the room.

The governor helps himself to a biscuit. 'Remarkable,' he says. 'I know a volunteer is worth ten pressed men, but I at least expected some resistance. He can hardly wait.'

The psychiatrist pipes up. 'The fact he's a first-timer has a bearing. They simply can't handle prison life. An experienced lag would cruise his sentence, but to him it's the curse of Sisyphus.'

The chaplain still has doubts. 'I can't help but feel concerned at this direction of travel. Allowing a prisoner to opt for voluntary end of life instead of serving out his sentence raises all manner of moral arguments. It's not as if he's a murderer or anything – he's only in for aggravated theft.'

The Treasury representative harrumphs at such lily-livered sophistry. 'He's a criminal, full stop. Serving ten years, which will cost the state upwards of a million pounds over the course of his incarceration. This initiative solves many problems: it lessens the economic burden on the taxpayer; it eliminates the prospect of recidivism, and it reduces the strain on our over-populated prisons at the same time. The public welcomed back capital punishment in the last referendum, and they're going to love this too.'

The chaplain remains unconvinced. 'The thing is, capital punishment is understood by the public – they get that murderers, terrorists and anti-government protestors deserve the ultimate sanction. Being sentenced to death as a convicted prisoner is one thing, but taking that decision for yourself? Some people might think it's not as voluntary as we claim.'

This point isn't of concern to the Treasury. 'Nobody would dare. In any case, ask yourself the question: does that prisoner we've just seen appear hesitant, or coerced? No, of course not. He's made a fully informed choice, based on personal criteria. He doesn't want to serve another eight years; he's happy to pay his debt to society, and he'll receive a considerable cash incentive worth what it would cost to keep him in prison for just half of one of those years, something for him to leave to his family. If I was in his position, I'd snap our hand off.'

The governor is a firm convert. 'I have to say, if the projections are right, it could make our job a lot easier in the future. Less prisoners for a start. A smaller staff requirement. Plus, we can slow down the new prison building programme – huge savings there.'

'Absolutely,' echoes the man from the government. 'For every one thousand prisoners taking advantage of this opportunity we'll save around one hundred million pounds per annum and, of course, that's multiplied by the total number of years those prisoners have left to serve. It's the biggest breakthrough in penal reform since the Victorians. It's visionary, it's huge.'

Several heads around the table nod in agreement. They're part of history, and it feels very satisfying indeed. The chaplain, however, still feels the need to unburden. 'What is going to happen to the prisoner now? We still have a duty of care, I assume?'

Treasury can hardly contain himself. 'You needn't have any concerns in that area, Reverend. He's going to be treated like royalty over the next few days. (He doesn't specify whether he's talking about Charles I or Henry VIII in this context.)

'He loses his prisoner status from this point onwards and will be accommodated in five-star luxury until it's, er, time. The equivalent of Civvy Street if the street was Mayfair, and beyond his wildest dreams compared to remaining here. No offence, governor.'

The prison chief smiles; none taken.

'I have to say, it does sound like a well-balanced trade-off,' chimes the psychiatrist. 'The stress and strain of prison life is intolerable to many, even with a short sentence. The mental toll, never mind the physical hardship, stretches for eternity. The package on offer is most appealing by comparison.'

The governor is quick to correct any misconceptions regarding the regime in his prison. 'I make no apologies for "intolerable". Never has the old adage rung so true: if you can't do the time, don't do the crime. We've spent years making a stay here is as unpleasant as it gets. A deterrent, an experience you wouldn't want to repeat.'

'Tough on crime and tough on the causes of crime,' adds Treasury.

'Is the scheme open to everybody?' continues the psychiatrist. 'You may get snowed under.'

'We've thought of that,' says the governor proudly. 'I've been assisting the government on the planning side and have proposed several safeguards. So, for example, the inmate must be over sixty years of age to qualify, and must have at least seven years of his sentence left to serve. We feel that's the right balance.'

'But, of course, we can adjust those parameters as we monitor the programme,' says the man from the Treasury, in case anybody thinks they're being too soft.

The chaplain, at the risk of annoying the governor, isn't finished yet. 'I don't want to be indelicate, but what is going to happen to him at the end? I mean, what form of execution is being used?'

There is a sharp intake of breath from around the table. 'No, no, no, Reverend,' tuts the man from the Treasury. 'We do not use the word "execution". Ever. Prisoners condemned to death have no choice in the matter and it is they who are executed. This, on the other hand, is completely different. This is an assisted action, carried out in accordance with the prisoner's – ex-prisoner by that stage – express wishes. Our partners call it the final journey, and that is the terminology we prefer.'

The chaplain is aware of several pairs of eyes bearing down on him and decides discretion might be the better part of valour at this point. He clams up.

'Actually,' says the psychiatrist, 'what method is being used? We're only really geared up for hangings here, but that's a bit, well, old-school? Lethal injection, I take it?'

Treasury hesitates momentarily as if unsure how to answer. He peers around the table, 'We're all signed up to the official secrets act here, I assume?' Nobody demurs. 'No, it won't be any of the old-fashioned methods. In fact, we feel the method of despatch is going to form a large part of the appeal for this scheme. I can't go into too much detail here, but I was advised just before we started this meeting that the secretary of state for wellbeing has come up with a new solution for the final journey that is quick, painless, and designed to relieve the user of anxiety. It also has the added advantage of being low-cost and mess-free. Mr Woodham is going to be knocking up a couple of major firsts in the next few days.'

This draws murmurs of approval from those assembled. Even the chaplain's conscience is slightly eased on hearing these reassuring words.

At last, Lawrence and Isabella can relax, having arrived home from a boring constituency fundraiser. It would be wrong to say it was an especially tedious evening, because to the Pestels any time they spend in the presence of the 'little people' is a chore to be endured.

As the Tiganello is quaffed, though, the minister is in high spirits – all down to the Peregrine Pod. He offers a toast: 'To Callan. Thanks to him, Project Doorway is finally ready to swing open.'

Isabella is aware of her husband's plans to widen his wellbeing programme through increasing the take-up of assisted dying, but has only just learned the details of the Peregrine Pod. She's impressed. 'Do remember it's your idea,' she reminds him. 'He's just come up with the means.'

Lawrence beams. 'Quite correct, my dear, as always.'

'And this pod can really see people off at a ridiculously low unit cost?'

Lawrence nods enthusiastically. 'For peanuts. It's a dream come true. I've solved the geriatric problem in one stroke: you either stay healthy and pay your way, or you sign up to be put out of your misery with the Peregrine. We'll even help fund it for you if you like. It's delicious.'

Isabella regards her husband with unfettered admiration. 'Genius, darling, genius. An "assisted" assisted demise.'

'I know,' he concedes, as he savours his wine. 'But the really clever bit is how I can use the Peregrine in the penal early release programme as well. The instant I saw that pod it just came to me – why not use it on prisoners as well, saving even more money. It's the double whammy of all double whammies. Plus, it means I can now go live with both programmes.'

'And dominate the headlines and conference for an entire week,' Isabella purrs. 'How convenient.'

'Oh, I hadn't thought of that,' he swaggers. They laugh and chink glasses.

Talking of his contribution to the party's law and order agenda, Isabella has a further question: 'What did those old farts at Requital say when you showed them how to do their job? They can't have been very pleased.'

It's true that the department responsible for law and order has been less than impressed with what they consider to be Lawrence's mission creep, but the idea of reducing the prison population and slashing costs through his radical early release plan was so compelling that cabinet had to listen. 'Oh, they'll get over it,' Lawrence sniggers, relishing the thought of their chagrin once more. 'The PM loved it when I laid the pod on cabinet earlier; he was all but creaming himself at the prospect. Of course, Requital wanted to launch it – claim it in other words – but I wasn't having that. No way.'

'Can they do that? The cheek,' Isabella cries, peeved at the prospect of such a double-cross.

'Don't worry. The PM is right behind me. And so he should be, after all I've done for him.' Lawrence has yet to twig the reason the PM backs him is so he can be blamed if these initiatives backfire while, if they succeed, he will take second billing behind the leader. So far, though, so good. The secretary of state for wellbeing has more than pulled his weight in reducing dependency on the state in recent years, spearheading the modernisation of an archaic NHS with an insurance-based replacement and masterminding the assisted dying bill. The slew of revolutionary cost-saving policies driven by Lawrence has saved billions while advancing the country forward from the bad old days. But this is only the start in Lawrence's view. It irks him he doesn't get the credit he feels he is due, and it is a source of frustration to him that his colleagues lack the same tireless energy and quest for perfection driving him on. What's wrong with them? Well, he isn't going to slow down in the face of their apathy and lack of imagination. He has further ideas, too, to ensure no individual will ever sponge off the state again, but to achieve these he needs the top job, the keys to Number Ten. There, he can decree rather than inveigle, and the prospect gives him goosebumps.

Isabella looks at her husband as if she could eat him, he really is a very clever boy. 'I can't wait to see their precious faces next week,' she says in anticipation of his impending triumph at conference. 'Then they'll have to take you seriously.' It is a source of considerable resentment to the Pestels that, despite Lawrence's many achievements, he is still not regarded as PM material by the party's upper echelons. Yes, they whisper, he's diligent, forceful and ruthless, but perhaps tries a tad too hard? Naked ambition is vulgar, and he lacks the natural authority a public-school education provides. Their nickname for him, 'Grammar', sums up his prospects as far as they are concerned. Isabella isn't exempt from this bigotry. Lawrence calls his wife his rock and his inspiration, unaware that many familiar with the pair refer to her as Lady Macbeth.

Still, tonight isn't a night for negative thoughts – they need to relish these landmarks. 'I'm telling you, Bel, Clay may come over like a *good ole boy*, probably because he is one, but that machine is the cat's pyjamas.'

Isabella can't argue with that assessment. 'We must have Clay and his wife over once conference is out of the way,' she says.

Lawrence raises his eyebrows at this magnanimous suggestion before conceding, 'Why not? Keep him sweet, maybe even find a wider role for you, now it's all taking off.'

Isabella is excited all over again, not least because she is besotted with Lady Margaret, the blue-blooded heiress Clay had the good sense to bag when he first fetched up on these shores. It's all she can do to stop herself from curtsying when they meet. Mrs Pestel loves being a stakeholder in Go Gently's funerals business and is only too aware her shareholding is about to enjoy another valuable boost on the back of the pod. Her husband arranged that too, and it's been the gift that keeps on giving. The association with Doctor Callan Clay has been a fruitful one for the pair since they first met the American, not that they would ever acknowledge it – gratitude equals indebtedness in their world, and they certainly wouldn't want Clay to think he had any hold over them. But there's no doubt they admire the American's 'can-do' approach.

Lawrence tops up their glasses, and remembers he's got another nugget to share. 'Talking about Cal,' he says, 'I took the liberty of getting Intel to do some background digging on our Doctor Clay. Just in case. Seems he's been very selective in his back story.'

'Ooh, do tell,' squeals Isabella.

'Well, you know he plays this "came up the hard way" self-made-man schtick? I thought it was all a bit of an act, but apparently, he *was* dirt poor and grew up on a hog farm in Tennessee.'

'Well, he did drag himself up by the bootlaces then.'

'Ah, but with a bit of help though. He left high school early, with virtually no qualifications and zero prospects. And then God intervened.'

'Don't be silly, Lawrence.'

'Seriously. Turns out his uncle was a renowned televangelist, Pastor Prentis Pfeiffer. He took Callan under his wing as his driver and assistant, mainly out of sympathy. The preacher's speciality was persuading people who were seriously ill to forego spending their money on medical treatment – told them it wasn't part of God's plan and to send their cash to him instead for prayers and an intervention.'

'Lucrative. Seems Callan absorbed that message well.'

'Yes, and it was Callan who apparently came up with all the marketing ideas that saw the pastor's business quadruple. Social media and rallies, that sort of thing.'

'Savvy, even then.'

'And then it all crashed.'

'You mean God forsook him, or the other way around?'

'The higher power in this case was the police. They arrested the pastor for burning down his own parsonage in an insurance scam – he got more than his fingers burned.'

Isabella laughs – the very idea. 'No doubt his defence was God told him to do it – He's a serial arsonist, I've heard. Was Callan arrested too?'

'No. But he was forced to move on, which was actually a good thing for him because that's when he set up his first business.'

'What, The Clay Method?'

'Yes. Made a fortune from health supplements and diet plans, before the US authorities shut him down.'

'That's when he came over here?'

Lawrence nods. 'He said it was because we provided a better business environment for men of ambition, but basically he was run out of town by the FDA.'

'And that's when he made a beeline for Lady Margaret and the family's chain of care homes?'

'Handy, that, wasn't it? That's when I first met him, when we were pushing the assisted dying bill through. He was a big supporter, mainly because the care homes were losing money as they weren't government supported any more after we scrapped the NHS. Bad timing and all that. But, with a little bit of help from yours truly, he comes up with Go Gently and using the homes for a different kind of care. He's a smart cookie is our Callan. Living proof that God works in mysterious ways.'

'Doesn't He just?' says Isabella. She raises her glass. 'A toast to the feats of Clay.'

They cackle at their peerless wit, at the sheer perfection of life. And at the promise that things are about to get even better.

Chapter Nine

A frustrated Geraldine screws the umpteenth piece of paper into a ball and tosses it into the bin. The Go Gently counsellor has recommended she writes down all the reasons behind her decision, which, she guesses, is both sensible and helpful. (As far as Go Gently is concerned it's also part of the legal consent process, but they don't really mention that.) No matter how many times Geraldine starts her account, it doesn't feel right, and she is compelled to begin again. Setting pen to paper is so damn difficult, which is silly really, as it's not like she'll receive a detention for not handing it in on time, or for it not being up to scratch. The big problem, she decides, is she doesn't really know who she is writing it for, who will ever get to read it. There is no one, and in a way, that's the heart of the matter. Go Gently has kindly supplied her with a crib sheet of prompts: *perhaps write about how you view your future years; describe how you feel about life now.* These are not the original suggestions that were conceived by a leading psychologist, because Callan angrily threw these into his own bin on reading them. *Goddam idiot. We don't want people changing their minds by looking back fondly; we want them to look forward, despair, double down and get it over with ASAP.* In any event, the guideline is failing to inspire Geraldine. She wonders if Dawn is having the same trouble, but doubts it.

Geraldine was shocked at how blasé Dawn appeared to be when recounting her reasons for being at Charon House. *I'm old, I'm knackered, the air has come out of my tyres. There's bugger all to live for and I ask myself is this life worth hanging on to at all costs?* Maybe Geraldine could write that down as part of her account too? But that would be cheating. In any event, Dawn has a daughter and a grand-daughter. Surely, they'd be worth hanging on for, even if her son-in-law is a pig? Admittedly, Dawn has cancer, but lots of people have beaten cancer, and lots have tried even if they didn't succeed. But she isn't here to worry about Dawn's reasons, she needs to articulate her own. Why is she finding it so difficult, as it's all she's thought about for months? Geraldine is a rational woman – too rational if she is being honest – and she's not fetched up here without weighing the pros and cons like a physics experiment. Reasons for living in this pan, reasons to end it all in the other and by the time she's finished the scales don't lie. (No artificial weightings either – she knows a kilogram of feathers exerts the same gravitational force as a kilogram of lead.) She shakes her head at how stressed she's becoming over this; should she simply write down her list of pros and cons here – maybe that would suffice? Her thoughts stray to Dawn again – it's a good bet, despite Go Gently's urging, she's not bothering to write anything down at all, so why is she getting so uptight about it? Another reflection strikes her: what about that poor man they overheard being discussed this morning? The one with dementia? He wouldn't be able to write down anything, or articulate his wishes at all, which is a whole lot worse. He could be depending on a living will, or preferences expressed earlier in life, leaving it to his son to interpret what he'd said. Maybe the son got to write his account in that case, but there would be no way of knowing whether he'd got it right.

But then it occurs to her that, in a decision of this magnitude, could there ever be a right or a wrong? Who'd be the judge? She twiddles the pen in her hand waiting for inspiration to strike. It's a Parker engraved with her name, presented on her retirement. An insufficient acknowledgement of forty-three years at the chalk face perhaps, but modest, reliable and practical all the same – just like Geraldine, in fact. A well-chosen token in other words. Who's going to write with this pen next? What will they be writing? A shopping list, a birthday card dedication, or perhaps a novel? Maybe, even, a Go Gently valediction like hers. She's leaving all her possessions to charity so she'll never know, but at least, unlike her, it will continue to have a use. She idly flicks away at the button at the top, releasing and retracting the ballpoint in rapid succession. According to the manufacturer this modest implement is guaranteed to last a lifetime. The ink in the cartridge will continue to run and run while the spring has been tested one hundred thousand times, without doubt possessing more bounce and snap than her. There it is again – she's the disposable one, the one that can be thrown away, the one that can easily be replaced.

Then she has the idea she's been searching for. She can write a letter. She can write a letter to herself because, let's face it, there's no one else to send it to. Express and share her innermost thoughts, lay out her reasoning in medium point blue characters on watermarked Basildon Bond. For posterity. For peace of mind. What was it Mark Twain said? 'I didn't have time to write a short letter, so I wrote a long one instead.' She thinks it would be as consoling to receive such a letter as it would to send one. She reaches for another piece of paper, sits up straight in her chair, and clicks her ballpoint.

Dear Geraldine,

I'd start by asking how you are, but I suppose the obvious question is: how am I?

I'm writing from Charon House in Stalybridge, which is a sort of sanatorium. Like that old joke, you don't have to be mad to stay here, but it helps. To be precise, it's also where I will end my life this coming Friday, with an assisted death. I've had to travel to this country to do this as the Irish government would never allow such a thing – they may be right, who knows?

So, I guess you want to know why I'm doing this; what's driven me to this decision? That's fair enough. You also probably want to remind me that life is precious, and give me a stern talking-to about all the good things I still have in my life. I understand.

Where to begin? Well, I'm not terminally ill or anything. Not physically ill either, other than the sort of aches and pains you'd normally associate with being in your seventies. But I am sick at heart, and to me that's as incurable as any terminal illness. It IS a terminal illness. Why do I feel like that? Let me explain. I've never had what might be described as an interesting or an incident-packed life. Sure, I had a steady job, security, and, for a period, even a husband. The latter didn't turn out too well and, if I'm being perfectly frank (and I suppose this is my last chance to be), I'd have to concede some of the blame lay with me. No, make that most of the blame. Kieran ran off with a daft schoolgirl, but looking back, if I'd have been married to me, I'd have probably done the same a lot sooner. Was I a good wife? What's a good wife, anyway? I hated the bedroom stuff, so that didn't help, and even in

74

this letter I'm not prepared to go into all of that. Suffice to say it still makes my flesh crawl to think of it. Nor was I what you'd call very social. I could never see the point of spending endless hours in the pub with the same people – I preferred a good book or my music for company. Kieran said I was a nag. Well, it's true I don't like untidiness or sloppiness so maybe I expressed that too forcibly from time to time. No, I was a nag. I like things being in the right place, I like dependability, and when Kieran left, I felt a sense of relief to be orderly again. Big question: if there had been children, would things have turned out differently? Well, there weren't any, and I'd call that a blessing in retrospect. I never felt maternal – maybe working in a school was part of that – and Kieran gave up on any ambitions in that direction early in the marriage. I wonder why? We co-existed is probably the best description, spending more and more time apart as the years progressed. And I liked it when Kieran went out and left me on my own – it felt liberating. Looking back, we did well to last twenty years before he strayed. I know I've cursed the man since, but realise in writing this that I judged him too harshly. I didn't make him happy, so at least I hope he's happy now. As they say, to err is human, to forgive divine (although I wish he'd have stuck to the legal age limit at the time).

The fallout from all that was embarrassing but it did lead me to a new start in Mayo, and I'd contend that the fifteen years I spent at The Institute of Technology there were probably the best years I had. By then, I knew I didn't need, or want, anybody else in my life. I was totally self-sufficient, could be my own person and, I don't mind saying it here, I was a very good teacher. Then I had to stop. The R-word. Retirement. The aim of most working people is to get to that finishing line, take up gardening, go on a cruise or two, spend more time with the grandkids etc. Not me. When I crossed that line, it was me that was finished off – nothing to get up for, not enough to fill my days and keep me focused. I didn't suddenly discover a new appetite for companionship, and I didn't want to fill my time with trivial pastimes or new discoveries. I had two things in my life, my twin gods as it were: The King of Heaven, and The King, Elvis.

Let's deal with the first one. The Catholic Church. Protestants – not that I know too many of them – often say being a Catholic must be great. You get to wipe the slate clean at confession, and then go out and do the same bad stuff all over again. Or, you lapse and don't bother for years, but then call for the sacraments on your death bed as an insurance policy. 'Just in case.' Well, I do have a confession – it took me seventy years, but one day I woke up to the fact it's all a load of mumbo-jumbo. Ever since I was five years old I had the catechism drummed into me, I lived by the holy sacraments, never missed mass and was in thrall to the parish priest. Duty. Obedience. Devotion. Did I feel spiritually uplifted? No, I felt unworthy. Did I ever express my doubt? Not a bit of it – I wouldn't have dared. Ironically, after retirement, the only thing I did change was to throw myself into the church even more as a way of being useful/having something to do. It was the only lifeboat left. Oh, I was a great organiser and fund raiser, all right, the best. And cleaner, chauffeur and general dogsbody. But being that close to it only made me see the hypocrisy of it all – the empty rhetoric, the feckless priests, the money grubbing, the whole magic show. It was like Toto going behind the curtain in the Wizard of Oz – nothing but a con trick. I wrestled with it, believe me, I did. When did I know? Well, you could say I knocked it on the head in Knock. I organised the annual pilgrimage to the shrine there, sometimes two coaches of parishioners, and three years back, my eyes were opened. Light a candle, say a prayer, buy a mass card, place a petition, make a donation, jump up and down and wave your knickers in the air. No one got cured – no one ever did – the entire delusion was justified as being 'enriching for the soul' and 'a reaffirmation of faith'. I mean, the whole shooting match is built on a will-o'-the-wisp anyway – does anybody really believe the Blessed Virgin Mary just happened to pop into a remote Irish village church for prayers in 1879? That was the trigger. The veil fell away, and from that moment I questioned everything. Virgin birth? Rising from the dead? Miracles? Transubstantiation? The scientist in me took over, I suppose. All I was left with was: 'You must believe'. A big lie to swallow, and I wasn't prepared to be taken for a mug anymore. Of course, true to form, I didn't share this with anyone at the church – I just stopped going, and soon tired of being pestered by the priests, prying and sticking their noses into my business, calling for divine interventions (which never arrived as if to prove a point). As soon as I'd thrown that off, though, I realised something else: the church – religion – is a prop, something to cling to, a raison d'etre. *Now I didn't want or need that reason, what was left? I concluded: not much. No family (well, that's not strictly true as there is my elder sister, Orla, who's been in the convent since she was eighteen. But she gave up on me – gave up on everything – and stopped returning my letters forty years ago. A bride of Christ. I hope she's made a better fist of her marriage than I did mine). No faith then, no friends, no job, no diversions – just a long, empty road reaching into the distance before the indeterminate curtain falls. Ah, I still had one thing though – Elvis. He still sang to me, made me smile and raised my spirits, like he's done ever since I was a teenager listening to Daddy's records. I could return to the music, the films, the concert recordings at any time, and I did – the only person in my life I could trust to never let me down. I'm not daft though – I might love Elvis, but I know that alone isn't a reason for living when everything else has faded to grey, when you're sick of life and have lived as much of it as you'll ever need. Elvis' job now is to help me leave the building, and that's enough for me. I'm lonesome tonight and every night, and there'll be no one crying in the chapel when I've gone. I'm not known for making jokes, and I'm not making one now. This is it. I've made my decision. I don't need to struggle on, face pain, dwindle away. I don't want to eke out the years for the sake of it, this black dog snapping at my heels. I don't want to have to rely on others to care for me (should anybody volunteer for the job). They always said I was a completer-finisher, that I saw a task through. So here we are.*

Writing it all down, do I feel any different now? No. I've not had as full a life as many, but a better one than quite a few. I've had my life, and that's enough. No regrets. I'm ready.

Chapter Ten

Callan Clay prides himself on his attention to detail and his ability to think three steps ahead. Whatever thoughts are occupying Callan's mind, his demeanour never betrays the slightest hint of effort or anxiety – he's Cool Hand Clay, the gunslinging card shark, the man you bet against at your peril. So how come he's on edge, feeling like the walls are closing in? Exactly what concerns have established squatters' rights in the polished state rooms of his mind? Two words: Lawrence Pestel.

Ideally, before hitting the start button on anything, Callan likes to work out every detail and angle, to anticipate – and smooth over – any wrinkles that may arise. He's invested heavily in the Peregrine Pod to drive the next phase of Go Gently's expansion, and he can't afford anything – anything – to go wrong. It's therefore a matter of great consternation that Lawrence has not only rushed forward the timetable for the launch of the pod, he's also lumped an altogether different idea on top of it with his early release prison initiative. Weeks of planning are being compressed into a few days and Callan's nerves are starting to jangle.

Over dinner, even Lady Margaret notices he's jumpy. She insists on pouring him a soothing snifter of bourbon to help him relax. 'This will take the edge off whatever's troubling you. I must say, it's not like you to worry.'

It's true Callan has skilfully cultivated a master of the universe public persona, but deep down he's never left the hog farm, and secretly fears it could all come crashing down at any moment. Even Lady Margaret hasn't tumbled to his well-disguised insecurity. Tonight though, unusually, he weakens and prepares to lighten his load. Taking a sip of his favourite tipple, Heaven's Door, he concedes, 'No, but I'm being rushed and when you don't plan properly, that's when mistakes creep in and bite you on the ass.'

Margaret attempts to rally him. 'But you've done dozens of launches; what could possibly go wrong?'

'How about we could lose the business?'

She laughs off such an implausible suggestion. 'No, seriously, darling.'

Callan has been compiling quite a list over the last day or so. 'The biggest problem is one of mixed messages. The purpose of the Peregrine Pod is to widen the market, to put assisted dying within the pockets of thousands of people for the first time. That was the deal I had with Lawrence, and he was driving it from a wellbeing and a legislation point of view. Perfect. Then he bolts on this altogether different idea of using it to reduce the prison population so it doesn't cost the state as much to run the jails.'

'But surely, that's a good thing, isn't it? It's scandalous how much it costs the taxpayer to keep miscreants in the lap of luxury.'

'Yes, but don't you see, it corrupts the Go Gently proposition. Positioning-wise, our pitch is to offer a five-star assisted death solution at a three-star price, but if the same method is being used to see off the scum of the earth, then it's hardly aspirational to a private client, is it?'

Lady Margaret gets it. 'Oh, I see what you mean. Awks. Have you raised this with Lawrence?'

Callan throws his hands up in the air. 'Fat chance. You know what he's like. It's not the prison reduction initiative that's the issue, it's the use of the pod. They could quite as easily have stuck to using lethal injections on those prisoners but Lawrence sees a shiny new toy and he has to have it. All he can see is the headlines. I sometimes wonder how they manage to govern at all – they never seem to think anything over for longer than sixty seconds.'

Lady Margaret shrugs as if to say 'tell me about it'. Her brother has been on the front benches for twenty-odd years. It's clearly a dilemma, but she may just have a solution. 'How about if you rebrand for the prison work? You know, call it something like the Terminator, describe it as a machine instead of a pod? Then you've got two completely different offerings – an industrial one and a consumer one. It's a simple question of badging.'

Callan is impressed. Of course, the oldest trick in the book: same, but different. 'Genius. That would solve a lot of problems. He'd surely have to go for that.'

Lady Margaret beams, glad to be of assistance, but she's only just getting warmed up. 'He will, and if he doesn't, I'll have to make him. You know he always turns to putty when I'm around.'

'Not as much as Isabella, though,' he laughs.

'Now, now,' she chides. 'Lawrence has been more than useful giving the business a lift, so we must forgive him his wife. He's coming to the launch I take it?'

'Try keeping him away. The Peregrine Pod is all his idea as far as he's concerned. In fact, he's doing a double shift, because we launch the pod on the Friday, and then he's doing his prison early release bit on the Saturday, to make the Sunday press.'

'There's a boy in a hurry. Clever, though. Double headlines too, especially before spring conference.'

Callan doesn't disagree. 'Obviously, I'm up front on the Friday, but not officially involved on the Saturday as the idea is the execution – oh, I'm not supposed to call it that – the despatch takes place at an undisclosed location. It's all part of testing the water to see what sort of reaction comes back.'

'Are they inviting the media to the actual… whatever you want to call it?' says a wide-eyed Lady Margaret.

'A pool feed for that. All sorts of dignitaries from across the spectrum too – prison service, the church, that sort of thing. And me, to make sure they don't cock it up. Friday's my big day – I just need to get that out of the way smoothly, and your rebadging idea could well be the perfect solution for the Saturday.'

'Problem solved then,' purrs Lady Margaret. 'Do you feel better now?'

Callan takes a slug of his bourbon. 'Yes. Lots. But there are a couple of other things bugging the hell out of me right now as well.'

'You are having a bad week, Cal,' she says, surprised her ultra-confident husband has fessed up to one dilemma, never mind alluding to a handful. 'Still, a problem shared is a problem halved, so do tell.'

Callan is unsure how to breach the second area of concern that has beset him. It's a totally new one in his experience, and one he very definitely does not like. He searches for the right

82

SHAKING HANDS WITH ELVIS

words. 'It's... well, I don't know how to describe it really. Insubordination? Mutiny? Or maybe I'm overreacting, and it's more a case of prissiness? I don't know, but it's sure as hell pissed me off.'

'What on earth are you talking about?'

'I briefed the team this afternoon on the launch of the Peregrine. They were surprised it was happening so soon, this Friday, but took it in their stride. We're ready. But I also brought them up to speed on, well, let's call it the Terminator programme now, and what was going to be happening on the Saturday with Lawrence. Obviously, that was total news to them. And – get this – I had two or three people "expressing concerns" as they so delicately put it. Crap like "were we exceeding our remit, was this truly complementary to our core business?" One even asked if it was "ethical". I mean, I don't pay these people for the benefit of their opinions or doubts. In my book that's dissent.'

Lady Margaret is fully aware her husband is unused to having his genius and decision making questioned in any way, and is stern in her advice. 'Well, you're going to have to nip that in the bud, Cal. No room for faint hearts and all that.'

'Oh, I did, and I will, but I've got to be careful, that's all. Can't afford any leaks at this point, but I also can't risk rot from within. I've made it volunteers only for Saturday to calm any ripples, but I've also made a note of who I'm going to sort out as soon as we're past this hurdle.' He bangs his fist on the table to emphasise the fate that awaits agitators.

That's more like my Callan, thinks Lady Margaret. 'You've got everybody tied up in non-disclosure agreements anyway. Nobody would be rash enough to take you on.' She tops up his glass. 'Do you want to make a clean sweep of your concerns then, seeing how well we're making light of them?'

Feeling altogether better for his pep talk, Callan reckons he may as well get this one off his chest as well. 'It's to do with the prisoner guy that's going to croak on Saturday. Lawrence has this idea he should have a few days at Charon before the end. He calls it a reprieve, a respite period, all part of the incentive to get prisoners to sign up. But, to me, that's nuts, 'cos then he's going to mingle with my normal clients and that can't be good for anybody.'

'No. Not at all,' says Lady Margaret firmly. 'It's like keeping raw meat and fish apart in the refrigerator. If you don't, you're asking for trouble.'

'Exactly. I've nothing against this early exit for prisoners scheme – I think it's a good idea – but I'd prefer to keep it totally at arm's length from our core business if we could. Jeez, we could install the pods in prisons and they could do it right there without all this free holiday stuff.'

Lady Margaret nods in agreement. 'Lawrence definitely needs to row back on that. It's like putting sun beds on death row. I remember reading a book by Albert Pierrepoint when I was a girl. He was the official hangman and saw off over five hundred crims. His boast was that it only took him twelve seconds from entering the condemned man's cell to pulling the trapdoor lever. That's the way it should be done – get on with it, no messing and certainly no pampering.' She coils an imaginary rope around her neck and jerks it for emphasis. 'Snap.'

Callan is inclined to agree. 'Besides the cross-contamination issue, the five days he wants for these prisoners isn't even that profitable for us as the state is paying. Granted, if there were enough prisoners signing up for the scheme, we could consider setting up some dedicated locations, prisoners only, very basic.

Honestly, I'd rather just supply the pod to the government to use at source. Then we can stick to our knitting.'

'And that's just what you'll propose in the debrief, darling. Common sense will win out in the end. And, you know Lawrence, he'll change everything after the debrief and claim any improvements as his own, and you'll be only too happy to let him take the credit if it means you get your way in the end. Just be patient and go along with it for now.'

Callan feels a huge weight being lifted from his shoulders. Margaret is right, of course. He's been here many times before, and he needs to continue to play the long game.

Margaret's mind is racing now though. 'So, the prisoner who is up for the chop on Saturday, is he at Charon House now?' Callan nods. 'Just wandering free?'

'Yes – it's crazy. He arrived at teatime – we were only given an hour's notice. Strict instructions from Lawrence he's to be treated like any other client, although we've got him under surveillance.'

'Well, you have everybody under surveillance, don't you? You're probably more secure than the prison he came from,' she quips. 'But is he fraternising?'

Callan shrugs his shoulders. 'Too early to say, but then we're back to the age-old argument of whether it's better for our clients to mix or not. The jury's still out on that one.' This debate has been raging ever since Go Gently took on its first customer. The shrinks continue to advocate integration, while Callan harbours fears social interaction could potentially influence people to change their minds over what they've signed up for. Still, they'd always managed to convince any potential backsliders to stick to the plan – he calls it talking them back on to the ledge. Not to mention some of the other techniques they'd introduced as a 'safeguard'. As Callan often jokes, Charon House is a bit like Hotel California – you can check out whenever you like, but you can never leave.

Lady Margaret's interest is piqued. 'Can you put me down for the Saturday as well as the Friday, Cal? This I just have to see.'

Chapter Eleven

Dawn presumes the man closely inspecting the giant shrub clinging to the rear of Charon House is the gardener. In a way, he is. 'Those white flowers are pretty, aren't they?' she calls out. 'What's this plant called?'

Slightly taken aback, he looks around nervously before answering. 'Er, it's a camellia.'

'Is it just coming out now, then?'

He shakes his head. 'This is the last of them,' he says. 'This particular camellia blooms from autumn onwards, so will be finished soon.'

'Really?' says Dawn, surprised. She thought everything botanical came up in the spring and disappeared, apart from Christmas trees, in the winter. 'Goes to show how much I know. I'm terrible with plants myself – could kill a cactus as soon as look at it.'

How often has he heard that? 'The thing with camellias is that they're not that difficult to look after. Put them in the right location, like this, sheltered from the wind, where there's a lot of shade, and they almost take care of themselves.'

'So that's where I went wrong,' she quips. 'Still, it's a shame they're on their way out.'

'But that's the beauty of nature, isn't it though, the cycles? These flowers will die soon, but will be replaced in time with something equally beautiful.' He visibly relaxes under her warm familiarity. 'Actually, this is a very interesting specimen,' he declares. 'I reckon it must be well over a hundred years old, quite possibly planted in the Victorian era. Imagine that.'

Dawn makes a closer inspection of the glossy foliage. 'How can you tell? It could have been planted yesterday as far as I can make out.'

He takes two steps back and points upwards. 'See that brick line, there? That would have been where the camellia house went up to. They used to build them out of stone and glass because, back then, they thought camellias were fragile and in need of warmth and light. But that structure has long gone and these camellias are still thriving.'

'Improving with age, then,' she says. 'Pity we don't.' Dawn takes in his features as they exchange niceties. Tall, whippet-thin, mid-fifties perhaps, although pale and sad-looking.

He nods, uncertain how to respond. He decides to stick to the flowers. 'The Victorians were mad for camellias. They attached all sorts of symbolism to them. White, here, depicted purity, or the love between a mother and a chid, or mourning if used in funeral flowers. If a white camellia was presented to a man, it was thought to bring luck.'

Dawn spontaneously reaches forward, plucks a bloom, and hands it to him. 'There,' she says, 'have one on me.' He blushes, which, Dawn notices, makes him look altogether better. She giggles at his discomfiture, and then reminds herself not to be such a tease. 'I never realised you gardeners had to know all this stuff. I thought you just had to be handy with a hover mower and not mix up the fertiliser with the weedkiller.'

The man's face drains of colour again. 'Oh, I'm not the gardener,' he stutters. 'I was just looking, that's all.'

Dawn grimaces. 'Oh, sorry. There's me, jumping to the wrong conclusion. I do that all the time.' She looks for a way out of the hole she has dug (without the aid of a trowel). 'So, you're visiting?'

He hesitates. 'Sort of.'

She looks at him quizzically. Surely, he can't be here for the same reason she is? It's so bloody difficult to tell. He's not in one of those coloured suits, so not staff. She glances at his wrist to see if he has a band like hers, but he is wearing a long-sleeved shirt. The thought strikes her people should wear more obvious lapel badges, possibly with the day of departure well to the fore. That would help. But he's not that old, mid-fifties? Is that ashen complexion a sign of some illness he's trying to beat to the finishing line? She feels a tinge of red encircling her cheeks now. 'I'm Dawn, by the way.'

He extends his hand. 'Wayne,' he says, 'although everybody calls me Woody.' He wants to spare Dawn any embarrassment, so continues, 'Actually, you weren't that far off. I used to be a parks gardener, back in London.'

Dawn rallies. 'See, I could tell you had green fingers.' She's reminded of the council gardeners that used to work in her local park when she was a girl. 'Did you like it best when it was sunny, or when it chucked it down so you could hide in the potting shed?'

Wayne's heard that one before, too. 'Come rain or shine, me. I loved it.'

'But you don't do it now?'

Woody hasn't had what could be called a civil – civilian – conversation with anyone for nearly three years. Although he quit the confines of Strangeways yesterday his brain is lingering in his old cell. Talking to Dawn reminds him he needs to catch himself up. 'No. I had to give it up.'

Dawn waits for him to continue, and there is an awkward pause between her not wanting to put her foot in it again, and him wondering how much information he should be volunteering. He breaks first. 'On the grounds of ill-health. Photophobia. A gardener's worst nightmare.'

'Photo…wotsit?' queries Dawn. It's a new one on her.

'Sensitivity to light, basically. Bright light – sunlight – gives me blinding headaches. The doctor said it was the other way round really – I was suffering from migraines and they triggered the light sensitivity, but it's all the same in the end. Stay out of the light and deal with it.'

'That sounds terrible,' says Dawn, sympathetically. 'Couldn't they do anything for it?'

Woody shrugs. 'You know how it is these days. The council got rid of me, I couldn't afford the anti-inflammatories or antibiotics, so all I could do was become pretty much nocturnal after that.'

'Like Batman. Or Dracula,' says Dawn before she can stop herself.

Woody laughs. He's not laughed in years and it's a strange sensation. 'Oh definitely. Batman Monday to Wednesday, Dracula at weekends, and Thursdays off.'

Now it's Dawn's turn to chuckle. She's enjoying their conversation but then it strikes her again it's an odd time to be making new acquaintances. A shiver runs down her spine and suddenly she's struggling for words. 'Right, well, I'd better be off. Nice to meet you.' And with that, she dashes inside the hall, leaving Woody to the camellias.

Ex-prisoner A1801MB seeks out a bench in the shadiest part of the garden, and tries to blend in with the surroundings. He's used to keeping his head down. The conversation with Dawn was unexpected, but delightful at the same time. It made him feel normal, almost human again, and that hadn't happened in a long, long time. Woody still can't get used to not being under lock and key, or under observation every minute of the day. He expected to be locked up and under surveillance here, but he's not even been electronically tagged. He's asked what the rules are for the next few days, but nobody appears to know. He's been told to make the most of his time, but not how to achieve that. Unsurprisingly, he's totally unaware of the politics that have preceded – and accelerated – his arrival at Charon House; this has been as much a blur for the government as it is for him. Yesterday morning this scheme was in embryonic form until Lawrence Pestel, with scant disregard for departmental boundaries, decided it was happening. Woody is the dry run, the bench test – he's the lab rat. It's no wonder details are sparse because they're making it up as they go along – not that they'd ever admit to that. Woody couldn't begin to guess at the intense arguments that have been raging over his final days. It was Pestel's idea to remove Woody's prisoner status and throw in the 'at leisure' staycation as an interlude between prison and the 'final journey', in his view part of the incentive for prisoners to sign up. Requital, on the other hand, contend that cons should be treated as dyed-in-the-wool villains and flight risks, not as hotel guests, and argue any prisoner signing up should be taken straight from the cells to final checkout. As if they needed any more reason to resent 'Grammar', they have also kicked off over his insistence on using an unproven despatch method over tried and tested lethal injection. They've been overruled for now, but everything could change.

All Woody knows is that when he'd been tacitly sounded out as a potential candidate – *what if, would he ever consider, if such a scheme existed etc* – a few months back, he never thought anything would come of it. Then, suddenly, it's happening, and it's happening this week. As he sits here, it's the first time since he left Strangeways he's had time to properly ponder what he's signed up for. This is for real, and it certainly feels different thinking about it overlooking the well-managed gardens of Charon House than it did staring at his green and cream cell wall. Is he getting cold feet? The first question is, could he change his mind now even if he wanted to? He's not saying he wants to, but he knows how the authorities work. He was told he could reverse his decision at any time when they explained it to him, but if his brief life as a con has taught him anything, it's never to trust what the officials say. The solicitor they assigned him couldn't wait to get him to put pen to paper – Woody wondered whose side he was on. But still, he signed, and he knows the reasons why. The last few years have been a disaster, he's hit rock bottom, and he has nothing ahead of him but more misery and woe.

How has it come to this? Well, for one thing, his age. Today is Woody's sixtieth birthday, a significant milestone for anybody but, in his case, also the age that qualifies him to become a human guinea pig, the pin-up boy, for the government. Except his age wouldn't have come into it if he hadn't been banged up for such a long stretch in the first place. Would his ex-wife and two children remember it's his birthday today? He didn't hold out much hope. He casts his mind back to his fiftieth birthday – back then the way things subsequently unfolded would have been unimaginable except in some sort of suburban horror tale on Channel 5. It had been a Sunday and they'd gone to the cinema to see the latest James Bond movie. After they got home, they argued. The next month Anita told him she'd met someone else. Two months later he left the family home. Six months later he lost his job due to the photophobia that suddenly afflicted him. One year later he was living in a crappy bedsit, watching TV all day, and delivering pizzas at night. If he thought that was bad, it was nothing on what was to follow. Prison. Ten years. He wasn't a criminal, only a no-mark, the fall guy. It made his stomach lurch to even think about the court case. As for prison itself, he'd had no chance: bullied and brutalised from the outset. The screws were as bad as the inmate bosses. Fear and despair were his constant companions; he couldn't see how he would survive. He thought of ending it many times only he didn't have the guts. But then they offered him this. What would anybody else do in his position? They'd take it too. And at least, this way, he could leave his daughters some money, hopefully help them on their way to a better life than he'd managed. No, he's not going back to prison.

He stirs himself and decides to explore the gardens. No point in moping; what will be, will be. It would interest Lawrence Pestel to know that, having made up his mind to pop his clogs, Woody would now prefer to get on with it rather than indulging himself with a mini-break. Not that he was given the option, but the next few days are only going to press heavier than the ones he's already had to endure. He understands he should be making the most of it, raging against the dying of the light, but it's like the condemned man's last meal: it sounds perfectly reasonable and attractive in theory but how many are ever eaten? After all, it's difficult to have an appetite for a multicourse feast when you know what's coming up for dessert. Well, staying here is that times a thousand.

He's attracted to a burst of colour in the far border and goes to investigate. Daffodils, an explosion of whites, oranges and yellows. Beautiful, cheering, and relatively easy to maintain. Perennials that, unlike him, thrive in the sun. Well, he's not going to need to worry about that for much longer. Neither sun, nor fortune, has shone on him for ten years – all he's known is shade.

Chapter Twelve

There is a gentle rap on the door and Geraldine admits to her room the same young woman who conducted the induction session on arrival. Same smart black blazer, matching skirt and crisp white blouse, same professional and attentive manner.

'And how are you finding Poppy?' she asks pleasantly of the accommodation.

'It's very nice,' says Geraldine. 'Lovely views.'

'Now, if it's all right with you, I want to take you through the plan for Friday, make sure that everything is just so for you.' She takes two documents from her leather folder and hands one to the client. 'You're obviously a big fan of Elvis.' Geraldine nods. 'Well, that goes a long way to explaining your preferences. We've found the Love Me Tender package to be very popular since we launched it and it's marvellous that you've gone for the deluxe option.'

Geraldine remains impassive. It's hard to remember everything she picked at the time, it being a couple of months back. It puts her in mind of the annual staff Christmas party where nobody could remember if they'd ordered the turkey or the beef.

'Let's start with the music, shall we? "Are You Lonesome Tonight", correct? Very poignant. And you've opted to have it sung live by our Elvis tribute artist, channelling the *'68 Comeback Special* era. Oh, he's marvellous. I'm sure you won't be disappointed.' They being girls together, she adds, 'And he suits black leather very well, I must say.'

Geraldine shifts uncomfortably. It's one thing ticking boxes online, but it feels awkward discussing her choices in the flesh. She'd be altogether more comfortable with a little less conversation.

'Attire next. You'll be wearing your favourite blue silk dress and emerald pendant necklace. Oh, and blue suede high heels. A lovely twist – I like that. You did remember to pack everything?'

Geraldine steals a look towards the wardrobe where her special outfit is hanging. She's not forgotten anything.

'Food next. You've gone for the Fool's Gold for your special meal, so I just wanted to check a couple of things with you on that. First, you're not a vegetarian are you, because it does contain bacon.' Nope. 'Now, we do make the actual sandwich much smaller than the original as we find some clients can be overfaced. One alternative – still on theme, of course – is the fried peanut-butter and banana sandwich that Elvis loved. It's slightly more manageable. Would that be preferable, do you think? There's still time to change it, kitchen is very flexible.'

Geraldine automatically starts to calculate the calorie intake of the competing snacks until a voice in her head reminds her it doesn't really matter either way. 'I'll stick with the Fool's Gold, thank you.'

'Now, the highlight. Have you ever used a gun before?' Geraldine admits such an experience has eluded her until now. 'Well, nothing to worry about as we will have a firearms expert on hand to show you what to do, and it's all perfectly safe. You'll be using a silver-plated Colt .45 automatic pistol, exactly like the one Elvis owned. So many of our clients tell us it's a deeply cathartic experience to shoot a bullet at the TV and see it exploding.'

Geraldine reddens on recalling she's agreed to – and paid a large amount of money for – these supplementary components to her package. One of those 'it seemed a good idea at the time' moments. Well, she'd paid for it, so she may as well have it.

'And lastly on the Love Me Tender package, I'm very pleased to tell you that I'll be your chaperone on Friday. Your Priscilla you could say. I was due to be off that day, but I've managed to swap shifts to be with you.'

When Geraldine had come to the part on the online form asking to name a friend or family member who might be in attendance, it had only gone to underline her decision for signing up in the first place. She could think of no one whose name she could put down, which is why, spending money like a drunken sailor, she'd ticked the box for Go Gently to provide an experienced escort to wave her off into the blue. (Like the opposite of a birth-partner she'd thought at the time.) She'd not reckoned on it being a 'Priscilla' (who she knew for a fact had been divorced from Elvis for four years at the time of his passing) but wasn't going to start arguing the toss now.

The remainder of the meeting is taken up with what 'Priscilla' describes as 'the boring bits', which she adroitly gets out of the way as quickly as possible. The times at which all of this will take place (*we pride ourselves on running to schedule to avoid undue anxiety*). Confirmation of the client's consent (*sign here and here*). The order in which the barbiturate package will be administered and how long it will take (*all perfectly painless*). Geraldine would be the first to admit she's a bit of a hard-headed woman but even she finds the exchange soulless and a tad perfunctory. It's like signing up for a new kitchen or double glazing without having to worry about the ten-year guarantee.

The meeting concluded, Geraldine is left to contemplate her selections. She frets that the Love Me Tender package may be a little bit over the top. No, it is over the top. Is she trivialising death by opting for such a – let's be diplomatic and call it 'theatrical' – way to end her life? Is she, in fact, making a mockery of her entire life by bringing the curtain down on it, almost literally, in Las Vegas style (minus the *Viva!*)? What would Dawn say if she knew? From what Dawn has mentioned, it appears she's going for the budget package. A no-frills medical procedure probably, in and out in ten minutes. It's consumerism gone mad; Dawn travelling steerage while she's in first-class. And what does it matter if, like on the Titanic, they both hit the iceberg five days into the voyage? No, that's not a suitable analogy, because in the movie Jack froze to death while Rose was rescued and lived to be a hundred. Is she a snob, a fraud, a hypocrite for choosing this way out? It's not like she's showing off; she's not even told anyone about it. It's a private decision, that's what it comes down to, and it's inevitable some people will have worse deaths than others (though choice doesn't normally come into it). She has always loved Elvis, he's been about the only constant in her life, so why not have this one last indulgence if she can?

She'd noticed how 'Priscilla' had skated over the final consent section, ticking the 'depression' and 'tired of life' boxes as casually as if making out a breakfast order. Maybe her form would be hung on the door handle overnight for all to see. But it's getting close now, and she had always figured this would be where buyer's remorse might strike. But no sign of that, yet, at least. She's Captain Smith, full steam ahead. She pulls open the desk drawer and extracts the letter she wrote to herself. She doesn't need to read it because she knows every word inscribed there. This is all she needs to remind her of why she's here, why she's going through with it.

A thought occurs to her – if Dawn was having the Love Me Tender, it's a good bet she'd have "Return to Sender" as her choice of final song.

As if Callan didn't have enough on his plate already, today is Go Gently's monthly management meeting. Under the circumstances he could postpone it, but that would only give his team a free pass to laze around for the next four weeks. He doesn't pay people to skive – he's a man who likes to keep the pressure on.

They start with the metrics, the figures relating to the past month and the year to date. The accountant proudly announces increased client numbers and record sales as if these achievements had something to do with him. Callan doesn't go as far as thanking or praising any of his team for these uplifts, but instead poses the central question: 'Good, but how can we improve on this?'

One brave soul has the temerity to offer a contrary view. 'The figures may be good, but we're stretched to breaking point in every department. The rivets are popping, and if we don't invest in new staff and training PDQ the whole thing is going to blow.' A couple of colleagues nod in agreement while avoiding eye contact with their boss.

Bloody ingrates, thinks Callan. 'In that case,' he says, 'perhaps we could take the staffing update now in response to that point?'

The HR manager is thrust centre stage considerably earlier in proceedings than normal and scrambles for her notes. Finally, she collects herself: 'We're doing our best to recruit, as you know, but face two major obstacles. First, we're churning staff at an unprecedented rate, while local recruitment has fallen off a cliff. It's like trying to fill a bucket with a hole in it – we never seem to catch up.'

These are mere excuses in Callan's view. 'Use more licensed guest workers to take up the slack in that case. There's no shortage of those, and they're cheap.'

They all look to HR to speak on their behalf regarding that suggestion. 'The thing there, Callan, is, well we're getting quite a lot of pushback from the various departmental heads over guest workers, because, how shall I put this...?'

'Because they're about as much use as a chocolate teapot,' ventures a gruff voice from the lower end of the table.

HR clears her throat before proceeding. 'It is true that we find the general aptitude, standard of work, motivation and communication skills of our guest workers tend to fall outwith expected parameters.'

'Well, train them better,' suggests Callan. 'It's simple enough.'

HR pulls a document from the pile in front of her, the better to illustrate her point. 'I've conducted an internal study on our training effectiveness, and the findings are revealing. Fifty per cent of guest workers don't last a month, which actually makes it uneconomical to train them in the first place.'

'Why are we struggling to recruit locally?' Callan wants to know.

'Pay and conditions,' interjects the gruff voice once more. 'They can get more elsewhere, and word has got around that Charon House isn't a very pleasant place to work.'

'They weren't so picky when we first opened, were they?' Callan protests.

'I think part of the problem is we've got competition now,' says HR. 'The new commercial waste incinerator plant in town is hiring scores of locals, and they pay way above our rates.' (So, it's true – the local inhabitants of Stalybridge now have two ways of earning cash for ash, and they are voting with their feet.)

Callan makes a mental note to ask Lawrence to get the plant closed down on environmental grounds and gives the team his considered advice, 'Well, sort it. That's what you're paid for.'

'Can I say something?' asks Mr Gruff, who it turns out is the head of operations. 'While we're trying to catch up, wouldn't it make sense to slow down on the sales and marketing side? Give us a little bit of time to fine tune; allow us to control the throughput more efficiently?'

'Are you serious?' comes the incredulous retort from the fashionably dressed young woman on his right. 'The whole point of marketing is to generate sales, which is a lot bloody harder than processing orders once we've dropped them in your lap.'

Callan couldn't agree more. 'Absolutely. The most difficult job in the world is getting people to sign on the dotted line and to part with their money. We can't just turn the tap on and off to match the weeks you've got a few people off sick.'

But Gruff isn't finished. 'Profitable sales, yes, but what about all the Clean Bill cases we're getting from the government? They pay peanuts and the margins just aren't there. Have we analysed if they're even worth doing?'

The accountant does, in fact, have in-depth data on how much Go Gently makes on each contract generated via Lawrence Pestel's department but, being a sensible man, chooses not to offer it to the meeting at this juncture as it will only prove Mr Gruff right.

'And that leads on to the next thing,' continues Gruff, who is in the right place for fulfilling a death wish. 'The Peregrine. Quick and easy, cheap. I get it – great. Saves money on costly barbiturates – fantastic. But won't we just end up swamping ourselves with even more low-margin budget-travellers? We could end up doubling our workload and losing money at the same time.'

Callan is unused to having his business acumen questioned in such a way. 'You've clearly never come across the term "loss leader", have you? It also appears you underestimate the importance of being first to market and establishing brand leadership. How about, instead of telling us what won't work, coming up with something that will?'

Gruff is in no mood to back down. 'When I came up with organ harvesting, you ignored it. We have a ready-made supply and no end of willing buyers – we could make a fortune.'

Callan has, in fact, already discussed this idea with Lawrence, and they agree it's a winner, a service they can float discretely to clients once Peregrine is up and running. He's put slightly on the defensive. 'Yes, but as you will recall, your initial proposal entailed not mentioning the removal of said organs to either the client or their families. At least I've not forgotten the strict ethical code by which we are bound.'

The head of operations' creativity is running wild and he doesn't mind putting it out there. 'OK. The Peregrine. It doesn't help you can only do one client at a time. Can I ask if there are any plans for a bigger, mass version? That would help, logistically speaking.'

There is a sharp intake of breath around the table, until Miss Marketing pipes up, 'You mean like a gas chamber?'

Gruff takes that in for a second before retracting his suggestion. 'Maybe not then.'

A fresh voice, that of the science officer, joins the discussion. 'On the subject of ethics, can I ask if the prison launch is still going ahead on Saturday? No last-minute U-turns from the government?'

'No,' says Callan. 'Why would there be?' (Gruff sniggers aloud at this response before quickly covering his mouth with his hand.)

'Because,' says the scientist, 'to my knowledge, this idea hasn't been fully tested, is morally questionable and could well lead to a public backlash, a backlash that could spell trouble for Go Gently.'

All eyes turn expectantly towards Callan – it's a fair point. However, the question – or is it more accurate to call it an observation? – causes Callan to all but detonate in anger. 'When I want advice from you lot on how to grow my business, I'll ask for it.' (A statement that rather contradicts the claim on the company website that he's a 'natural team player'.) He's into his stride now: 'Are you mice or men? We stand at the forefront of history and all you can come up with is a trivial concern over what a few bleeding hearts might think? Are you suggesting the government doesn't know, or doesn't understand, what people want? Maybe you'd like me to tell them to take this opportunity to a competitor? I can, you know, but then I'd have to sack the lot of you because we wouldn't have a business left to pay anybody.'

He shakes his head in frustration. They don't know it, but the point about low profit margins is closer than they think, and everything is now riding on the Peregrine. As soon as we get past the weekend, he thinks, I need to do some heavy surgery on this senior team. Lady Margaret has often said it's a failing of his that he's too soft on his staff; well, next time there will be no more Mr Nice Guy.

Chapter Thirteen

Adil gently steers Jeffrey towards the residents' dining room tucked away off reception. He could have called for room service for his charge, but that would be a cop-out. Stimulation and movement are the best two things in a situation like this – for both carer and cared-for. It's taken half an hour to make the short journey from Jeffrey's room. They've stopped to take in all the diversions along the way – every picture frame, ornament and view has been pointed out by Adil for Jeffrey's delight and wonder. As they enter the small, four-table dining space there is only one other occupant. Adil is aiming for an empty table until the lady already seated politely moves along to free up the two end chairs. He can't interpret whether her gesture is a deliberate or unconscious invitation for company, but not wishing to appear rude, takes up the seats.

'It's Adil, isn't it? Hello,' says Geraldine, who remembers the grinning and stuttering helper from her arrival. She was always good with faces and names.

He smiles and nods back at Geraldine saying only, 'This is Jeffrey.'

Jeffrey no sooner has his feet under the table than he turns to her and says, 'Have you seen Rosemary? She said she was only popping out for a minute.' No, she's not seen Rosemary. By the time Jeffrey has repeated the same question five times, and declared he never says no to a cuppa, she recognises the signs. This is the gentleman she and Dawn overheard being talked about. She almost winks at Adil to let him know she understands the situation.

Adil peruses the menu as Jeffrey continues to chatter to no one in particular. 'Ooh, fish and chips,' he coos. 'Do you like fish and chips, Jeffrey?' He's met with a firm shake of the head. 'OK, then. How about shepherd's pie? That's tasty.' Jeffrey pulls a face. 'You could have lasagne if you like. We could go all-Italian.'

'Fish and chips,' decides Jeffrey. 'I like fish and chips.'

Geraldine smiles benignly as Adil checks his charge's preference a few more times before finally placing the order. 'You handled that very well,' she whispers. 'I used to volunteer at my church and we had a few old dears in the same boat. It's very sad, isn't it?'

Adil is slightly taken aback to hear one aged client express sympathy with another when, by the end of the week, they will be as level-pegging as it gets. She mentioned church, so this must be a Christian thing? Since he's been working at Charon House, he's noticed that the clientele is predominantly white. Perhaps that's not such a big surprise, as his faith, for example, would never allow an action to end your own life. On further study, he realised there were finer distinctions at play, for example, you didn't spot many practising Catholics signing up. If Adil could have gained access to the company's filing cabinets – and oh, how Sacrosanct would love that – he'd find Go Gently's customer base was essentially split into two distinct groups: Anglicans and the godless. 'Yes,' he replies to Geraldine's sentiment, 'but on the other hand, he doesn't have a care in the world. That's a blessing of sorts.'

'It is, surely,' says Geraldine. A puzzled look crosses her face. 'I must say, your English is a lot better than I'd given you credit for. I hope you don't mind me saying so.'

Shit, thinks Adil, (whose extensive command of profanities would no doubt confound Geraldine even more). It's not like he can play dumb while he's looking after Jeffrey. 'It's just that I'm not always confident in my conversation, especially with guests,' he counters.

'But it's not your native tongue?' she says, her question falling, she realises on launching it, midway between casual racism and downright nosiness.

'No. I'm from Syria originally.'

'Well, you speak the language better than most of the locals,' she concedes. 'And how long have you worked here?'

Adil's heart sinks. This is exactly what he's been warned against by both his employer and Sacrosanct: talking to clients, establishing any kind of bond. It brings his fear at being discovered bubbling to the surface. Frankly, he's sick of it, having to mask his natural congeniality under a cloak of ignorance. He hates working here. He doesn't want to be here. He's caught in a vice, squeezed between his bullying employers and his activist controllers with their competing demands and strictures. None of them gives a damn about him. All he wanted to do was help, but instead he finds himself at the bottom of a deep, dark pit, a reluctant enabler of euthanasia. He's at cracking point – he needs to get out.

'Not long,' he concedes.

Now Geraldine stalls, at the realisation that further platitudes along the lines of 'Do you enjoy your work?' and 'Still, you must meet lots of people,' would be misplaced. What *do* you say to someone like Adil who, quite literally, is in the ultimate dead-end job? She swerves away from trouble with a hollow, 'Well, you seem very good at it.'

Adil is viewing Geraldine with a similar degree of curiosity. She seems perfectly nice, normal, and doesn't seem to be suffering from any obvious physical ailment, yet to his certain knowledge she's signed up to join the choir invisible in two days' time. (Another plus for Adil on the English language front: his knowledge of euphemisms for death has soared since joining Go Gently thanks to the staff's shop-floor humour.) He can't understand it. Why would she want to end it all? What's compelling her to take this ultimate, drastic step? How has she managed to reconcile herself to a self-inflicted fate? It's a mystery, one that he will never understand.

His thoughts are interrupted as Jeffrey perks up and asks Geraldine, once again, if she's seen Rosemary. She still hasn't, but avoids answering directly and changes the subject instead. 'My name is Geraldine. Ger-al-dine. That's a lovely shirt you're wearing, Jeffrey. I like the colour. It's a very nice blue, just like the sky.'

Jeffrey studies his shirt as if searching for the lost chord, before confirming, 'Blue.' He points upwards... 'Like the sky.'

The exchange continues along similar lines for a minute or two until the fish and chips are served, at which point they can all focus on the battered cod and thick-cut chips. 'I like a nice piece of haddock,' Jeffrey declares as Adil helps to tuck in his napkin. They don't bother to correct him (it's hard to tell the fish apart at the best of times). He pulls the plate in close, and stabs at a chip – no assistance required. Adil passes the salt and vinegar across only for Jeffrey to recoil in horror, as if he's been handed a fizzing bomb. 'No salt,' he cries. Shaking his head with increasing agitation, he repeats his mantra as if warding off an evil spirit: 'No salt. No salt.' Adil whips the offending condiments away, and soothes the diner by diverting his attention towards the apple pie and custard that awaits him when he's finished.

Geraldine is as surprised as Adil at Jeffrey's aversion to sodium chloride, and feels a wave of sadness sweeping over her. Rosemary was obviously a stickler for healthy eating – since Geraldine guesses she won't be turning up again, such fastidiousness doesn't appear to have done her any good. Her heart goes out to Jeffrey. Poor man, lost his wife, lost his wits, but still apparently ruled by a list of inviolate dos and don'ts. She wonders how and when his world came tumbling down. He has a pleasant face, he's well-dressed, and it's apparent, even behind the current smokescreen, that he's well-spoken and polite. She conjectures he would have had a good job, provided for his family, been a good husband. He has a few years on her, but he's not in the worst of shape physically – Rosemary obviously maintained a hard line in the kitchen. And now? He's heading for an appointment with Doctor Barbiturate, like she is, but somehow it feels different. Would Jeffrey be meeting up with Rosemary again in the great health food store in the sky? Geraldine doubts it. All this, and he's worried about salt on his fish and chips? If only he knew. She lightly places her hand on his arm, and says: 'You treat yourself, Jeffrey. Fish and chips don't taste the same without salt and vinegar. We won't tell anyone, will we, Adil? It's our little secret.'

Jeffrey considers this concession to his tastebuds for a moment, then reaches for the salt. He shakes the cellar vigorously, abruptly upends it, and continues to shower his meal with a white crystal coating until an alarmed Adil intervenes with, 'I think that's enough now, Jeffrey.'

Geraldine squirms. They've ruined his meal. Jeffrey, on the other hand, takes his knife and fork, shovels a large piece of cod into his mouth and leans back, his eyes closed in pure ecstasy. 'Lovely,' he purrs, and proceeds to polish off the lot in double-quick time.

Chapter Fourteen

Adil is on a late shift tonight. Two hours after he's deposited Jeffrey back in his room, he makes his way over to Harmony Wing (known colloquially to the staff as 'The Business End'). It's the first time he's been allocated duties in this area and he's apprehensive. His brief tonight is to cover for an absent workmate and oversee the loading. His heart sinks as his manager outlines the simple task 'that's impossible to cock up'. It annoys him that his first thought is he may be able to gather fresh information for Sacrosanct given he's venturing into new parts of the building; after all, he's just told himself he's had enough and has to get out of this hellhole as soon as he can. Maybe nothing to do with barbiturates, but anything that may earn him a passage out of here would suffice. Perhaps this could be his swansong.

His upgraded pass allows him access deep into the interior of the building and he finds the supervisor he's to report to. He is told to stand at the loading bay at the rear of the building and wait. Soon, a white van appears out of the darkness and approaches. He notices the name on the side: Wash 'n' Go Laundry (*We Clean up After You!*). It's soon followed by another van. Then a third. Then a fourth. The roller shutter above the bay inches up slowly to reveal a stack of uniform, rectangular, cardboard boxes. He realises with a start he's not looking at laundry baskets. They're coffins.

Now the supervisor explains his duty – tick the coffins off the list as they are loaded, and account for each one. The day's reckoning is neatly typed out on two sides of A4, sixteen names in total, in alphabetical order. The drivers work together to load four coffins apiece into the vans as Adil crosschecks the name tag on each one and ticks it off against his manifest. Adil has a glazed expression on his face as he performs this baleful duty, totally ignored by the drivers who josh each other about City and United's varied fortunes. As he wields his pen, he cannot help but notice the dates of birth recorded against each name and mentally calculates the ages of each occupant: *Seventy-five. Sixty-six. Forty-four. Eighteen.* Two names jump out: Marshall and Marshall. On closer inspection of the respective tags, it dawns on him this is a married couple who have taken advantage of the Go Gently couple's discount. United in death, if newly parted into two separate coffins now being loaded into different vans. He has a lump in his throat as he consigns each one to their final rinse. Before long, the coffins are all loaded, the drivers bang the rear doors shut and drive out in the same order they arrived, leaving Adil to his clipboard and his thoughts.

'What time do you finish?' It's the supervisor, stirring Adil from his reverie.

'Midnight,' replies Adil, who is staying over in the dorms tonight.

The super looks at his watch, and shrugs. 'A quick load tonight. No point in going back – they'll only find you something else to do. Grab a drink and take it easy.'

Adil follows him inside as the roller shutter descends. Two battered armchairs and a small table with a kettle and tea things are set up in the corner, a nice little hidey-hole. Adil's head is swimming with regret at the addition of this new role to his CV, that of tallyman in a charnel house.

His new mate brews up and takes a seat next to Adil. 'First time backstage, then?' Adil nods. 'It's a lot easier this side. We don't get as many complaints from the customers.' He cackles. 'Not like Cassius and his lot, there's a different matter.'

'Cassius?'

'You're not a boxing fan I take it. Clay. Callan Clay. Nothing's ever right for him.'

'Oh,' says Adil, not getting the reference, but understanding Doctor Clay was as much a stickler for standards back here as he was front of house.

'It's been all go this week, I can tell you. Cassius has been here every day, keeping everyone on their toes. Had that smarmy government minister in, too. We'll be glad once it's done – he might leave us alone then.'

Hardly able to contain himself, Adil remembers why he's been parachuted into Charon House. Eyes and ears. This is the moment. Don't screw it up. 'What's being done?' he says as casually as he can.

'Some big launch or other. Everybody on standby Friday and Saturday, but it's ruffled a few feathers, I know that.'

'What are they launching?' asks Adil, his excitement mounting.

The supervisor takes a slurp of his tea, unsure how much information to divulge, but like most gossips is only building up to his reveal. 'A death machine,' he says conspiratorially, enjoying the shocked expression on Adil's face as he absorbs the news. 'Some fancy way of bumping people off, apparently. That's what I'd heard anyway.'

'What's wrong with the current method?' enquires Adil, genuinely baffled as to why a new solution might be needed.

'Well,' says the supervisor, warming to his role of expert summariser, 'cost, for a start. They say he's getting stung on the price of drugs, so he's come up with a different way of doing away with people. Something that's still attractive to the punters, but quick and cheap as chips.'

Fighting the revulsion he's experiencing, Adil presses on. 'How does this death machine work?'

'God knows. We'll have to wait for the launch, but it's not gone down well with some of the techs. There's been mutterings over "ethics" – there's even been a couple of walk-outs.' The supervisor delivers this last observation with scornful relish before adding, 'He likes to sail close to the wind, does Cassius, but most people know that when they join.'

The disclosures hit Adil like a thunderbolt. Just as he has decided his presence here is a fruitless mission, it appears he has struck gold – *they say he's getting stung on the price of drugs.* Hence cancelling the barbiturates order. Such information, surely, will be of vital use to Doctors Ruth and Andy and, more importantly, herald his own release from this burdensome responsibility. But replacing the barbiturates with what, exactly?

How far can he push it? 'Have you seen it, this death machine? It sounds mad.'

The supervisor shakes his head. 'Not me. Authorised access only down there.'

He must ask, so he does, as innocently as he can. 'Down where?'

The supervisor laughs. 'Why, are you thinking of going down for a look? I wouldn't get too close if I were you, they might think you're a customer.' Such wit. 'No, it's down in Zone Z – or Zone *ZZZZ* as we call it.' He erupts in a coughing fit at his little joke. 'You'll just have to wait like everybody else to see it. Won't be long now.'

As Adil takes his leave to head back to the dorms, his head is spinning. Is this the best science can come up with – a new, improved way of killing people more quickly and at lower cost? Obviously, he must report this to Sacrosanct. But report what, and how? It's just a rumour, casually tossed aside by a co-worker. If he really wants to find out more, he'll have to find Zone Z and get inside, establish some facts. Well, that's way beyond his remit and there is no guarantee he'd find anything either, other than himself in deep, deep water. For a start, he could be deported if he was discovered. Who was he kidding? He could be deported – or worse – now if they stumbled on the truth about him. It occurs to him he'd very much like to leave Charon House by the front door rather than the back. A familiar emotion sweeps over him, one he's experienced many times in his relatively short life: terror. Fear of the unknown, fear of punishment, fear at being completely at the mercy of others. As he tramps aimlessly through the darkened corridors he wrestles with the conflict within. It's fight or flight time, but which one? Coming to a set of double doors blocking his way, he realises he is completely lost. He's been wandering aimlessly, with little sense of direction, and missed the turning that would have led him back to the dormitories. The doors stand before him, defying him to try his luck. He fingers the new pass around his neck and makes a deal with himself: *if these open...* Gingerly, he swipes the card across the wall-mounted key pad and is startled

SHAKING HANDS WITH ELVIS

as a loud buzz is followed by a click as the lock retracts. Pushing through, he takes in the large sign hanging from the ceiling: Phlebotomy, turn right. Pharmacy, turn left. Zone Z straight on. He was hoping for heads and landed tails. His instinct is to turn back, to get as far away from here as possible, but he's placed his bet now and must see the race out. If he can verify, add any detail at all, to what he's just heard, he will have done his tour of duty and earned his discharge, and an honourable one at that. From here, there is only one direction he can take.

Dawn is getting ready for bed when a wave of pain sweeps over her. She slumps to the vanity stool and stares at her ashen reflection in the dressing table mirror. 'What a mess,' she pronounces. Kimberley has been arguing with her mother for months now over her aversion to potent painkilling drugs. It's one thing to refuse surgery, but why suffer unnecessarily when it's avoidable? At first, gritted teeth, over-the-counter medication and a Yorkshire determination helped to mask the pain, or at least make it endurable, but there's little doubt it's getting worse by the day. 'Stubborn old mule,' Dawn confides to her twin image. 'At least we won't have to worry about it after Friday.'

She picks up the framed photograph of Mark from the bedside cabinet, and pulls herself together. He wouldn't like to see her struggling. 'Well, love, not a pretty sight tonight, eh?' she says to his smiling face. 'What was it you used to say? Pretend it doesn't hurt and then it won't. Well, I have news for you, darling: it bloody well does.'

A lot has changed in the eight years since Mark passed away. For years he'd gobble down whatever opioids they threw at him for his hip, the cheaper alternative to expensive surgery according to his employer's insurance company. By the time they accepted surgery was unavoidable, he was hooked: difficulty with his breathing, stomach ulcers, internal bleeding – the lot. Dawn had worried about how they'd wean him off the pills following the operation, but then they managed to kill him anyway. Problem solved! 'I know you think I'm a silly bugger,' she tells him, 'but one of us had to go cold turkey.' Even if Dawn could have afforded to buy strong analgesics, never mind surgery for her cancer, it would have taken every penny she and Mark had ever earned. No insurance, no national health scheme these days. No guarantees. She thinks back to her own mother's death – she'd been on palliative care, and spent the last few weeks of her life in a hospice, dwindling away, but at least not in pain, or so they said. No, the pain was all theirs, watching her fade away like a portrait left in direct sunlight. But that was twenty years ago, no chance of that now unless you had money to burn. Mark hated the government for all the cut-backs they'd imposed on normal people's lives, but what would he have made of events since he passed away? He used to say, 'We'll get rid of this lot at the next election', but there was no chance of that now. Not ever. 'You got out at the right time, love,' she tells him. *As I am,* she thinks.

What would Mark say to her if he was here now? If he *knew*? Mark loved life, and so did Dawn, but what was the alternative, really? There was a lot to be said for living a long and healthy – a long and wealthy – life, but what about people like her? She was going to die anyway, so she might as well pass jail and go straight to Go. Lots of other people were. It was the easy option all round. They'd made it so simple; it was almost an obligation to go along with it. She feels his eyes boring into her. 'You're in no position to lecture, so don't start,' she chides. 'You'd laugh at the paperwork, though. I think we had to sign more forms when we got Milo from the cat's home. Basically, three questions: *do you consent to an assisted death?* Tick; *do you agree to allow us to liquidate your assets?* Tick; *who do you want the balance to go to?* Insert name and bank account details here.'

That's another thing about growing old and getting ill. The longer you leave it, the lonelier you become. And think of your funeral if you were the last of the gang to die. It was a fact: the younger you died, the more people there were at your funeral. She's not saying it's a reason for her decision, but it's comforting to know they won't need to hold hers in a Wendy house. Mark had a big turnout for his, not that anyone foresaw his end as he died a week before he retired (brilliant timing, Mark). Dawn had seen off many loved ones in her time, her mother, her father, her husband and her two closest friends. She'd suffered with them, cared for them, grieved for them and been there for them, but who was there for her now? Kimberley? Dawn can't help but suspect she'll get over her mourning the day the government coughs up the final settlement on her mother's life. 'I know I'm being unfair about Kimberley,' she confesses to Mark. 'But what prospects has she, and especially Ava, for the future? It's a shitshow. People today have so much less than we had in our day – at least I can help them in my own little way.'

Kimberley is visiting tomorrow, the last time she'll see her as she doesn't want her here on Friday, and she's full of apprehension at the thought of it. Was she being selfish baling out on her and her grand-daughter? No, she was doing them a favour if you thought about it. Mark would no doubt frown at her decision – all her decisions – but that's how it had to be. 'It's all very well for you to dole out advice,' she scolds, 'but you're not here, are you?'

It's comforting to talk, to share her thoughts with her husband, and she feels the pain easing. 'Hey, do you think we'll be reunited by the weekend? That would be a turn-up for the books, but I'm not getting my hopes up.' Mark and Dawn had never been religious, didn't even get married in a church, preferring the register office. She casts her mind back to occasional conversations regarding the afterlife, where Mark maintained religion was a great big con and a way of controlling and getting money out of people. Of course, they were much younger then, and had endless years ahead of them, or so it seemed. When Mark passed away, she'd been gripped with an almost comic panic that he might have got it wrong. How would he be explaining it away up there, promising to make amends? But that was only a passing fancy, a reaction to his sudden demise. As she approaches her own great reckoning all she anticipates is a great, big, black nothing (which, if you think about it, is a relief, and certainly better than an eternity of reparation or regret if heaven and hell turned out to exist and she failed to make the cut). It reminds her that most religions (except for the one she had been schooled in as a girl) remained steadfastly opposed to the type of end she's chosen for herself. 'Sort of proves your point, Mark,' she muses. 'Our lot reckon assisted death is OK, as long as you sign up for a blessing before you go and please could you leave us a legacy in your will.' Should she be joking about faith or the lack of it? No, particularly as they say you should never close the door completely.

'This is your last chance, Mark. If you are out there, you'd better send me a sign,' she teases.

After five seconds, 'No? Thought not.'

She tenderly strokes his cheek. 'We should have gone together, really. That would have been a much better plan, but beggars can't be choosers. It's been rotten without you – I bet your head is swelling to hear that. What would you have done if I'd gone first, and you had to fill in for eight years on your own?' She grins. 'I hate to imagine the state of the kitchen by now.'

She plants a warm kiss on his glossy 8 x 6 image and replaces the frame on the bedside cabinet before climbing into bed. 'I'm all right, really, I'm all right. Don't fret.' Mark looks back adoringly, but she perceives the look of concern in his eyes.

'Tell me I'm doing the right thing, Mark. I've been over it so many times, I'm sick of it.' He gazes deep into her being but says nothing.

'Don't do this to me, Mark.'

She reaches for the light switch and the room is plunged into darkness, causing her to start. She stares into the void and is gripped with a sudden panic.

'Mark,' she whispers, 'I'm scared.'

Chapter Fifteen

Late night phone calls by their very nature suggest something can't wait. Callan has been trying to get hold of Lawrence throughout the day and it's taken until nearly midnight for the secretary of state to call him back. 'Been a bit busy running the country, Cal,' is his laconic, non-apologetic, excuse.

Callan mouths a silent expletive under his breath and hoists his middle finger at the speakerphone. 'Sorry to bug you, Lawrence. It's just that there are a couple of items we could do with nailing down.'

'Really?' comes the indifferent reply. 'I thought we were good to go?'

Callan surveys the written list of points in front of him. 'A few loose ends we can put to bed now, if that's OK?'

Lawrence wearily resigns himself to another Callan mither. Why does he have to do everything for these people? 'Fine. But let's make this quick, shall we?'

Callan doesn't need a second invitation. 'First, have you had any more thoughts on rebadging the Peregrine for the prison work? So we don't cross-contaminate the different markets?'

'Oh, the Terminator thing?' When Callan first mooted this change, Lawrence had been against it, most decidedly. Go Gently were worrying about nothing in his view. But since the subject has come up again, he has to concede it sort of makes sense. 'Right, Callan, here's what I think. I can live with a different brand for the penal programme, but calling it the Terminator? No, that's too Hollywood for me. And it might be too Hollywood for their lawyers too, if you see what I mean.'

Callan knows exactly where this is heading. He cues up Lawrence accordingly: 'OK, a different name, but not Terminator?'

'Exactly,' says Lawrence who will now come up with a new name and rebadge the rebadge idea as 'copyright Lawrence Pestel'. 'How about something like, let me see now…' – he feigns searching for inspiration before testing the titles he jotted down earlier – '… I know, how about the Transporter?'

Callan coughs. 'I like it. Yes. It's … punchy.' A slight pause. 'But maybe it evokes the days when prisoners were shipped off to Australia?'

Lawrence had, of course, thought of that, which was part of the attraction. But this is merely playing games. 'You may have a point. I know, what about Voyager?' He doesn't wait for Callan to respond because he immediately dashes his own suggestion. 'No – make that a non-starter – it's a bit overused.' As a long established – and successful – politician, Lawrence knows very well how to play the three-card trick. First suggestion: good, but we can improve on it. Second – not as good as the first, so be decisive and jettison it, which makes the third suggestion the winner by dint of having been built on the back of a rigorous thought process. Callan know he's being played too. 'Got it,' says Lawrence finally. 'Polaris. Redolent of power, suggests science, and invokes the infinity of the heavens. What do you think?'

By this point, Callan doesn't give a stuff. Anything will do. 'That's the one, Lawrence. Love it.' He ticks the item off his list.

'Now, the point I raised over building dedicated sites for the penal programme, away from Go Gently's day-to-day activities? Have you had any further thoughts on that?'

There is a brief silence on the other end of the phone line as Lawrence strains to recall what he's supposed to be deciding here. Then, 'Dedicated sites?'

Callan feels his hand forming into a fist. 'Yes. Where I suggested that we create dedicated sites for the penal programme, away from our core centres, or even build facilities within designated prisons to streamline the activity and minimise the logistics. Including whether the five-day relief period for prisoners is strictly necessary? You were going to think about it?'

Given the weight of responsibility thrust daily upon the minister's shoulders he could simply say no, he's not thought about it, but such an admission is not a function of progressive governance. 'It's a valid point, Cal, but I think maybe you're leaping ahead of yourself. We must remember there are two core messages at stake here. Point number one: the Peregrine Pod, a joint project between the department for wellbeing and Go Gently, is bringing a quick and easy painless assisted death within the reach and the pocket of millions of citizens for the first time. Point number two: Polaris will provide a humane solution to the rise in mental health disorders caused by extended incarceration while at the same time reducing the prison population. There. The first rule of communication: keep it simple, stupid.'

'But what if we're asked about the detail?'

'The detail will be shaped, in due course, by the response we get once the headlines are printed. That's how it works. Calm down, Cal, for Christ's sake.' He softens: 'Listen, about these dedicated sites, let's just get Friday out of the way – that's your gig, that's where your focus should lie. You don't have to worry about Saturday because that's our responsibility; you're just the uncredited host, so no worries. All you have to ensure on the Saturday is that Peregrine – Polaris that is – does its job and offs our man like he's having a filling or something.'

Callan knows it's futile persisting with his list, and resignedly crosses out the next five points. At least he's got a rebrand agreed for the early release initiative and Go Gently won't be linked directly with it come the weekend. 'You can depend on me for that,' he says.

Lawrence relaxes. 'Good. All sorted. How is dead man walking anyway? You keeping an eye on him?'

Callan grimaces at the mention of surveillance on ex-prisoner A1801MB, his unwelcome guest at Charon House. How's he supposed to keep abreast of every little detail? 'Yes, he's fine,' he replies. 'No trouble at all.'

'See, I told you. The leisure break is all part of the package.'

'Well, he's only a sample of one, so a bit early to predict how others will react,' says Callan defensively.

Lawrence laughs. 'Chillax, will you? You're making me nervous. Nothing else bugging you is there?'

Callan chews his lip. Now would not be the best time to mention his growing anxiety over the pace of these launches, several operational hitches he's dealing with at Charon House caused by the rapid expansion of his business, the dissent some of his staff are showing towards the prison programme, and his growing resentment at being treated like a lackey by the secretary of state. 'As happy as a tick on a fat dog,' he says by way of reassurance.

'Very good, Cal, says the minister. 'You can take the boy out of Tennessee but you can't take Tennessee out of the boy. I'll see you on Friday morning.'

And with that, the line goes dead.

Adil inches slowly down the corridor, expecting to be apprehended at any second. He dearly wants to turn back, scarper, before it's too late, but this is his mission, his passport out of Charon House if he can discover what Go Gently is planning for Friday. He ignores the passages to the left and right and heads on down to Zone Z. With every step his heart rate quickens – what if there are people still working late, how far will this pass get him? Finally, his way is blocked by a set of double doors and he presses his ear to them desperately hoping for silence on the other side. He can hear what sounds like air conditioning whirring away, but little else. This is it. He takes a deep breath, almost praying his pass won't work, but no sooner does he grip his key card than he hears a loud click and the doors start to swing inward of their own volition. He stands frozen to the spot as a voice rings out: 'Are you coming in or not?' The voice is speaking to him. Looking up, Adil sees he is being addressed by a dumpy young man, dressed in an ill-fitting suit, just inside the dimly-lit room. Well used to taking orders, Adil obediently steps inside and hovers uncertainly as the doors close behind him. The man turns to two similarly-clad office type workers and says, 'Fingers out.' They appear to be hurriedly collecting their things. 'You,' says the man in charge, pointing at Adil, 'don't leave this place in a shit tip like you did this morning. You're paid to clean, so do your bloody job.' He punches the door release button and, without a second glance, the trio march out, leaving Adil alone in what looks like a giant operating theatre. He lets out a huge sigh of relief, grateful for the gift of anonymity, being the lowly minion who doesn't count. It looks like they're not coming back but the real cleaner will be along before too long. He takes in his surroundings, wondering what to do, where to start. Surely, a death machine can't be that easy to hide? As his eyes become accustomed to the low-level lighting it's apparent the room is set out for a presentation of some sort. Around forty chairs are lined up in four rows facing a lectern. Six huge monitors on stands, three on each side, frame the walls. Beneath a giant screen mounted on the far wall stand two bulky covered shapes, each the size of a small car. Adil catches his breath as he makes his way over – exactly what kind of infernal apparatus is lurking under these sheets, ready to unleash yet more woe on mankind? He lifts the corner of one of the fitted silver neoprene covers and peers inside, taking in the machine beneath. It's like a cigar-shaped spaceship, made of glass and aluminium. He needs to work quickly, so boldly pulls at the cover to reveal the full sinister outline in full; a conveyance of some sort, but what does it do, and how does it work? Inside, he can see a flat screen, but other than that there are no evident controls or features. Quickly, he makes his way around the fuselage, running his hands along the contours. The machined metal is smooth and seamless, offering no clues. With rising dread, he pulls at the corner of the second shape – it's identical. He can't hang around, so, committing the visual image to memory, replaces the covers as neatly as he can, already anticipating the grilling he's going to receive from Ruth if he ever gets this information to her. He takes in the area behind the machines, searching for any other signs of preparation. There, in the darkest corner, is a wire mesh cage full of bottles. As his eyes adjust in the dim light he gasps – not bottles, but canisters. Gas canisters. He looks back at the two large shapes behind him as the realisation hits home. The cigar-shaped spaceships are gas chambers. A room for one, with no wake-up call required. A distant memory of his childhood is evoked with men, women and children uncontrollably crying, vomiting and soiling themselves after the planes came; ten minutes of violent and helpless convulsion before the point of no return. He, too, starts to feel nauseous and light-headed at the grim reality of his discovery. People would volunteer, pay for this? He tries to read what's on the side of the canisters, but it's too dark to make out the writing. They look like miniature fire extinguishers in this light but it's not flames they'll be putting out. In the opposite corner he spots another wire mesh cage that on closer inspection turn out to be full of identical-looking cylinders.

Adil is desperately trying to order, to collect, his thoughts. He has no phone, so cannot take photographs. He has no paper or pen, so cannot make notes. He must take all of this in and not forget a single detail. He must get out of here undetected. He must get news to Sacrosanct. He must, above all, keep calm. Satisfied he has put everything back in place undisturbed, he steals back towards the double doors. He's just about to hit the door release when he notices a desk to the side, with a large desktop computer, printer, and two mixing consoles plonked on top. As he follows the direction of the cables floorward he alights on an overflowing wastepaper bin, rammed with coffee cups, sandwich wrappers and numerous screwed up balls of paper. His hand hesitates over the exit button. His subconscious is screaming at him to get out, leave while he can, but he's not finished yet. Kneeling, he pulls one of the balls of paper from the wastepaper basket. Flattening it out in the gloom he recognises it's a bar chart of some description. He reaches for another and just about makes out the heading: *Draft Intro.* A third: *Further Reducing the Burden on the Tax Payer.* A fourth: *Draft Q and A.* Whatever they're presenting it's all in this bin, carelessly tossed away, not even shredded. Adil randomly grabs more balls of paper from the treasure chest, ignoring the handwritten sandwich order and photocopied crossword puzzles in among the trash. Some pages are covered in coffee and yoghurt stains, but as he wipes and smoothes the surfaces he knows he not only has a way of explaining what he's seen, but also hard proof for Doctors Ruth and Andy. When he calculates he has enough he rolls the pages together and places them inside his waistband. What was it the supervisor said? *Some big launch or other. Everybody on standby Friday and Saturday.* Well, first things first: he will work out what to do with these pages, how to get them to Sacrosanct, how to get as far away from this bloody place as possible as soon as he gets back to the safety of the dorm. The priority now is how to get out undetected, before the real cleaner arrives. He makes one last sweep of the theatre and reaches for the exit button again. That's when he sees the small red light blinking away in the corner: a CCTV camera. His blood turns to ice.

Chapter Sixteen

Geraldine jerks awake with a dread sense the walls are falling in: *has it started?* It's with some relief she realises she's in her room and still in one piece. It strikes her such a reaction on waking from an anxiety dream in Charon House could best be described as 'ironic'. Ever the pedant, she muses over a more appropriate adjective – would 'contradictory' or 'idiosyncratic' be more apt? As she dresses, she tries to rationalise the sense of foreboding that's clouding this beautiful, sunlit morning. It's only natural, she tells herself, to be conflicted once you've made your mind up and set the clock ticking on a one-way, irreversible journey. The spirit is willing but the body has yet to cease its protests (or maybe that should be the other way around). She rips yesterday's page from the desktop calendar to reveal today's date. Wednesday. Getting closer. Against her better judgement she reads the inspirational quote reproduced beneath the large red numerals, the *bon mot* for the day: 'Life is like riding a bicycle. To keep your balance, you must keep moving.' Albert Einstein. Geraldine dismisses the sentiment with a shrug – *easy for him to say*, she thinks. *My handlebars fell off years ago.*

Once she's ready, she sets off for Ground Swell. It does a lovely latte she's found, although her primary reason for going is the hope Dawn has the same idea. As she approaches the elevator a door to one of the rooms swings open, and she holds back out of politeness. Jeffrey emerges, accompanied by an orderly she's not seen before. 'Good morning', she trills. 'And how are we today?'

Jeffrey smiles back at her and in a poor attempt at an Irish brogue, says, 'Top of the morning to you, Geraldine. Or should I say Ger-al-dine?' He laughs heartily and almost skips down the corridor pursued by his helper. How strange, thinks Geraldine – this is the same man she saw struggling to hold a knife and fork and put two words together last night. And how did he remember her name – even how to enunciate it? Confused, she makes her way downstairs.

Dawn is already in the coffee shop when she arrives, looking as white as a sheet. 'You look terrible,' volunteers Geraldine. 'Couldn't you sleep?'

'Thanks a lot,' replies Dawn. 'You certainly know how to make a girl feel good about herself.'

Geraldine's face and neck redden in embarrassment. 'Sorry. Me and my big mouth. It's just, well, you do look a bit peaky.'

'No, you're right,' says Dawn, 'I had a bit of a rough night. I'll be fine. Latte, I take it?'

'Not for me, thanks. I just made myself one in my room. I'll have a croissant though.'

'I don't know how you can resist the coffee – I wish I had your willpower.'

They order and settle down. Instead of engaging in social chitchat, Dawn dispenses with the niceties and opts for a very direct question: 'Do you ever get second thoughts, about, you know, your decision?'

Geraldine is taken aback. Is her new friend getting last-minute nerves? She figured, before arriving at Charon House, that her own resolve would only be reinforced through the presence of like-minded people. Such as Dawn, who hasn't betrayed a moment's regret at any stage. Has it all been an act?

'I think it's only natural to question yourself as the event gets closer,' replies Geraldine cautiously, as if she's a Go Gently counsellor.

'Yes. But have you thought about, well, changing your mind?'

Geraldine feels her face flushing again, fazed at being put on the spot. She deflects the query: 'Are you having doubts?'

Dawn fidgets and stares at her coffee cup before brushing the question away. 'Oh, don't pay any attention to silly old me,' she says. 'I had a bad night, that's all.'

Geraldine decides it's safer to duck this topic of conversation. Nodding sympathetically, she digresses. 'You know the gentleman we overheard being talked about in here? The one with dementia? I met the poor fellow last night. Jeffrey.'

Dawn pulls a face. 'That doesn't sound like too much fun.'

Geraldine smacks her playfully on the hand. 'You're awful, Dawn. Although he did keep asking me where Rosemary was, whoever Rosemary is.'

'Well, at least he's not fretting over whether he's made the right decision,' says Dawn ruefully. 'That's something.'

Geraldine ignores the observation. 'It's a terrible affliction. I had to deal with quite a few sufferers back home. But then, the curious thing is, I saw him again this morning, and he seemed altogether… well, more lucid. Very odd.'

'Aren't their moods supposed to go up and down?'

'Yes, but it wasn't his mood that struck me – he seemed to be as normal as you or I.'

'Steady on, Geraldine. You're assigning us super powers now. Normal? How nice would that be?'

It's a well-made point. 'When I said he was normal, I meant in an old man "Aren't I witty?" sort of way. But the change did strike me as being very unusual, that's all.'

Dawn is altogether more at ease now – it's not like her to overstress, and she feels her worries subside now Geraldine has appeared. Losing her train of thought and forgetting they're discussing dementia, she makes a confession: 'I made a bit of a fool of myself yesterday,' she titters. 'I was in the grounds and thought I was talking to the gardener until I twigged he must be here for the same reason as us. He was younger than us – I just never thought. I could have died of embarrassment. As it turns out, he did know a lot about gardening – I had a lesson about the history of camellias, not that I'll ever be able to put it to use.'

'Young young, or just not as old as us?'

'Oh, definitely a babe in arms. Fifty-something? He said he had migraines, a problem with sunlight. Photo-something-or-other.'

'Photophobia,' Geraldine corrects her. 'Sensitivity to light. They can treat that relatively easily, so I wouldn't have thought that was the reason he was here. Are you sure he wasn't working or visiting?'

'That's what I guessed at first, but the more he talked, I just got that feeling, you know? He seemed quite jumpy and sad. Poor thing.'

Geraldine nods. It really shouldn't come as a surprise that the majority of people in a place like this are sad and jumpy. What else could you expect?

Before they can resume their conversation, there is a loud crash as the door to the coffee shop swings open and bangs against the wall. *They should really put a door stop on the floor there,* thinks Geraldine as she turns towards the source of the commotion. There, framed in the entrance, like Samson between the two pillars of the temple, stands Jeffrey, wearing a look of complete bewilderment on his face. Catching sight of Geraldine, he directs a plaintive enquiry in her direction: 'Rosemary?' Before she has time to respond, the orderly she'd last seen trying to keep up with Jeffrey appears and gently ushers him away.

Dawn points at the now empty doorway and mouths, *Jeffrey?*

An astonished Geraldine manages a weak affirmative nod.

'Well, who's to say what's normal and what's not these days,' ribs Dawn.

'I don't understand it,' is all Geraldine can muster in reply. If she thought Jeffrey's earlier greeting to her had been bizarre, this sudden relapse was even stranger. Something's not right and she can't quite put her finger on it. However, no sooner has Jeffrey been led away than a new arrival in the doorway of the coffeehouse commands their attention. He, too, looks like a man who has lost his bearings, although in his case it's whether to enter or not, rather than the erosion of his mental faculties. 'Woody,' exclaims Dawn on spotting him and excitedly beckons him over. He stands rooted to the spot. 'Come and join us,' urges Dawn, pulling the chair next to her out from under the table. 'It's the gardener,' she whispers in a rather loud aside to Geraldine. 'From yesterday.'

Unable to resist the gravitational force otherwise known as Dawn, Woody slowly and hesitatingly makes his way over. He still doesn't sit down until he's been fussed into it. Introductions over, the conversation teeters awkwardly on the edge of collapse as they each search for appropriate icebreakers. (In reality, the first thing that pops into most residents' minds on meeting a new acquaintance at Charon House is: 'when are you down for the chop then?' Fortunately, decorum steers most exchanges in a more anodyne direction.)

'Dawn says you're a very accomplished gardener,' offers Geraldine brightly (as if to prove the point).

Woody shakes his head in embarrassment. 'Not really,' he stutters. There's another strained hiatus as it becomes clear he's nothing further to add to that qualification.

Geraldine shifts uneasily, wondering why Dawn, acting like a giddy teenager, called Woody over. Surely, it's better to not get involved with new people in here – it's not like they're on a cruise. Then she remembers how she and Dawn have struck up a relationship like a couple of new girls at big school and ticks herself off for the contradiction. Well, Dawn called him over, so let her run with it. Except, it appears that the ever-garrulous Dawn is struggling to keep it flowing here, which must be a first. Even in the short time she's known her, Geraldine imagines Dawn wringing people's life stories out of them in five minutes flat. She pictures her in a hairdresser's or in a shop queue, the questions rolling off her tongue: *Where do you live? Are you married? Do you have kids? What line of work are you in? Going on holiday this year?* Dawn has been as open as an all-night deli telling Geraldine how she's fetched up at Go Gently, while she hasn't offered a specific explanation or justification in reply. *Always the quiet one, that Geraldine. Taciturn, you'd say.* Not that Dawn has made her feel rude over her lack of disclosure. Her new friend's phraseology is also well short of the self-censorship you notice around this place. Take that *'I could have died of embarrassment'* from a minute ago – delivered without a flicker. Geraldine tends to weigh every word before uttering it, which is probably another reason no one is going to miss her when she's gone. Dawn is warm, chatty, engaging, positive – full of life. Yes, that's it, full of life. She's ill, granted, but it's hard to imagine that spark being extinguished within a few short hours. Her own spark – make that 'dull glow' – yes, but not someone whose spirit burns as brightly as Dawn's. But then again, didn't Dawn just ask her if she was having second thoughts? That's telling. This is all starting to weigh heavily. Maybe she should just get up right now and leave them to it. Two's company, three's a crowd after all.

Geraldine is on the verge of excusing herself when Dawn pipes up. 'We were just talking about you a minute ago, Woody, trying to guess if you worked here, were visiting, or if you were here for the same reason as us.' Geraldine nearly falls off her chair. So much for diplomacy – she's gone from nought to a hundred in five seconds.

Woody, on the other hand, remains composed, looking from one to the other as he considers his reply. 'I'm afraid it's the latter,' he says flatly. 'No sugar-coating that.'

Geraldine doesn't know where to look. She should leave, but perhaps not just yet.

Dawn reaches out and softly places her hand on his. 'We're all in the same boat, love. We understand.'

Woody's eyes moisten as he searches for some words, any words, to express himself. No one has shown him any kindness in such a long time, it's overwhelming.

'It's our choice,' Dawn continues, 'but not our choice, if you get my meaning.'

Woody nods in agreement; he gets her drift. 'All I ever seem to have done is make bad choices. At least I won't be making another one after this.'

Now Geraldine feels the tears welling. It is her choice, one hundred per cent her choice, but for the first time since she made her mind up, she hears the ghost of doubt whispering in her ear.

Chapter Seventeen

The hospital cafeteria in central Manchester is full of tired faces, stretched over drinks that have long gone cold. Nobody stirs or pays any attention as Adil enters – people here have their own crosses to bear. He picks a table in the corner, out of the way, and sits facing the door, his hand patting his inside pocket every five seconds to check the papers are still there. Doctors Ruth and Andy are late. When the doctors do appear, having agreed to meet during their break, Andy is clearly grumpy and spends five minutes fussing over his lunch order before he's ready to pay attention. Ruth is visibly irritated at Andy's lack of urgency – she knows Adil wouldn't have insisted on seeing them at such short notice unless it was important.

Finally, they're ready. Looking round to make sure he's not overheard, Adil solemnly cuts to the chase. 'I've found out why Go Gently has cancelled its barbiturates contract.'

That gets the attention (even from Andy) it deserves and Adil goes for broke in an urgent hushed tone. 'They've developed a new death machine, capable of killing people more cheaply and quicker than a lethal injection.'

He doesn't quite know how they'll react to this disclosure – shock, admiration at this sleuthing, revulsion perhaps – but nothing prepares him for Andy's dumb response. 'Unless they're bringing back the rope or the axe, I don't see how it makes that much difference. They're still killing people, just with an alternative method.'

A clearly exasperated Ruth cuts off her partner with an irate '*Shhh.*' Andy is about to defend himself, but thinks better of it and tries to rescue the situation instead. 'Remember we're talking about Go Gently here. They hype the shit out of everything. It's probably just a different drug formula they're using or something. "Death machine"? That doesn't sound like it will be much of a winner in their sales literature.'

'Go Gently aren't calling it a "death machine",' says a frustrated Adil. 'One of the supervisors called it that. They're calling it the Peregrine Pod, but the point is they're going to kill even more people with this than they currently do.'

Ruth lets the gravity of the disclosure sink in. 'This is serious shit, Andy,' she chides. Her abashed companion lowers his gaze and contemplates his half-eaten tuna mayo sandwich, leaving her to takes over.

'How does this machine work, Adil?' she asks. 'Were you able to find that out?'

'I've seen it,' he nods. 'In a theatre they've got set up. It's like a small rocket ship built of steel and glass. They put the patient inside, and they reckon they can see off the occupant in a few short minutes.'

'But how do they kill the patient, Adil?' urges Ruth. 'With what?'

'Liquid nitrogen. I saw that too.'

Andy perks up. 'Liquid nitrogen? That was very popular for suicides back in the day, if you could get your hands on a supply. It was very difficult to prove cause of death with it, especially if you had someone clear up the canister and whatnot after you.'

Ruth doesn't respond for a few moments as the implications soak in. 'Because the liquid nitrogen converts to gas inside the capsule.' Then the stark realisation: 'They're gassing people!'

Andy shakes his head in mild wonder. 'Well, it just goes to show, there's nothing new under the sun.'

She ignores him. 'This is… barbaric,' she cries. 'A crime against humanity. Has history taught us nothing?'

Even Andy gets it now. 'Like the Nazis, you mean?' He too lets out a horrified gasp. 'The monsters.'

But Adil hasn't finished yet. 'There's more,' he declares. 'The launch of this pod is in less than forty-eight hours. Then, the next day, it gets even worse.' Ruth and Andy brace themselves at the prospect of the next disclosure. 'The government is launching a new plan to reduce the prison population by paying prisoners to opt for an assisted death using the pod instead of rotting in jail for years. They start on Saturday with some poor unfortunate.'

The doctors' disbelief turns to incredulity at this juncture, forcing Adil to press the dumb-struck duo. 'So, the question is, what are you going to do about it?'

Andy looks to Ruth – she's the one who will have to answer that, although at this exact moment her expression is one of helpless stupefaction. They can almost hear her thoughts creaking as they slowly turn over.

Adil fidgets nervously waiting for her to speak, until a searing flashback of that blinking CCTV red light prompts him to be assertive. He hasn't endured the hell of Charon House and risked his liberty to make these discoveries only for Sacrosanct not to act on them. 'You have to stop this before it starts,' he barks. 'Or it's all been for nothing.'

To clinch his argument Adil reaches inside his coat pocket and, in a sweeping gesture, bangs down sheet after sheet of rumpled paper on the table between the red and brown sauce bottles. 'There. There's the proof. Everything they're planning. What more do you need?'

Andy and Ruth pick at the corner of various sheets, sifting through *Project Doorway, democratisation of death, Requital early release programme* and a 3D drawing of what looks like a car for a new fairground ride.

'Where did you get these from?' asks Ruth, astonished at the detail. She's even more astonished when Adil tells her.

But there's still no hint of an action plan from the two doctors. Adil is beginning to despair. 'Come on, I've done my bit, you're the activists – how are you going to stop these murderers getting away with it?'

Andy has turned a sickly shade of green on realising the size of the challenge being thrust on Sacrosanct's – and his own rather narrow – shoulders. 'I'm sure we can do something with it,' he says. 'We just need to think it through first, not jump straight in. Don't you agree, Ruth?'

I'm sure we can do something with it. That's his response? A deflated Adil turns to Ruth for support, help – anything. It doesn't have to be an on-the-spot masterplan, just a promise of action that can be classed under the category of 'definitive'.

Ruth appears to recognise that Sacrosanct has met its moment of destiny. She takes a deep breath, pulls herself up to her full five feet two inches and makes a solemn vow: 'We're not going to let these bastards get away with it.'

Adil takes the bus back to Stalybridge as it will give him more time to think before he arrives at Charon House. *What on earth is he doing going back? He must be mad.* But as Ruth pointed out, he would be in more trouble if he didn't return. That's easy for her to say, of course, because she didn't have to endure a night of terrors waiting for the clatter of boots in the dormitory corridor as security came to apprehend him. Even now, on the top deck of the bus, he can feel the strobing red light of the CCTV camera assaulting his retinas, blinking out a message he didn't need a morse manual to understand: he'd been caught bang to rights. On spotting the camera last night he'd bolted down the darkened corridors in blind panic, imagining a thousand demons, eager to devour him, at his back. But there was no alarm. No pursuit. No sign of anything untoward. Scarcely believing his luck, once he reached the familiar territory of the dorm he had taken care to hide the purloined papers in a linen cupboard and sneaked into his bunk. Surely, it was only a matter of time before they came for him? Resigned to his fate, and cursing Sacrosanct, Go Gently and his own judgement in equal measure, he'd finally fallen into a fitful sleep.

Waking at first light, he took stock. Security might have missed his presence in the theatre in real time, but that didn't mean last night's footage wasn't being zoomed through and inspected for irregularities this morning. In fact, that's exactly what would be happening. His reprieve would be short-lived. And he still had his mission to fulfil. He made a mental list of what he had to do and his heart missed several beats: pretend everything was normal, clock out, retrieve his phone, contact Ruth and Andy to arrange an urgent meeting, rescue the stowed papers, get into Manchester, show Sacrosanct the evidence, hand over the responsibility to them. *Do all of that?* And then what?

SHAKING HANDS WITH ELVIS

Well, miracle to behold, he'd done it. It was up to Sacrosanct now, but the big problem remained: what was *he* going to do next? He'd pleaded with Ruth not to send him back, but to no avail. He'd left only on the undertaking they would make a formal application to have him transferred back to the age-atorium as soon as possible. *As soon as possible.* Whatever that meant. After all he'd done for them, that's all they could offer? But what choice did he have? Not going back to Charon House wasn't an option. If he fails to turn up for duty today, he'll be reported to the department of organised labour and his licensed guest worker status will be revoked. The hell of Charon House or the abyss of immediate deportation? A beggar's choice, and the same choice he'd always had in this country: none. Do as he's told, be grateful.

And once he walks through those doors, who is to say security – or worse still, immigration – won't be waiting for him with handcuffs and a hood? They've had all day to review the CCTV. Would it be any consolation in that eventuality that he'd at least delivered for Sacrosanct? Was it any concern of his what action the activists might take given the information he had furnished them with? No – he didn't want to think about that. He was no hero: survive today, and get out of Go Gently – that's as far as his ambition stretched.

Despite the fifty-four stops the bus makes between Manchester and Stalybridge, it nevertheless finally delivers a reluctant Adil to his destination. Adil steels himself, and clocks back in at Charon House, wondering how many more times he'll have to do this (wondering how many more times he'll be allowed to do this). He checks in his phone and makes his way to the staff changing room without mishap, but as soon as he's spotted by a fellow-worker, he's given the message to report to the supervisor. He doesn't ask the reason why.

The duty supervisor, a pleasant enough fellow, has a smile on his face as Adil enters the office. 'Ah, Adil. A question for you.' He waits for the axe to fall. 'What do you reckon the cushiest job is in this place?

Adil doesn't know where this is going but before he can stop himself blurts out, 'Watching the CCTV?'

The supervisor bursts out laughing. 'Well, yes, I'll give you that. Especially as none of 'em work. Nothing works in this shithole. No, Adil, the easiest job in these parts is mixologist. And you've just qualified.'

Adil is struck dumb. The CCTV cameras don't work? Can he just curl up and die on the spot, please?

His boss breezes on. 'Ever made a cocktail? No, thought not. Well, your good work has been noticed and you're about to be assigned new duties. I think you'll be pleased – more responsibility, and less running around the place.'

Adil tries to gather himself, but can only stutter his response. 'Mixologist?' Normally, he'd be delighted to be adding a new noun to his expanding lexicon, but somehow the thrill of this new one is passing him by.

'A bright lad like you will soon learn the ropes. Finish up your duties as normal this week, and on Monday report to Dr Ivy in anaesthetics. Her nickname is Lucretia, but don't let her hear you use it if you catch my drift.'

Adil is puzzled. This sounds way outside his scope of reference. 'But I don't have any science background. How can I possibly help?'

'You're not making anything. Your job will be to administer. Dosage and all that.'

Adil is still in the dark. 'Administer what? And who to?'

The supervisor is enjoying the naivete of the greenhorn guest worker and can't help showing off. 'Benzodiazepines. Or tranks or downers to the likes of you and me. Mother's little helpers, to stop our guests freaking out and having a change of heart. Because that would be bad for business.'

Adil considers this for a moment. 'So, I basically administer whatever dosage the client has requested?'

The supervisor snorts in derision. 'Well, yes. And no. They don't *ask* for the tranks – they're given them from the off. They don't know they're having them – they're normally slipped into their drinks. It's for their benefit, see.'

Go Gently are drugging their guests against their will? So that's why nobody ever changes their minds. He can't possibly be party to this, but what if he already has? 'I've not slipped anything in people's drinks. Is it everybody?'

'You're on Alzheimer's, that's why. They don't need any help to charge off into the great unknown. But everyone else – all part of the service. Even in the cafeteria – there's a barista there they reckon can work out exact dosages just by eying up somebody's weight.'

Adil's horrified reaction to this new revelation is to somehow get the news to Sacrosanct. But he's finished with them. And, as he's just reminded himself, he's no hero. He nods to acknowledge he understands his new role, but can't help asking one last question: 'But what if somebody refuses the drinks they're given, or insists on leaving?'

At that, the supervisor's merry demeanour is replaced with a solemn headshake. 'Well now' he says, 'that's an altogether different kettle of fish.'

144

Chapter Eighteen

Dawn and Woody stumble across an appealing stone arbour on their stroll around the gardens and decide it warrants a break. They squeeze on to the two-seater, glad of the shade and the tranquility the resting place provides.

'Did you know that the word "arbour" comes from the Latin word for tree?' Woody asks. 'Arbor.'

'I feel another masterclass coming on,' she teases. Seeing his face drop she quickly adds, 'Don't be daft, Woody, I'm only joking. No, I didn't, because I know nothing about gardens, but I do like you telling me.'

Reassured, he continues. 'Man has always needed shade from the sun, and what better solution than a tree. So, when the Romans started to build permanent sun shelters the name must have stuck. Classic gardens have had arbours for centuries, the more ornate the better.'

'Kimberley bought a pergola from Argos a few years back. It only lasted one summer before it fell apart.'

'Ah, a pergola isn't an arbour though. Quite different. That's basically a trellis covering a walkway, not something as sturdy as this.'

'Yes, it is nice,' Dawn concedes. 'Makes you wonder how many people have sat here over the years and what thoughts they had.' They relax and enjoy the serenity, content to breathe in the view without speaking.

It's Dawn who finally breaks the silence. It's something that's been on her mind since yesterday. 'Can I ask you something, Woody? A personal question?' He knows what's coming but doesn't raise any objection. 'I know it's none of my business but you're young and seem to be in good health, so if you're here for the same reason as Geraldine and me, then I just can't fathom it.'

'It's complicated. A long story,' is all he can muster.

'I like long stories. And I've nowhere else to be.'

He sighs. Dawn has shown him such kindness since he arrived. How best to explain his predicament, if explain it at all? He decides he can at least relate the background to his woes. 'Are you sure you want to hear this?'

She pats him gently on the knee. 'I'm sure.'

He stares directly ahead in order to avoid eye contact, and addresses his tale to the verdant landscape. 'I had a normal – boring some might say – life until ten years ago. Married, two kids, a steady if not very well-paid job as a parks gardener. An ordinary Joe. How it all went downhill so fast is frightening.'

He falters and Dawn silently urges him on, not wanting to break his train of thought.

'I suppose it started around my fiftieth birthday. The old story – my wife left me. Another bloke. We'd not been getting on and I got my marching orders, as simple as that. I moved into a small flat, tried my best to see the kids, attempted to stay friends with her, but all she wanted was to get on with her new life.'

Dawn thinks of Mark and all the happy years they spent together, and her heart goes out to Woody.

'Then, about six months after we'd split, I got this photophobia. Could have been related, I'll never know, but not clever in an outdoor job. And like I told you yesterday, the council got rid of me, no messing. So, there I was, a handicapped, unskilled, divorced fifty-year-old – not the most attractive proposition in the jobs market.'

Dawn does some mental arithmetic – he can only be around sixty years old, if that.

'By now I was living in a crummy bedsit, and the only job I could get was delivering fast food, not so much because it was at night but because they'd take anybody who'd work for slave rates. I did that for a few years, and it was a bloody grind. I thought life back then couldn't get much worse, but I'd give anything to be back in that bedsit now.'

He steels himself as he approaches the next part. Strangely enough, it feels liberating to relate his story, particularly as no one has shown the slightest interest in his misfortunes up to now. 'I'm embarrassed to tell you how the nightmare really started – a stupid bloody penalty notice three years ago for driving my moped in a bus lane. A one hundred quid fine. I don't even remember doing it, but I knew I couldn't pay it. So, and this is the crazy bit, I ignored it. I got a few reminders and threats, but I threw them in the bin and hoped it would somehow go away.' He sighs. 'Eventually, the bailiffs arrived.'

Dawn squeezes Woody's shoulder in a gesture of sympathy and support.

'They demanded a thousand quid – the original fine, interest, costs and what have you, and I had to laugh. The only thing I had that was worth a bean was my moped, so the bastards took that. So now I can't work. I was desperate, so desperate I even went to my ex-wife to see if she'd help me out, enough to get my wheels back, but she gave me short shrift.'

Dawn senses he's nowhere near finished and wonders what's coming next.

'On the way back from getting the hard word from her, I'm walking home, in the pouring rain, when I run into a bit of trouble outside an Indian restaurant. A guy with a bib on – the delivery guy – is running out screaming 'Stop, stop' at some pillock who's just stolen his electric bike. The bike's heading towards me so – I don't know why – I react and jam my umbrella through the spokes and down he goes, crunch, into the pavement. He's motionless, stunned by the looks of it, and that's when my troubles really begin.'

Dawn braces herself for the next grisly chapter.

'I suddenly get mobbed by a load of posh yobs whose mate I've just decked. Turns out they're students on the piss and he's the son of a politician. Before I know it, I've been arrested. Aggravated theft.'

'But…'

'I know. The delivery guy. They paid him off to say he'd lent his bike to this Hooray Henry for ten minutes to deliver flowers to his girlfriend. Then they come up with three witnesses – his mates – to say I'd violently attacked him to steal the bike. And on top of that, they produce a medical expert to testify the real tea leaf suffered a cracked skull, which I know fine well he didn't. Course, they had a great line in court as to why I needed a new set of wheels. Simple as that – ten years inside.'

Dawn's hand flies to her mouth in shock. 'You poor thing. That's…' she's going to say 'criminal' but stops herself just in time '…awful. Didn't you appeal?'

Woody shakes his head. 'Tried that, but didn't get very far. No money, nobody interested. You've done the crime, now shut up and do the time.'

'And they call that justice? It's outrageous.'

He's not looked at Dawn once as he recounted his story, but he turns to her now and shrugs his shoulders, 'It is what it is.'

Dawn considers this broken man, and the cruel fates that have brought him low. There's no question of not believing him, she knows instinctively he's telling the truth, but then she is struck by another couple of thoughts. If he was sentenced to ten years, shouldn't he be in jail still? And even if he was let out early, the same question she asked him earlier still applies: what on earth is he doing here at Charon House?

Despite the debate raging in her head over existentialism and her impending date with destiny, Geraldine's thoughts, somewhat implausibly, have been returning to Jeffrey all morning. *Something's not right and she can't quite put her finger on it.* As a good science teacher should, she has been preoccupied in defining the variables and pondering the relationship between cause and effect in a bid to reach an explanation. Finally, just as she's about to give up, she notices one of the cleaners freshening up the cut flowers dotted around the place by pouring a sachet of plant food into each vase. *Eureka! Could that possibly be the explanation?*

She therefore finds herself in two minds on spotting Jeffrey in reception. He has company, his son Simon, and daughter-in-law Vicki, whom she recognises from her coffee bar eavesdropping. Should she say anything?

Before she knows it, she's zoning in on the group. Jeffrey spots her first, and squints in her direction. 'Rosemary?' he enquires hopefully. Simon and Vicki smile benignly by way of explanation, but none is required.

'Hello, I hope you don't mind,' says Geraldine, 'but I wondered if I might have a brief word?' Simon and Vicki assume she's a member of staff, and look expectantly towards her. 'It's just I couldn't help noticing that Jeffrey's condition seems to... well, it's puzzling.'

Simon is immediately on the defensive. 'Dementia is a puzzling condition,' is his curt response. 'And you are...?'

'Oh, I'm staying here,' replies Geraldine. Simon rolls his eyes. 'Look, I know it's none of my business, but while Jeffrey is demonstrating all the symptoms of acute dementia, this morning he appeared quite lucid.'

'I don't want to appear rude,' says Simon testily, 'but it is none of your business. And fluctuations in clarity are a common feature of dementia.'

Vicki, however, wants to hear more. 'What did you notice?' she asks tentatively.

Geraldine draws herself up, as if addressing a new class after the summer holidays. 'Look, I know Jeffrey is here for his dementia, but how certain are you that it is dementia? Could, for example, a misdiagnosis have occurred?'

'Are you serious?' sneers Simon. 'A misdiagnosis? As if.'

Geraldine pushes on. 'All I know is that I had a conversation with Jeffrey yesterday evening where, shall we say, he wasn't present, yet this morning he knew who I was and even made a joke about my name. Yet, now, he's absent again.'

Simon bristles. 'I assume you mean well, but do you realise how painful this is for us as a family? How your interference is unwelcome, not to mention deranged? What do you know, anyway? You're not a doctor.'

SHAKING HANDS WITH ELVIS

Vicki reddens – there's no reason for Simon to be so mean towards this little old lady, but he's been like this for months, anytime his decision regarding his father has been questioned. 'What do you think a change like that could be down to?' she asks of Miss Meddlesome in a bid to calm the moment.

'No, I'm not a doctor, quite right, I'm a science teacher – or was,' she concedes. 'But, and here's what I think you should be checking out, has Jeffrey ever been tested for sodium deficiency?'

Simon is fit to explode. 'What sort of people do you think we are? That we'd casually ship my father off to Stalybridge if there was a single doubt? He's had every test under the sun. I don't know what your situation is, or what's motivated you to interfere in our affairs, but can I please ask you to leave us alone before I report you.'

Vicki isn't quite so quick to dismiss Geraldine. 'What makes you think it could be that? And what is it anyway?'

Geraldine prepares to deliver the first lesson of term to her new pupils: 'Low blood sodium – hyponatremia – occurs when you have an abnormally low amount of sodium in your blood, or when you have too much water in your blood. Electrolyte imbalance in other words. It's more common in older adults, and one of the symptoms is cognitive disorder – confusion and memory loss. When Jeffrey seemed almost normal this morning, I recalled how he had a lot of salt on his meal last night and it occurred to me that might be the reason he temporarily gained something approaching clarity.'

Simon springs out of his chair and almost squares up to the elderly ex-teacher. 'What total bollocks,' he bellows, almost spitting in her face.

Vicki pulls him back with a stern reprimand, and takes over. 'But Jeffrey has always been very careful over his diet – he doesn't put salt on anything.'

Geraldine holds her ground. 'Exactly. He kept saying "no salt, no salt", which is why you should investigate further given the difference it made when he did. Don't you see? I know it sounds improbable, but the body can lose water and electrolytes so easily – not just because of diet, but through medications that have a diuretic effect, diarrhoea, and the like. The impact can be devastating. Isn't it at least worth making sure?'

Vicki, jolted into recalling Rosemary's concerns over her husband's blood pressure, Jeffrey's use of antidepressants and her father-in-law's illness just prior to succumbing to dementia, is struggling for any meaning in all of this. Not so, Simon. 'Utter crap. Absolute tosh,' he barks. 'If you don't leave right now, I'm going to have them lock you up. I don't care who you are, or why you're here, you ought to be ashamed of yourself gate-crashing other people's grief.' His hand literally forms a fist as he hisses a warning to her: 'Don't come near me or my father again.'

Jeffrey, who has spent the past few minutes transfixed by the shadow cast by the giant oak tree in the middle of reception, comes to at the sound of 'father'. Seeing Geraldine standing there, he appears to want to say something to her but instead screws up his eyes in silent bewilderment. A distressed Geraldine turns on her heel and dashes for the stairs, leaving the family unit in her wake.

At the first-floor corridor she rests on a large windowsill seat overlooking the garden and waits for her heart to stop racing. *I was only trying to help.* No, Simon was right, it was none of her business, and what did she know in any event? What if she'd jumped to the wrong conclusion entirely? It was only a theory, one piqued by her curiosity. Or should that be a gross distortion conjured up by her nosiness? Simon said fluctuations in mood and clarity were common, and it stood to reason that Jeffrey must have had all the tests going. No matter what her thoughts were, she had no right to drop an additional burden into the family's lap. God knows what they were going through without her adding to their uncertainties and doubts. What had she done?

Not only that, why had she done it? Wouldn't it have been better to have kept her mad theory to herself? She herself wasn't going to be here the day after tomorrow, so why the obsession with somebody's else's problems? She had hours to live and here she was fretting about somebody she didn't know, hadn't even encountered, before yesterday. It was crazy. What had got into her?

As she calms down, however, she begins to remonstrate with herself all over again. Yes, Jeffrey displays all the classic symptoms of dementia, but she'd been around many other sufferers and knew, just knew, something wasn't right. *Evaluate the evidence.* She'd witnessed Jeffrey consuming a substantial amount of salt last night, and hyponatremia is a real condition, with the risk of serious disorders, and you can't disprove the science of that. Would they have tested him for sodium deficiency? In this country, who could be sure the way things had been going? She'd elected to come here precisely because of the laxity of controls and checks, but was that necessarily a good thing?

But say she was right over a potential misdiagnosis, what right did she have to stick her oar in? Jeffrey was far from the only person in this place heading for the exit. Yes, but what if you weren't the one making the decision? This was a human life after all, not something to be casually jettisoned early because of an incorrectly dated 'best before' sticker. Her own resolution to come to Go Gently had only been taken after hours – days, months, years – of soul searching. Surely that made it more justifiable – defensible – in a way?

The thought also occurs that this might be a distraction she's fashioned for herself, a means of not having to cope with the enormity of her own impending demise. As she gazes into the distance looking for an answer, a bright light seems to call to her, to beckon her. Instinctively, she moves towards it. It's a vending machine, at the end of the corridor, selling soft drinks. As she surveys the range of beverages on sale, one brand in particular jumps out at her: Red Bull Energy Drink, with the assurance that it 'gives you wings'. Another Eureka moment hits her: of course, trust to science – the answer lies in a controlled experiment. She sets off to her room in search of her purse.

Chapter Nineteen

D awn has been so transfixed by Woody's story she only just makes it back to her room minutes before Kimberley arrives. She checks her face in the mirror and gives herself a ticking off: *Bloody hell, Dawn. Pull yourself together.* She applies a quick coat of lipstick, some rouge to her pallid cheeks, and straightens her hair. *You still look a bloody mess* is her final take on the result.

Kimberley arrives with a large bouquet of flowers, and tears in her eyes. Where to begin? Tea. A nice cup of tea. As her daughter fusses with the kettle and cups, Dawn suppresses the pain threatening to crush both her body and spirit. She realises how the adrenalin of the week, and the diversion Woody has provided, is keeping her afloat. Now she needs to find extra reserves for Kimberley.

Kimberley comes straight out with it on dishing the digestives: 'I've left him, Mum.'

Several thoughts flash through Dawn's mind. Is this a ploy to make her abort her plans? A farewell present to send her off without having to worry about her daughter's future? A cry for help? Does she even need to know about this development? 'Well, you took your time, love. It must be like taking a really tight pair of heels off.'

'I didn't know whether to tell you, but I know you never liked him. I've been so unhappy, I was at a loss what to do.'

Dawn ignores the first point. 'If it's any consolation, why put up with unhappiness and continuous pain when you can make it stop,' – she clicks her fingers – 'just like that.'

'Like you're doing?'

'I didn't mean that, no. I meant persisting with a marriage that has run its course. You're young, you still have your life ahead of you and Ava too.'

'You've still got me and Ava, Mum, but you're not persisting, are you?'

Another wave of pain washes over her – she's forgotten to take her painkillers in all the rush. 'Let's not go into all that again, shall we?' She squeezes her daughter's hand, 'You'll be better off without him.'

'But I won't be better off without you, Mum,' says Kimberley, tears running down her face. 'Please, please, don't do this.'

Dawn feels she might expire on the spot with a broken heart, depriving her – and Go Gently – of two extra nights. She's light-headed, in pain, not thinking straight and wants to lie down. Despite the creeping doubt now stalking her, she is determined not to show any sign of vacillation to her daughter. *I've made my mind up. Don't try and make me change it now.* 'You know why I'm doing this. You don't want to see me dwindle away, never knowing the day, do you? It's better this way.'

Kimberley drops to her knees and grasps her mother's hands. 'Every minute longer you're here would be like a year to me. I'd rather see your light fade gradually than have it snuffed out in a flash.'

Dawn persists with her practised script. 'I'm ill. A goner. And it's not just me – I don't want you to suffer every day.'

'You think I won't suffer every day when you're not here? Do you?' Dawn starts to weep too. She doesn't answer. 'I can help care for you; you know that. Let me.'

'Oh, Kimberley, you don't want your last memories of me to be a helpless bag of bones praying for it to end. You'd be praying for it to end too if we did that.'

Kimberley shakes her head. 'No, that's where you're wrong. I wouldn't.'

Dawn knows she is struggling in this exchange. 'There's a reason people take this way out. There's plenty of people in here doing exactly the same. It's not like it's just me.'

'I don't give a shit about anybody else. I just care about you. If I could swap places with you now, I would. I don't want you to die, Mum, not like this.'

Dawn, reeling from this onslaught, calls for a time out. 'Pass me that tea, will you? All this arguing is making me parched.'

Kimberley does as she's asked and returns to her chair. They sit in silence until Dawn circles back to the point they started on. 'When you say you've left him, what exactly do you mean? Tell me in full.'

Kimberley dabs her wet cheeks with a sodden handkerchief, and takes a deep breath in preparation. 'I've kicked him out. On Monday night when we got back. I spoke to a lawyer yesterday, and I've started divorce proceedings. He can't contest it under the new rules, so that's it as far as I'm concerned. I never want to see him again.'

'And how's Ava in all of this?'

157

'I've tried explaining it to her as best I can. He'll have access, but he's so selfish, I wonder how hard he'll try after the first few weeks.'

Dawn nods knowingly. 'So, what happened to make your mind up?'

'We argued over everything, you know that.'

'Yes, but there must have been a trigger point?'

Kimberley fidgets, unsure how truthful or detailed to be in her explanation. Finally, 'It was to do with you, actually.' Dawn could have guessed as much. 'He was so callous about…' she throws her hands in the air '… all of this.'

'It's always the mother-in-law's fault.' They laugh.

'And, well this is what really got to me, he couldn't wait to get his hands on your money. That's what it was all about to him. Flogging you off to the knacker's yard for a few lousy quid. He kept going on and on about what we could do with the cash – a new car, a new kitchen, a holiday. I can't believe I ever saw anything in him.'

Dawn knew Ben was a wrong 'un from the start, but Mark had been quite clear she wasn't to say anything: *give him a chance, don't upset Kimberley, it's her choice and nothing to do with us.* Mark, of course, was right. Anything she might have said back then would only have made her daughter dig in her heels more. Well, she wasn't the first woman to sign up for a bad marriage, and she wouldn't be the last. 'Well, it's done now, and that's the hardest part.'

Kimberley rises from her chair again to hug her mother. 'You could come and live with me now, don't you see? I know it was difficult with Ben, but you can move in and I'd be there for you. There's nothing to stop you now.'

Dawn is wilting under the pressure. 'It's not the answer, love. It sounds like a good solution, but we've both got to be brave and face the inevitable.'

Kimberley still isn't having it. 'If you're brave enough to do this, you're brave enough to take every breath you can until nature gives up on you. And I'm strong enough to be with you every step of the way.'

Dawn strokes her daughter's hair, and smiles. 'You beautiful, beautiful, girl. Thank you.'

Kimberley, determined not to give up, delivers her ultimatum. 'I'm coming here Friday and I'm not taking no for an answer. You pack that bag and come on home with me or we say goodbye properly. Am I clear?'

When Geraldine calls in at Jeffrey's room after lunch, the departing orderly tells her not to be too long as he is due a nap. Four hours later there's fat chance of that. Jeffrey is licking his lips as she hands him his fifth can of Red Bull. She's been administering the sodium-charged solution (without the aid of a prescription) on a strict hourly basis after ascertaining, from the nutrition label, the exact amount of sodium in every 250ml can – it's important she build ups the dosage slowly so as not to overcook her patient. She is also aware that the other ingredients could cause Jeffrey to experience nausea, rapid heartbeat or even a seizure, and the last thing she wants to do is accidentally kill him (which would be a dismal fail on her report card). Has she seen any change in him? Well, he's been quiet all afternoon, his mind orbiting the far side of the moon from where no signals can reach earth, but compliant enough to her ministrations.

She needs to see the experiment through. She's not expecting Jeffrey to suddenly spring up and recite *The Rime of the Ancient Mariner*, but any indication that the haze is lifting will be proof enough. She's got all day and nowhere else to be. She doesn't try to engage Jeffrey in conversation as the hours unfold – experience tells her you never rush a lab test.

She briefly dozes off and finds Jeffrey staring at her in bewilderment as she comes to. 'I know I know you, but I can't seem to place you.'

Geraldine tenses. Is that Jeffrey being vague, or *vague vague?* She reminds herself she must take this slowly. 'We were only introduced yesterday. I'm Geraldine.'

'Of course. Ger-al-dine.' He leans forward and politely shakes her hand. 'And I'm Jeffrey. Very pleased to make your re-acquaintance.'

Geraldine almost punches the air in delight.

He looks around uncertainly. 'Sorry, I'm a little confused. Where exactly are we?'

Confused? God, if he only knew, thinks Geraldine. 'You're a client at Charon House, Jeffrey. So am I. It's like a hotel.'

Jeffrey brightens. 'Of course. I like to get out and about, you know.' His face falls slightly. 'Ever since my good lady passed away.'

'Rosemary,' says Geraldine.

'Oh, you knew her?'

'No, Jeffrey, you mentioned her to me. She sounds like a wonderful woman.'

He smiles at the memory. 'She was a cracker. Miss her every day.'

Geraldine resists the temptation to fill in any gaps for him. She needs to discover how much he can recall. 'You go on a few trips, do you?'

He nods genially. 'Oh yes, city breaks, coach tours – I've even been on a couple of cruises. It's a wonderful way of meeting new people. No point in just pining away at home, is there?'

'When did you arrive here, Jeffrey?'

He knits his brows. 'Yesterday? Yes, yesterday. My son will have brought me. Simon. He's a good lad, looks out for his dad. He's always arranging things for me.'

'You're lucky to have someone caring for you.'

'Do they do golf here? I used to play a bit myself, but I skip the first eighteen holes these days and go straight to the nineteenth.' He cackles at his own joke.

'I don't think so. How long are you staying?'

Jeffrey is thrown again as he discovers he doesn't know. 'I'm not sure. A weekend-break?'

'A mini-break I think they call it.'

He takes this in, and then suddenly remembers his manners. 'Are we dining? How rude of me to keep you waiting.' He strains to get up. 'Shall we?'

Geraldine doesn't want him to leave the room just yet. 'Maybe later, Jeffrey? Room service?'

'Ooh, yes. Just the ticket.' He yawns. 'Might just grab forty winks first. Simon's wife, Vicki – lovely as she is – says I mustn't overdo it. She's a fusspot, but means well.'

He sinks back into the comfort of his armchair and his eyelids begin to droop. 'Yes, a fusspot, but means well,' he mutters. And with that, he's fast asleep.

Geraldine lets out a massive sigh of relief before trying to make sense of what she's just seen and heard. She assesses the results. First, Jeffrey is cogent. He knows who he is, is aware his wife has passed away, and he acknowledged his son and daughter-in-law. He was civil and courteous towards Geraldine, as he no doubt was towards other 'new friends' he met on his trips. However, he was confused as to where he was, why he was here, and when he arrived, which is only to be expected as he'd had all the pages ripped out of his diary since the day he fell ill. One thing she can be certain of is that Jeffrey does not have dementia. Her hunch that he could be suffering from sodium deficiency has been upheld, albeit in the crudest of manners. Poor Jeffrey may be sickening from age, loss, creaking bones and hardening arteries, but the symptoms of dementia he's displaying can be reversed with appropriate treatment.

Jeffrey begins to snore, causing her to smile. Look at him, she thinks, in the land of Nod. Except there they wouldn't have put a label on him specifying his expiry date. No, you only find that in this God-forsaken country. He seems a pleasant old cove, jocular, amiable – larger than life; what a crime to bring the curtain down on him before the finale.

She gathers her senses. This is all very well, but what is she to do about it? Simon gave her short shrift earlier, but if he could see his father as she'd just seen him, this dreadful mistake could be avoided. Yes, that's what she must do – get a proper medical diagnosis, arrange appropriate treatment, and grant him the gift of a few extra years. He looks like he'd make good use of them too.

The irony of her situation isn't lost on her. Here she is, trying to save Jeffrey's life, when she's about to toss hers to the wind without a backward glance. The question flashes across her mind: Why?

She shudders at the thought, knocking a can of Red Bull to the floor. Jeffrey stirs at the noise, and jerks awake. Spotting Geraldine, he has but one query on his mind: 'Rosemary?

Chapter Twenty

Geraldine prays she will find Dawn in the coffee shop the next morning. Beset with doubt and worry, who else can she turn to? Her heart leaps when she spots her new friend seated in the corner, idly contemplating an empty cup. She looks terrible: ghostly pallor, puffy eyes, vacant stare, despondent.

'Are you all right?' asks Geraldine as she sits down. 'You don't look it.'

'Caffeine overdose, I think,' Dawn replies. She doesn't try to dress up what's on her mind: 'I think I might have made a dreadful mistake coming here.'

The news hits Geraldine like a kick from a mule. She thought Dawn was wobbling earlier, but this confirms it. And haven't similar misgivings been gnawing away at her since she started investigating the true state of Jeffrey's health? She squeezes Dawn's hand consolingly. 'Do you want to talk about it?'

Dawns blows her nose and fiddles with her handkerchief as she wonders where to start. 'I had it so clear in my head, but I'm all confused now. I couldn't afford treatment and didn't want to waste away in pain, didn't want to be a burden. I'd had a full enough life, so couldn't complain – what was there to live for anyway? Nobody but Kimberley and Ava would miss me, and at least this way I could do something for them, leave them some money. But now…'

Geraldine's heart goes out to her. A day or two ago she'd have tried to bolster her companion's fortitude, tell her such thoughts were inevitable, remind her to rely on the thought process that had led to her decision. She'd have been mainly reassuring herself, but nevertheless the common bond they shared would help them towards their final goal. But now…

'Did something happen?' is all she can come up with.

'Kimberley. Kimberley came to see me. She pleaded with me not to go through with it. She's left her useless husband and said she'll help care for me. She loves me and needs me.' She brushes a tear away. 'I love her and need her.'

Geraldine, with no family of her own to speak of, suddenly feels even more alone in the world. 'So, you've made your mind up. That's good. You've got to do what's right for you.'

Dawn shakes her head. 'I don't know if I have or not. Am I being selfish, or just scared? I've been going back and forth and back and forth.'

Geraldine had long known this final twenty-four hours would be the worst, the day when you would attempt to talk yourself out of it, the time to convince yourself you never really meant to do this. She's steeled herself not to succumb to false sentimentality, not to pull a handbrake turn at the last minute that she would subsequently regret as the emptiness of her old life reasserted itself. She doesn't know what to say.

'And something else,' says Dawn, 'which you'll think is crazy.' Geraldine is starting to think she is long past the point of being surprised at anything. 'I can't get Woody off my mind.' She immediately realises she may not have expressed that as clearly as she intended and moves to avoid any misinterpretation. 'Not in that way, it's… I can't work out what he's doing here.'

'The same as the rest of us, Dawn, surely?'

'He told me yesterday about being sent to prison for something he didn't do. He's had such rotten luck, poor man, he's at the end of his tether. But ending up here is, well, there's something not quite right.'

Something not quite right. Just like Jeffrey, thinks Geraldine. Maybe, just like them. 'We all have our reasons, Dawn. Woody may not be able to work out what you're doing here, either. Or me, certainly.'

Her words impact deep with Dawn. The one thing she's never truly squared with herself in coming to Charon House is her self-denial of medical treatment. What if her cancer could be beaten, giving her a reprieve and more years to spend with Kimberley and Ava, then wouldn't that be worth fighting on for? A life weighed against the equity of some modest bricks and mortar? The other thing that jumps out is Geraldine's reference to her own reasons for being here. In the few short days she's known Geraldine, she's never really explained. Dawn has been curious, of course, but it's not exactly the sort of question you can come straight out with, is it? *Tell me, why are you ending it all?* You have to wait for people to volunteer that type of information, like she did, gabby, gobby Dawn, on a mission to explain to all and sundry. A mission to explain to herself, more like. 'You're right,' she says, 'I'd not thought of it like that.'

'Well, I've got a bit of an issue, too,' says Geraldine. 'You remember Jeffrey, the man with dementia? Well, he's not got dementia at all, but he's still going to be euthanised unless we can stop it.'

'What?' This is totally left field and Dawn is struggling to get her head around this new development. 'We've seen him, Geraldine. He's obviously got dementia.'

'No, that's where you're wrong. I think he's suffering from sodium deficiency which can cause similar symptoms to dementia, but in his case it's totally reversible.'

'Who told you this?'

'Nobody. I did my own experiment, gradually increasing his salt intake, and he was pretty much normal for a spell. If he's treated properly, he'll be fine.'

Dawn knows Geraldine isn't a doctor and can't help wondering if the strain of the week is getting to her. 'Are you sure about that?' she asks. 'Have you told the staff or his family?'

Geraldine shakes her head. 'Not yet. The trouble is he's relapsed again, so I need to top him up and then pick my moment. The other problem is I mentioned my suspicion of a misdiagnosis to his son, Simon, and he hit the roof. He said I was a mad, interfering busybody.'

Dawn bursts out laughing.

'What's so funny?' asks a bruised Geraldine.

'We must have a weakness for strays, that's all. I'm agonising over what I should do, and Woody keeps interrupting my thoughts. And here you are, Supervet, planning on rescuing Jeffrey from the dog's home. It doesn't feel like we're finished yet, does it?'

Geraldine's serious demeanour cracks for a second. 'No, it doesn't,' she concurs. 'The question is, what are we going to do about it?'

Dawn's answer springs fully formed from her lips without the need to engage her brain. 'Get out of here,' she says defiantly. 'Are you coming with me?'

Geraldine doesn't wait for second invitation – it's as if she's simply been waiting to be asked: 'Yes,' she replies. 'But there are a couple of matters we need to attend to first.'

Upstairs, Adil has just finished helping Jeffrey dress, and is showing him the results in the mirror. 'Very sartorial' he comments, as proud of his new word as in his ability to tie a necktie around someone else's collar. He himself has never worn a tie. Jeffrey doesn't comment one way or the other (but if he could he'd no doubt advise Adil he usually favoured a Windsor knot).

Since learning of his new duties yesterday, Adil is lower than ever. His mind is clear: he must leave Charon House and get out of this accursed country as soon as he can, to one where humanity and decency still holds currency. Yes, he's relying on Sacrosanct for that, but he's buggered if he's going to administer tranquilisers to unwitting guests in the meantime; he's simply not prepared to do that – he'll pour them down the sink if it comes to it. Why, it's asking him to be an accessory to murder. But then the thought crosses his mind: isn't that what he's been doing anyway? Manslaughter, at least, whether voluntary or not. He takes in Jeffrey's full reflection in the mirror – whatever fate awaits Adil in the next chapter of his life, at least he's got one, unlike this tragic old figure in front of him.

He's not expecting the knock on the door that precedes the arrival of Geraldine and Dawn. Inter-room visits are rare in his experience, not that these two wait for an invitation to enter. They swiftly close the door behind them, giving the impression they're throwing a pursuer off their scent. Now Adil is sporting the same perplexed expression as his charge.

'Adil, thank goodness,' says Geraldine breathlessly on seeing who's attending to Jeffrey. 'You have to help us.'

The poor put-upon licensed guest worker feels his stomach churn. Here we go again. Does anybody in the country ever say 'please'? He *must*, he *has to,* instructions are to be *complied with,* guidelines *observed.* What fresh hell does this most simple of sentences – *you have to help us* – presage? Especially coming from this kindly old lady who has treated him decently during the week. He looks from Geraldine to Dawn and back again, waiting for the inevitable bad tidings.

Geraldine ushers him to sit down, and begins. 'Adil, what do you know about who's in charge here, the head doctor in particular?'

'It doesn't work like that,' replies Adil, wondering where this is all going. 'There are no doctors on site. Once people are through those gates, they're not really in need of one. Why are you asking?'

'Because Jeffrey here doesn't have dementia. He's been misdiagnosed, and unless we do something it will be too late.'

This is news to Adil. 'How do you know? It looks to me like he's got dementia.'

As Geraldine hands in her elementary science homework, Dawn purses her lips – Geraldine's theory doesn't sound any less absurd the second time around. Looking at Jeffrey staring off into space, she can't decide if her friend is barking up the wrong tree entirely, or simply barking.

'Look, I can prove it,' says Geraldine, realising she's on the verge of losing the room. She reaches into her handbag and produces a can of Red Bull. 'If we give Jeffrey this, you'll see for yourself.' She is met with silence. 'It contains salt,' she says shaking the tin, as if that will clinch the argument. 'So, Adil, the first step is to get a doctor to do the appropriate tests, and to get Jeffrey's son to cancel the arrangements.'

Adil doesn't know what to think. It hardly matters if Geraldine is right or wrong, because, as he has learned from the supervisor, as far as he can tell Jeffrey's fate is signed, sealed, and will be delivered on time and as per spec. 'I don't know if Jeffrey has been misdiagnosed or not but, from what I've found out, they won't be willing to investigate or tell the relatives anything. They don't like people going back on their agreements.'

Dawn harrumphs. 'Don't they? Well, we'll see about that. I've changed my mind, as I have every right to do, and I'm going home.'

Adil, who had earlier convinced himself that not wriggling would pull him clear of the quicksand, feels the ground give way beneath his feet, dropping him right back in it. He has no option but to tell her. 'They won't let you change your mind. The ones who try never succeed.'

Geraldine is busy administering Jeffrey's medicine as Dawn bristles. 'I'd like to see them stop me. It says I can change my mind right up to the last second.'

How far should he go? He's torn. But these people are directly affected. 'Are you on a government package?' he asks.

'Yes,' Dawn replies. 'Clean Bill.'

'Giving you a cash sum on the value of your assets with a ten per cent bonus on top?'

'Yes, that's the one.'

'Do you realise that if you cancel your contract now, you could forfeit those assets, that sum?'

Dawn freezes. 'Rubbish. Where does it say that?'

'In what you call the small print.'

'Just let them try it,' says Dawn defiantly.

Geraldine, taking a break from being drinks monitor, chips in. 'Well, I've not signed a Clean Bill contract or whatever you call it, and you know what? I'm leaving too.' Dawn high fives her in solidarity. But the main problem remains.

Adil sighs. He's had enough of aiding and abetting this monstrous concern – these people need to know the worst of what he's discovered. 'Your Go Gently contract, Geraldine, as per Dawn's, empowers them to "administer appropriate care subject to circumstances". What that means is, if you tell them you've changed your mind, even if you're prepared to honour the forfeits, they will pronounce that you are suffering from stress and knock you out with sedatives. They'll then keep you under right up to the moment they wheel you into the theatre and you'll never wake up again.'

'They can't do that,' says a horrified Geraldine. 'That's murder. It's illegal.'

'It's not illegal here,' says Adil, shaking his head. 'They've been sedating you since you arrived. Have you not noticed anything?'

Dawn and Geraldine stare open-mouthed at Adil as they mentally retrace their beverage consumption.

Infused with renewed courage, Adil decides the moment for full disclosure has arrived. 'Listen, I hate Go Gently and I detest Charon House. I was sent here to do some spying and now I've got to get out too. If you only knew what goes on in this place.'

'Worse than murdering us against our will?' says Dawn scornfully.

'Spying for whom?' is what Geraldine wants to know.

'People who are opposed to assisted dying. They've put me in here to see what I could find out. And I've made some horrendous discoveries.'

'Like what?' Dawn exclaims.

Adil, relieved to get some of this weight off his chest, solemnly lays out the full extent of what he's learned. 'They've invented a new killing machine, a pod to gas people to death, one at a time.'

'Do you mean, like the Nazis?' Geraldine gasps.

Adil shrugs. 'They wouldn't put it like that. They're going to claim it makes assisted death cheaper and quicker so more people sign up for it. They're calling it science, they're calling it progress, but the basic goal is to eliminate entire generations who have outlived their usefulness and who are a burden on the state.'

'Well, they can try to dress it up any way they want, but it sounds like the Nazis to me,' says Geraldine.

But Adil hasn't finished with the bombshells yet. 'It gets worse. They're also going to use this killing machine to get rid of prisoners who are costing the state money to keep in jail. They're calling it a voluntary early release scheme.'

Dawn's mystery is solved at last. 'Woody,' she laments. 'Oh no. That's why he's here.'

'You should never have come to this place, ladies. But the last thing you should do is let anybody know of your intentions to leave. Your final appointments are scheduled for tomorrow?' They nod. 'So, you have your final psychological assessment later?' Correct. 'Then my advice is to play along and don't create any suspicion.'

'But how will we get out?' asks Dawn.

Adil takes in the sight of the grey-haired fellow travellers and decides: 'I will help you,' he says.

Geraldine reaches into her handbag for another can of Red Bull. 'And Jeffrey too?'

'And Woody,' says Dawn. 'We can't just leave him here. We've all got to make a break for it.'

'And when we do,' adds Geraldine, 'we need to let the world know exactly what's going on in this hellhole.'

Adil, not entirely convinced the world will want to listen, doesn't respond to that. Dawn's mind, however, is occupied with far more practical matters: 'Can we worry about that when we get out? First things first.'

'Yes. Exactly,' agrees Geraldine. 'Let's focus on our escape. How *are* we going to get out?'

Jeffrey suddenly snaps to attention as if he's been connected to the mains. 'Hello, Geraldine,' he says on spotting her with two other visitors. 'Are we having a party?'

Chapter Twenty-One

Adil and Dawn watch with renewed interest as Geraldine engages with Jeffrey. Could she be right and he's been misdiagnosed, or is she clutching at straws?

Channelling her inner-game show host, she kicks off with a soft, 'Can you remember where you are, Jeffrey?' (At least she doesn't ask if he's animal, vegetable or mineral.)

Jeffrey views her with suspicion as if she's trying to catch him out. 'Yes, of course. I'm on a mini-break.'

'Can you remember the name of the place?'

Jeffrey strains for an answer, before coming up with, 'Sharon Something. Whoever she is.'

'What are you planning to do here, Jeffrey?'

He contemplates for a few seconds. 'Golf? Having said that, I tend to skip the first eighteen holes these days and go straight to the nineteenth.' He cackles at his own joke.

Geraldine persists. 'And are you here by yourself?'

Jeffrey's face falls. 'My good lady wife died some years back, I'm afraid. I find these excursions help to keep up the spirits – there's life in the old dog yet.'

Dawn and Adil are astonished. Whatever Jeffrey is suffering from, it certainly doesn't appear to be dementia. But if Adil is right, Go Gently won't want to hear about, or act on, Geraldine's discovery.

Geraldine needs to get Jeffrey out of the way briefly in order to consult with Dawn and Adil. 'When did you last have a shave, Jeffrey? Can't have you looking like Desperate Dan if we're going to have dinner tonight, can we?'

Jeffrey rubs the stubble on his chin, and exclaims, 'I must look like a pirate. Right – give me ten minutes,' and with that he slips off to the bathroom.

The three of them huddle together for an urgent, whispered conversation.

'Do you believe me now?' asks Geraldine.

They nod. 'It's remarkable,' says Adil. 'Never seen anything like it.'

'Me neither,' Dawns adds. 'You've done a better job than his doctor, that's for sure.'

'So, what do we do about it?' Geraldine asks. 'Especially as you said Go Gently will deny the truth of the situation.'

'Don't you think we should speak to his son?' says Dawn.

Geraldine shakes her head. 'He thinks I'm a lunatic, and even if he did believe us, which I very much doubt, he still has to get past Go Gently.'

Adil agrees. 'They'll say a flash of clarity in a dementia patient isn't out of the ordinary. Terminal lucidity, or an awakening, in a dementia patient is often taken as a sign that death is near.'

'Well, they're not wrong there,' Dawn ventures.

Geraldine queries Adil: 'Are you saying Jeffrey *does* have dementia?'

'No, not at all. I'm saying that's what they'll say. I believe you, because his clarity is obviously linked to his sodium intake. We've just witnessed it.'

'Good. We must get him out of here, then, at the same time we escape. Agreed?'

'And Woody, too. Don't forget Woody.' Dawn certainly isn't about to.

Geraldine gets to the point. 'So, are we going to tell Jeffrey the truth about why he's here, and who put him here? And why he is going to have to make a run for it with us instead of simply walking out of here?'

'What if he doesn't believe us, or doesn't want to go with us?' asks Dawn. 'What do we do then?'

'Then we'll just have to persuade him,' says Geraldine, who'd pit herself against a reluctant schoolboy any day.

Jeffrey chooses this moment to re-enter the bedroom. 'Smooth as a baby's bum,' he declares proudly.

Geraldine makes him sit down for their 'intervention'. 'I'm not in trouble, am I?' he jokes.

She resumes. 'Jeffrey, do you know who we all are?'

He looks at her. 'You're Geraldine.' He turns his gaze to Dawn. 'I'm sorry, but I don't think I've had the pleasure.' And finally, to Adil. 'Pretty sure we've not met.'

His chief interlocutor presses on. 'Jeffrey, you've been poorly. So much so that people were really worried about you.'

He snorts in bemusement. 'Rubbish. I've been a bit dicky, that's all. What am I supposed to have had? Ebola? Lassa Fever?'

'Dementia.'

'Dementia? That's a good one. I used to say to my lad, Simon, if I ever got dementia take me straight to Stalybridge.' He draws his index finger across his throat in a cutting action. 'No messing.'

Geraldine wasn't expecting such a convenient tee-up, and isn't about to waste it. 'You are in Stalybridge, Jeffrey, at Go

Gently. That's the whole point.' Jeffrey looks so confused she wonders if he needs a saline top up. 'We've pieced it all together,' she says. 'You became ill, displaying classic symptoms. You were diagnosed with dementia, so your son, Simon, following your wishes, went ahead and arranged an assisted death for you here in Stalybridge.'

Jeffrey explodes. 'He what? Arranged to have his own father put down like a pet hamster? The little shit.'

'In fairness,' Dawn chips in, 'he does only seem to be doing what you asked him to do.'

'Bollocks,' declares a defiant Jeffrey, before quickly adding, 'Pardon my French.' Rattled, his face a study in shades of red, he tries to explain. 'I was talking hypothetically, isn't that obvious? I didn't mean for him to actually do it. What sort of child signs a parent's death warrant? It's unnatural.'

Dawn is about to repeat her earlier point, but bites her lip instead.

Geraldine, at least, is placatory. 'I'm sure he meant well,' she says by way of mitigation.

'Wait a minute,' says Jeffrey, 'when are they supposed to be, you know…' he draws a finger across his throat again.

'Tomorrow,' comes back the answer in triplicate.

'You're bloody joking, aren't you? Tell me this is a wind-up.' From the looks on their faces, he perceives that he's not on *You've Been Framed*. He shakes his head in exasperation. 'Hang on a minute, there's a bloody great big elephant in the room here: how can I be euthanised for having dementia, when I don't actually have dementia?'

Adil joins the fray. 'No, you don't, but for much of the time you've been here that's exactly how you've presented.'

'And who are you?' Jeffrey demands to know. 'A doctor?'

Geraldine needs to get the whole story out before things disintegrate. 'This is Adil, who has been looking after you most of the week. See, you can't even remember. To clarify, you don't have dementia, but you have been suffering from sodium deficiency which can look exactly like dementia, only in your case those symptoms can be reversed.'

'Oh my God,' he groans as he takes all this in. 'Sodium deficiency? Thank goodness the doctors picked up on it – I could have been dead meat.'

'The doctors didn't spot it. It was Geraldine,' says Adil, keen to set the record straight. 'And she's the one who has come up with the treatment, which is why you're pretty lucid now.'

Jeffrey's shoulders slump. 'Thank you, Geraldine. You're a life saver. Literally.' He takes a deep breath. 'Right, a plan of action. I'm going to tell them I don't have dementia, check out of this place, and go home. And just you bloody wait until I give that Simon a piece of my mind.'

'Listen,' says Dawn to the others, 'you'd better fill him in on why we're here, and why we've got to take matters into our own hands. I'm going to find Woody, and then we need to plan the great escape.'

Dawn is in a tizz as she makes a dash for the gardens. In choosing to live, she has turned her own world on its head, but getting out of Charon House may prove less easy than she'd anticipated, having stupidly authorised Go Gently to act as her judge, jury and executioner, with no right of appeal. Poor Jeffrey was in the same boat without even being aware. But that was only the half of it given Adil's news about the death machine and the plan to deploy it on prisoners. Prisoners like Woody, who she believed when he said he hadn't committed the crime he was accused of in the first place.

She spots him under the camellias – she'd known exactly where to find him. She charges over and comes straight out with it. 'I know why you're in here,' she declares, 'and I'm not bloody going to let them do this to you.'

Woody is alarmed at being accosted by a clearly agitated Dawn and steers her over to the stone arbour so they can speak in privacy.

'You're not here out of choice, are you, Woody?' she continues once they are seated.

Woody hesitates before answering. 'I am,' he says guardedly. 'I'm here of my own free will, just like you.'

That throws Dawn. Has Adil got it wrong? Has she jumped in with two feet when discretion was called for? As for him citing free will, wasn't it true that she had hidden behind that line, only realising at the eleventh hour how hollow it rang? The idea of free will, autonomy, was a cruel deception, a pretence that you were in charge as you were herded like cattle: first to pasture, then to the marketplace and, ultimately, the slaughterhouse.

She shakes her head. 'No, Woody. You're here because of an insane government and its callous disregard for human life; they think your life is worthless and they want to make you think it is too.'

Woody bows his head. She *does* know. 'I was offered a way out and agreed to it. Prison is a living hell – I couldn't take it anymore. You've made a similar decision, Dawn. You know when the game is up.'

'That's not true, Woody. They tell you the game is up because that's what they want you to believe, and they make it easy for you to go along with. But I'm not falling for it anymore. I've changed my mind and I want to go home.'

Woody feels his heart lift as if it's him, not Dawn, who's been granted a last-minute pardon. Whatever brought her to Charon House, he's glad she has rejected self-sacrifice in order to live and love a while longer. If only he could. 'I never asked your reasons for coming here in the first place, Dawn, because that's your business, but I'm really pleased you're not going through with it. It's just that I don't have any choice.'

'You don't know half the story, Woody. Listen to me and then tell me you feel the same.'

'I'm listening.'

When she gets to the part about the death machine, Woody is immediately put in mind of Ming the Merciless. 'That's truly sickening,' he says.

Dawn falters. He's not twigged. 'You're the first person they're using it on, Woody.'

Up until this moment, Woody has been under the impression his method of despatch was to be lethal injection. 'Are you sure? They implied they were using a chemical cocktail, but that details were subject to change. I thought that might mean the date or the time.'

'Typical,' says Dawn. 'Lies, lies, lies. No, of course they didn't tell you. They're launching the machine tomorrow as the latest thing to have in assisted death, and on Saturday they'll announce the early release prison scheme with you as the poster boy. Is that what you want?'

This is not what a shocked Woody wants, but it does lead back to the earlier question. 'No, it's not, but as a prisoner I don't get a say. Not unless I pull out and go back to Strangeways. I'm damned if I do, and damned if I don't.'

Dawn has doubts over the promises made to Woody. 'I think you'll be given the same option as people here, that is, no option at all.'

He buries his head in his hands. 'I'd only ever looked at it from my point of view, a way of ending a personal hell.'

'I know. We all look for ways to rationalise the decision. I was diagnosed with cancer and convinced myself ending it early was a way of avoiding months of pain; that nobody would miss me anyway.'

Woody is shaken at this revelation. 'Cancer? But you can be treated for cancer.'

Dawn thinks back over numerous dark nights of the soul, valuing her life so cheaply it wasn't worth saving or preserving. 'Yes. Treatment doesn't always work, but that doesn't mean you don't try. I'm ashamed to admit it, but I was prepared to give up far too easily.'

Woody grasps her hand. 'Never give up.'

She squeezes his hand in return. 'Same goes for you, too. The only way out of this for you is coming with us – me, Geraldine and Jeffrey. Time to join the great escape, Woody.'

'But where would I go even if we did get out? I'd be a prisoner on the run.'

'You still think that's worse than being gassed to death on Saturday?'

'Not when you put it like that…'

'Good. When we get out, we're going to bring this place to its knees. You can hide – stay – at mine until we get your name cleared. It's time us old fogeys struck back.'

In his revolutionary zeal Woody can almost hear "La Marseillaise" being struck up, feel the waft of air from the swaying *tricolores* on his face. He's in. *Marchons, marchons.*

Chapter Twenty-Two

Geraldine returns to her room to put together some homemade saline solution for Jeffrey. Her bag is bulging with salt cellars and water bottles she's pilfered from Ground Swell and the spa, and she is more than pleased with her efforts. *I'd have made a damn good shoplifter* she tells herself as she prepares her lab.

There is so much to do, she needs to concentrate. She has no way of knowing how to control Jeffrey's behaviour with any accuracy. She needs to prevent him relapsing again, but at the same time can't say for certain how long she can keep administering her crude DIY remedy without causing some other form of damage. They need to get him to the doctors as soon as possible, but to do that they first need to get him out of Go Gently's grisly grip. Never mind not reporting Jeffrey's misdiagnosis – if Adil hadn't told them what goes on in this place the game might already be up for her and Dawn. If, as they intended to, they had informed Go Gently they'd changed their minds and wanted to leave, they could already be under forced sedation, never to wake again. And as for poor Woody? None of this bore thinking about – it was a complete nightmare.

So much has changed in such a short time. A few days ago she'd taken Adil for a poor guest worker – shy, awkward, and hardly able to talk. How wrong she'd been, when he's put everything at risk to work undercover at Charon House. Put, even, his own life ahead of theirs, because without Adil, how were they going to get out of here?

Dawn, too, was a revelation. She'd come here with the same objective as herself (and possessing a far more justifiable cause if the truth be told), to end it all. Dawn hadn't tried to whitewash her reasons and had been matter-of-fact about the whole thing. All the more incredible then that she'd had the self-possession to change her mind, not out of fear, but out of courage. She had tackled her demons, and cut them down one by one. Hadn't Dawn opened her own eyes too, making her realise life wasn't something to be undervalued, exchanged for oblivion, without a fight? Maybe it was being here at Charon House and staring death in the face that sharpened the mind and made you re-visit your choices? Forced you to re-evaluate life itself? But what was the point of that if U-turns weren't allowed? She wonders how many people had changed their minds once they'd arrived, only to have their wishes ignored, or were drugged against their will to ensure their fate? Why were there no checks, how come the government didn't intervene? No, who was she kidding? Geraldine considers herself to be a sensible and pragmatic woman, yet she'd fallen for the whole shooting match, hadn't she? You could hear Go Gently trotting out the excuses: *We just needed to make her more comfortable in her final hours. She was in a highly distressed state so we gave her a little something to calm her down. We see people* thinking *they've changed their minds from time to time – it's quite natural.* If a friend or family member wasn't present in the final hours – as in her case – they wouldn't even have to pretend.

She busies herself with her mini-production line. She considers boiling the water first to purify it, but that would take too long to cool and, in any case, the filtered mineral water should be safe enough. Her idea is to taper the level of salt in each successive bottle, start big and go small, as if she's weaning a patient off an addictive drug, but she can't really be sure if that's the right thing to do and has no way of checking. It's a simple enough process in the end – she tips out the top half inch of water from each of the bottles, then measures in the salt using a rolled-up sheet of paper for a funnel. After vigorously shaking each bottle she then writes #J1, #J2, #J3 up to #J10 on the labels and packs them back in her bag. Will ten be enough? She has no way of knowing. She's allowing for twenty-four hours, but will they really be clear this time tomorrow and have delivered Jeffrey into safe hands? They've yet to come up with a plan.

Adil, cautious over being missed by his supervisor, has returned to his designated duties, leaving Jeffrey to re-acquaint himself with his thoughts for the first time in months. He has plenty to get his head around. As he strains to piece together the discarded fragments of his memory, the pre-eminent recollection is one of stumbling blindly in the dark. It was as if he'd been dropped into the deepest reaches of an impenetrable ocean, with no light or sound. He recalls flashes of memory darting past – a fish and chip shop, a hospital bed, a schoolyard, Simon calling his name. Above all, a profound sense of having mislaid something, only it's not a something, it's a somebody. Rosemary. She materialised through the murk from time to time and his joy and relief were unconfined as he stretched out to take her hand, only, damn it, he could never quite grasp it and would have to watch helplessly as she receded into the blackness once more. You'd think it would be exhausting, but it wasn't like that at all; his senses were in abeyance and time was immaterial. But he's back in the present now, Lazarus, risen from the dead, facing a new reality, a renewed life. Except he doesn't recall Lazarus having a son as keen as Simon to see the back of him. All that stuff he'd said about 'Send me to Stalybridge' – how could Simon have taken him so literally? Jeffrey loved life, and his son knew it. Another curious thing about having dementia – or what passed for dementia – is that it hadn't actually been that bad. Of course, he had no real way of knowing, but he wasn't aware of any pain, stress or concerns while he'd been AWOL – for the first time in his life he'd had no cares or problems to worry about. (Actually, make that the second time in his life because it was like being a small baby, where if you were clothed, fed, and distracted from time to time, you were as happy as Larry.) There'd been no reason at all for Simon to hasten things along to such an abrupt conclusion, like he's straightening the cushions on the settee in a tidy-up. He was going to have serious words with his son for calling time on him just as he was planning last orders.

What to make of this Geraldine? Rosemary always said he needed organising, as if he was a pile of ironing or the contents of a fridge, so he feels she'd have approved of this kindly Irish lady who had come to his aid. She'd taken charge (he liked a woman who took charge) and had restored his wits above sea level for the first time in months. He was no fool, and knew what Charon House was, but he hadn't quite worked out what had brought her here. He must remember to ask her. Whatever it was, he was glad she'd changed her mind. The spot of bother they found themselves in, this need to escape rather than just call Simon to pick him up, was all a bit hush-hush but if these Go Gently people were really as beastly as had been made out by the young boy, then there was no point in taking chances. He was going to kick up a stink about their shenanigans when he got home, just you wait and see. Once he'd sorted Simon out that is.

All this thinking is making him tired. Geraldine said she'd be back soon, they'd all be back, to form a plan. He's a good planner himself so will have a big role to play in getting that off the ground. Hadn't he been top salesman year after year? You don't lose the magic overnight. May as well have a nap while he waits. His eyes start to flicker, and he feels himself dipping below the water line, down, down, down, until a voice, like an arm reaching through the waves, pulls him back to the surface.

'Rosema…?' he stutters, before refocusing and trying again: 'Rosemary?'

Geraldine sighs and looks heavenwards: *Not again.*

Chapter Twenty-Three

It takes bottle #J1 and another half an hour for Geraldine to bring Jeffrey round, by which time Adil, Dawn and Woody have re-joined them. Geraldine is already worrying she's going to fall short on her cache of pick-me-ups. 'I can always make some more,' she whispers to the others.

Remarkably, Jeffrey is straight into action mode on reviving, totally unaware his brain has been on furlough. It's as if some unseen hand is using a remote control to switch from pause to play and back again. 'Right,' he says, rubbing his hands together, 'let's call this meeting to order. Item number one on the agenda: knotting the bedsheets.'

Adil is confused – he thought they were here to plan their escape. 'Knotting the bedsheets?'

'Doing a bunk,' explains Dawn. That doesn't seem to be any clearer, so she adds, 'Getting out of here. Escaping.' Adil shakes his head in wonder – English is such a peculiar language.

Jeffrey is a stickler for protocol. 'All present and correct, and may I welcome Woody to our gang of five.'

'Gang of four,' Adil interjects. 'I'm not coming with you.'

'Why not?' Jeffrey fires back.

'Because I can't. I'm a licensed guest worker and if I get caught, I'll be deported or worse. Plus, I have nowhere to run, and you'll be in trouble if you shelter me, so I'll keep my head down, wait for a transfer, and then I'll look to move to a different country.'

Their attempts to persuade him to change his mind don't last long. They know he's right.

'But you are going to help us, Adil,' insists Geraldine, making sure his earlier offer stands.

'Yes. I think I know a way. Can I ask, though, did you do your psychological assessments?'

Dawn's hand shoots up. 'I did,' she cries. 'Told them I was all set.'

'Are you sure that didn't raise any suspicions?' says Geraldine, concern etched on her face at the apparent flippancy of Dawn's reply. 'I emphasised how I'd come to terms with my decision and confirmed I was in a state of preparedness.'

Dawn laughs. 'Same thing, Geraldine. I got my big tick anyway.'

'Pity they didn't ask me,' says Jeffrey bitterly. 'I'd have bloody told them. But, of course, Simon has already given me my big tick, hasn't he?'

Woody hasn't had an assessment at all as nobody is bothered if wants to change his mind or not.

'It's strange to think,' giggles Dawn, 'that by this time tomorrow we're all supposed to be dead.'

Woody corrects her. 'That's not entirely right. I'm Saturday. And Adil isn't, you know…'

Jeffrey needs to bring the meeting back on track. 'Yes, well, that's not going to happen, as we're leaving under our own steam and without giving Go Gently a chance to stop us.'

'Exactly,' echoes Geraldine. 'And then tell the world all about this place.'

Adil stirs uneasily again. Sacrosanct and these four oldies – what chance do they really stand against the might of Go Gently and the government? 'You may feel differently once you get out. These people have a long reach.'

'Hmm,' says Jeffrey. 'My daughter-in-law, Vicki, has a friend who works in radio, and she certainly owes me, but I can see your point. Assisted dying is old news, and it's not as if this lot won't be announcing the death machine and the prison early release scheme to the media themselves, so where does that leave us?'

'They're not telling people how you can never leave once you check in,' says Geraldine forcefully. 'That's one angle to push.'

'And how poor people are being brainwashed into thinking they're helping themselves and their families by jacking it in as soon as they've nothing left to give,' says Dawn ruefully.

'And how bad the prison system has become that prisoners would rather die than serve their sentences,' adds Woody.

Their mood is on the verge of insurrection at the realisation of the fate that awaited them.

'People have sleepwalked into this,' says Dawn. 'In the beginning, assisted death was an option for the terminally-ill, to avoid unnecessary suffering. Now the state is actively encouraging it, not least by making sure you won't get any care at all if you're ill, unless you can afford it.'

'While fat cats like Callan Clay screw every last penny he can out of people's misery,' an indignant Geraldine adds. 'Selling you things you don't need and making you feel selfish or an eejit if you resist.'

Jeffrey interrupts their list of cavils. 'Calm down everybody, please. We need to get on. OK, Adil. Please continue. What's your plan?'

Four pairs of eyes fix on the guest worker. (Why is everything depending on him all of a sudden?) 'They're launching the pod in the morning, so that will provide perfect cover as all normal business is being backed up to the afternoon. They use vans disguised as laundry trucks to move the coffins and I know where they keep the keys. I'll nab one, park it around the back, get you all on board and off you go.

'So, we are going out of here in a box?' Dawn sniggers. Nobody smiles. 'Oh, take no notice of me – I always get giddy when I'm nervous.'

'If we time it for nine o'clock, everybody will be preoccupied,' Adil continues. 'I'm assuming one of you can drive?'

Jeffrey raises his hand. 'No problem there. I once drove the family all the way to the South of France without a single stop.'

The suggestion is met with a collective grimace. It's Dawn who breaks first. 'Can you drive, Woody?' He nods. 'Well, no offence, but wouldn't it be better if you concentrated on the planning side of things, Jeffrey?'

Geraldine, taking stock of her saline stash, is quick to back her up. 'If Woody wouldn't mind driving, that would allow you to keep an eye on things, Jeffrey, react to any unforeseen circumstances.'

Their unelected leader dismisses that suggestion with an airy wave of his arm, 'No, no, I'll be fine. I'm the man to burn some rubber.'

Nobody mounts a challenge, so it's left to Adil to expand on his plan. 'The rest of you will have to hide in the back – I'll make sure there's room. Two minutes to pack you in, and then it's on to the main gate and out.'

This sounds simple enough. *Too* simple.

'You should just get waved straight through at the gate, but if by any chance they stop you, I'll put a manifest on the front seat. It will be an old one, but they never check them properly. I doubt they'll stop you in any event.'

'But where do we go then?' asks Dawn. It's a good question. Before Adil can make a suggestion, Jeffrey pipes up. 'All back to mine, I'd say. Once we're out, I'd like to see the buggers try to drag us back. Then we can expose them for what they are.'

'Where do you live, Jeffrey?' Geraldine asks.

'Peterborough.'

'That's miles away,' says Dawn. 'We'll never get there without somebody trying to stop us. Remember, we'll have an escaped convict with us.' The answer is suddenly obvious to her. 'I'm less than an hour away and I still have my keys. We'll go over the moors to Yorkshire, hide Woody, and then split up. They'll have nothing on us three once we're out of here.'

'Except aiding and abetting a prisoner to escape,' interjects Woody. 'You should drop me as soon as we get clear of here.'

'Rubbish,' says Dawn. 'The gang of four, remember. All for one and one for all.'

'That was The Three Musketeers,' says Geraldine, a self-confessed pedant.

'Whatever, we're sticking together,' says Dawn. 'No point in getting Woody out of here if he's dragged straight back in the day after.'

Jeffrey endorses this defiant line. 'Hear, hear. Quite right. We'll get Woody a top lawyer to fight his corner. I know a few chaps at the golf club.'

Adil still has a few points to iron out. 'It's important that you lie low tonight, especially you, Woody, and be ready on the dot in the morning.'

Dawn has an idea: 'Why doesn't Woody stay at mine tonight? Nobody will think of looking for him there. Keep him out of harm's way.'

It strikes Geraldine that a similar arrangement will allow her to keep an eye on her patient. 'And if you hide out in my room, Jeffrey, I can make sure we keep your saline level balanced.'

Jeffrey hesitates. He's not sure Rosemary would approve of that, and besides, 'Right as rain, now. No need to worry about me, I can assure you.'

'No, Geraldine's suggestion makes a lot of sense,' Adil agrees. 'Quicker and easier to meet and get to the loading bay in the morning. Jeffrey and Geraldine go out the back way, pick up Dawn and Woody on the way, and then you skirt the grounds to the van.'

'What do I do about Kimberley?' queries Dawn. 'She's coming tomorrow to take me home, or so she thinks. Could you call her, Adil, and explain?'

The question sets Jeffrey off again. 'I suppose my beloved son will be planning to turn out too, making sure I shuffle off my mortal coil. Well, he can whistle as far as I'm concerned.'

Adil shakes his head. 'I wouldn't recommend that, Dawn. Best if you call her from a phone box when you're clear. She won't have arrived by the time you leave. That way, she won't panic and there's less chance of word getting out.'

'A phone box?' says Dawn. 'Do they still have those?'

'Sure they do,' confirms Woody. 'Well, they do in prison.'

'If you're only an hour away you should be home before Kimberley sets off, so I really think you should play it safe,' advises Adil.

Dawn nods. 'OK. So that's the plan.' She pauses. 'It's not exactly sophisticated, is it?'

191

Adil is just about to suggest she should come up with something better if she's unhappy with the arrangements, but Jeffrey chips in first. 'Not so fast, now. These stories you've told us, Adil – they aren't conclusive proof of diddly-squat, you know. Do you have any documentary evidence to back it up?'

Adil is starting to think he preferred Jeffrey when he was *gaga*. He sighs. 'No. I've given Sacrosanct what I found. I really think you should be concentrating on your escape, and leave all that stuff to them.'

Jeffrey considers for a moment, 'No, it's important that we are able to bear witness.' Suddenly he has it. 'I know what will swing it,' he says. They look to him expectantly. 'Take me down there, Adil, tonight, and I'll take a peek. Nobody would dare doubt my first-hand testimony,' he adds confidently.

Adil's heart sinks. He's not going back there again. But before he can say anything, Woody nips in. 'I want to go too. See what they were going to do to me. And back Jeffrey up as well, of course.'

Adil, Geraldine, and Dawn all protest at the same time: *You can't. It's too dangerous. You might get caught. It's too big a risk.* But Jeffrey has decided. 'Yes, two is better than one in something like this, and as you don't really count Adil – nothing personal – then Woody coming with us would be most wise. Agreed?'

The poor Man Friday bites his tongue. Here we are, the same old story – he doesn't count, he's going to have to do what he's told and, if anything goes wrong, take the rap as the fall guy. But even under the weight of his disappointment he recognises a valid point has been made – Jeffrey has more chance of being believed than a lowly factotum, and a separate account will help endorse whatever Sacrosanct comes up with (assuming they come up with anything at all). Could he get Jeffrey and Woody into the theatre and back out again without being detected? Security is lax and the CCTV cameras don't appear to be working – it's possible. Is bossy boots Jeffrey up to the task, though? Half an hour ago he was spark out of it again. Whatever this elderly whistleblower subsequently reports to the world, Go Gently will smear him, and say he's away with the fairies anyway. As for Woody, he's a convicted felon, and registers only slightly above Adil on the social scale – another one who doesn't really count. The entire plan is crazy, dangerous, foolhardy, and rash.

Adil shakes his head in resignation: 'I suppose so,' he sighs.

Chapter Twenty-Four

Just before midnight, Geraldine passes bottle #J4 to Adil for safe keeping and tells him to administer it to Jeffrey if he shows any sign of a relapse. 'He should be fine without it,' she says optimistically. 'He only had one an hour ago.' It's not exactly the most encouraging of send-offs for the wary guide.

Jeffrey is holding forth on their mission. 'Your job is to show the way, Adil. Straight there and straight back.' He turns to Woody, 'We'll survey the landscape, taking it all in before beating a quick retreat.' He taps his temple for emphasis: 'Important to memorise everything, then we'll debrief on our return, writing all the key points down. A contemporaneous account no less.' It all sounds so simple the way he describes it; nothing could possibly go wrong.

'Are you sure this is strictly necessary?' protests Dawn, who has spent the past few hours fretting over them being caught and foiling their escape plan for tomorrow. 'Once we get out of here, they won't be able to drag us back against our will, and we can tell people what we know. Woody can say he doesn't want to be part of their horrible early release scheme, and they wouldn't dare force him once it's public.'

'I'd still have to go back to prison, though, and I don't want that,' Woody reminds her.

A stronger justification for the midnight raid comes from an unlikely source: Geraldine, in full-on combat mode. 'I have to say I agree with Jeffrey – we have a duty to bear witness, because the more we've seen, the more credible our account will be when we come to relate it. A lone voice like Adil's can be silenced. They will say Jeffrey is suffering from his so-called dementia. They will accuse me and you as being two mad old bats. They'll stop Woody from saying anything at all. But together, we are harder to ignore. If Jeffrey and Woody can confirm what's in that theatre, it will carry weight, reinforce our narrative, and lend credence to the evidence Sacrosanct put forward. Go Gently staff who've experienced the rumours Adil has heard about might be encouraged to come forward and confirm them. Relatives who smelled a rat but said nothing in the past might start to ask the questions they wished they'd raised at the time. This is bigger than us now. We cannot leave this stone unturned.'

'Bravo, Geraldine,' shouts Jeffrey, well and truly stirred, as Woody nods his agreement.

Dawn, borne along on her friend's passion and resolve, is thus moved to bestow her blessing on the sortie: 'Well, what are you waiting for then? The sooner you start, the sooner you'll finish. Just don't get bloody caught.'

Under cover of night, the three set off, imagining they are commandos on a mission deep behind enemy lines. In fact, they only need to cross the lawn and skirt the shadows of the undergrowth before entering Harmony Wing via the deserted loading bay. Five minutes tops. When, without encountering a soul, they reach Zone Z, Adil makes the other two wait off the corridor before trying the double doors. If anyone is working late, he will claim to be a cleaner. He can hear the air-conditioning unit whirring away, but no voices, as he hesitates at the entrance to the theatre. He suddenly imagines what Dawn would say if she was behind him, and hears her words ringing out loud and clear in his ear: *Get a bloody move on, Adil. We haven't got all night.* He suppresses a smile as he passes the card over the reader and the lock disengages. The doors part like reluctant lovers until he can see fully inside. Empty. Nobody home. He lets out a sigh of relief.

Within seconds, he ushers Jeffrey and Woody inside and closes the door behind them. 'Be quick,' he urges. The dimly-lit theatre doesn't look much different from the other night, just tidier, all set for the morning. Rows of seats, flanked by three monitors on each side, are set out while there, at the front, directly beneath a giant screen, stand two bulky covered shapes. He looks up towards the corner where the red light of the CCTV camera continues to blink like a poker player with a poor hand. Can he be sure it's not working or being monitored? He pulls his collar up and beckons Jeffrey and Woody towards the front of the room. A quick look and they can leave. *Straight there and straight back* is what Jeffrey had said. He'd better not be kidding.

Jeffrey and Woody immediately begin to peel back the silver neoprene covers to expose the cigar-shaped vessels beneath. Within seconds the fitted sheets are cast to the floor.

'They're both the same,' hisses Adil, annoyed it will take more time to re-cover two machines instead of one.

Jeffrey ignores him, and whistles in wonder under his breath at the sleek contours of the space-age conveyance. 'I've had my head under a few bonnets,' he says, 'but nothing like this. It's a beauty.' He scratches his head. 'How does it work?'

Adil points at the canisters standing in the wire cages in each corner of the room. 'Gas'.

His voice is so low, Jeffrey repeats, at full volume, 'Glass? How do you mean?'

'No. Gas,' Adil shrilly repeats.

Woody and Jeffrey approach one of the cages and retrieve a shiny cylinder apiece. Jeffrey (clearly the type of man who thinks instruction manuals are for wimps: *Self-assembly is obvious, isn't it? King of the flat pack, me),* immediately starts to work out how it all fits together. Returning to one of the cigar-shaped cylinders, he starts to feel around the fuselage until he hears a click. 'There, knew it.' He reaches underneath, disconnects the canister that's already in place and holds both aloft. 'Ingenious,' he announces (a tad too admiringly as far as Adil is concerned). 'Hop in, secure the cabin, turn on the tap – blast off.'

He nods at Woody to try it on the other pod. 'Flick the small lever just under the belly.' Woody copies Jeffrey's action, but then makes the mistake of staring into the cockpit only to see his own face gazing back at him from the reflective surface. Pale, motionless, lifeless. Was this really to have been his end? A cold, clinical deprivation of life, devoid of any compassion; a cruel negation of the years he's spent on this earth. Images begin to flood his consciousness – his mother, the schoolyard, his wedding day, kids, their first days at school, working in the park gardens, family holidays – in an uncontrolled showreel of hope, loss and yearning. Even in this light Adil can see the blood drain from Woody's face as he takes in how his last moments on earth, scheduled less than thirty-six hours away, were to unfold (and still could if they get caught). Without warning, ex-prisoner A1801MB involuntarily doubles up and retches, causing him to drop both his canisters on the floor with a resounding, metallic clang. Alarmed at the noise as much as at his companion's condition, Adil rushes to his side.

'Take deep breaths,' says Adil as he vigorously rubs the unfortunate's back. Woody's response is a second, prolonged dry heave – *huurrrrahuur....*

'We have to get out of here,' says a frantic Adil, wishing he'd never embarked on this madcap endeavour (wishing at this point he'd never been born). He looks around for Jeffrey to signal the retreat, but he's disappeared. *Where the...?* Letting go of Woody for a moment, he peers over the two gleaming glass and steel chariots to discover Jeffrey is flat on his back, staring up at the ceiling with that familiar look on his face. Adil's first thought (second, really, after the one Geraldine wasn't kidding when she said she was no doctor) is to make a run for it. He owes these people nothing. They're putting everybody at risk. This was a crazy idea to start with. But he's stuck. It's like crossing the channel with his parents all those years ago: once you've gone so far, it's harder to turn back than it is to press on – danger lies on both sides of the divide. He pulls himself together and shakes Woody's shoulders. 'Get a grip,' he scolds, and runs over to Jeffrey. Relieving Jeffrey of the two canisters he's somehow still caressing like prize marrows at the village fete, Adil props the sodium deficient soldier of fortune up against the nearest wall and starts to unscrew the top from the saline Geraldine had the foresight to give him. A sheepish Woody, his stomach eruptions subsiding, comes around to help. Adil thrusts the bottle in his hand. 'Give him this – slowly though, don't choke him.'

The put-upon guest worker takes in the scene of mayhem around him, the two uncovered shiny ships of death with canisters scattered on the floor beneath them. Quickly and nimbly, he locks two canisters back into place in the bellies of the beasts, returns the others to the wire cages, and stretches the neoprene covers neatly back into place. There, done. He runs to the door and listens – nothing. *Please, please, let us get away with it.* The red light of the CCTV camera appears to be blinking at him even faster now – *no, it's just an illusion* he tells himself. Beads of sweat pump from his brow as he takes stock of the situation. Two choices: either make a break for it now, with an incapacitated Jeffrey, or wait until the saline takes effect? Both carry enormous risks.

He checks how Woody is doing – the bottle is down to halfway. He decides. 'OK,' he whispers. 'Give it ten minutes and then he should be able to make it back on his own two feet. Agreed?'

Woody nods. 'I'm sorry I freaked out,' he says. 'I imagined myself in there and my whole life flashed before me.'

Adil brushes his apology aside. 'The main thing is you and Jeffrey have witnessed all of this now. It exists; it's real.'

'Will he remember, though?' says Woody, indicating the slumbering figure nestling his bottle like an overfed baby.

'He'll remember the important bits,' says Adil coolly. 'Just not the parts where he nearly got us all caught.'

As if on cue, Jeffrey splutters back into life. 'Right, you two. Key objective achieved. Time for a secure and orderly withdrawal.'

Dawn's room has been selected as their HQ given its proximity to Harmony Wing, and she and Geraldine are mightily relieved to see the intrepid trio return unscathed.

'Told you there was nothing to worry about, didn't I?' Jeffrey boasts as they are welcomed back.

'What did you see?' asks Dawn. 'Was it worth the risk?'

'I'll tell you all,' replies their self-appointed leader, 'but let me and Woody collect our thoughts and make some notes first. Wouldn't want anything to slip our minds, would we?'

Woody is beckoned over to the small desk where Jeffrey has requisitioned Dawn's set of Charon House stationery to write up the official debrief.

The real third-degree takes place at the other end of the room, out of earshot of the executive arm.

'Were there any problems?' is Geraldine's opener to Adil.

Were there any problems? Where does he start? Or should he pretend everything was tickety-boo (another expression he'd been planning on introducing into his vocabulary)? No, they need to know. 'The good news is we weren't intercepted, and we got back in one piece. Jeffrey and Woody have now seen the pod and can speak with authority on the goings-on here.'

Geraldine waits a few seconds before the obvious, 'And the bad news?'

Adil checks that Woody and Jeffrey are preoccupied before proceeding. 'I'm afraid Jeffrey had a relapse while we were in there, and Woody also had what I think you would describe as an episode.'

Both women looked shocked. (Dawn more so than her Irish friend if it was a competition.) Geraldine groans. 'Oh, Jesus, he didn't?' She begins to count off on her fingers, trying to re-run all her earlier computations. 'Maybe it's the dilution? I reduced the salt content in each successive bottle so as not to overdose him. Could it be that, do you think?'

Dawn and Adil are in no position to offer scientific advice. 'It could be,' says Adil, noncommittedly, 'but the thing is, what about tomorrow? He could go again at any time.'

'And he's insisting on driving,' Dawn reminds them. 'I knew that wasn't a good idea. We'll have to get Woody to do it.'

Adil wonders whether the self-appointed driver will readily give up his position: 'It strikes me, with Jeffrey, he's a man who is very…'

He searches for the right adjective, until Dawn beats him to the punch with a whole Thesaurus to select from: 'Stubborn? Patronising? Cocksure?'

Geraldine feels she should intervene. 'I agree that he's… single-minded… old school… but he means well. I think he must have been in a job where he thought that was the way to get things done. We can't really say for sure what's going on in his mind, but he really does want to help and some of his suggestions are quite good.'

'The other thing,' continues Adil, 'is that he doesn't realise when he's drifted off. He zones out when you don't expect it and then comes back in a flash, without remembering a thing, and just carries on as if nothing has happened. It could be a big problem for you in the morning.'

'We are not leaving him behind,' says a resolute Geraldine. 'All for one and one for all, isn't it? We know if we leave him, he won't last the day. Nobody will believe he doesn't have dementia and nobody will care. I'm not having that on my conscience.'

Dawn speaks to her softly in response. 'Nobody is suggesting we leave Jeffrey behind, Geraldine. But Adil is right – we should be firmer with him, and not let him dictate everything.'

Geraldine nods. She understands it's down to her to remind Jeffrey of the principles of consensus. After all, she's the one who is looking out for him, the one who has his ear. She also intrinsically knows he's a good man at heart. 'I'll try,' she concedes, 'but first I've got to do something about his saline dosage. We can't have a repeat blackout tomorrow.'

'All you have to do is get him to Yorkshire in the morning and out of harm's way,' says Adil. 'If Woody drives then you're only an hour from safety.' (Surely, he thinks, that shouldn't be so difficult to achieve?)

Enough of Jeffrey. 'What happened with Woody though? Is he all right?' Dawn asks.

Adil completes his report. 'He lost it in there and had a bit of a panic attack when he saw the pod and realised that was to have been his fate. He came round quickly enough though, and he's OK now. He'll be fine.'

Dawn looks over to where Woody is struggling to get a word in edgeways with Jeffrey. *Poor lamb*, she thinks. She guesses she'd have freaked out too under the circumstances. 'Listen, Geraldine,' she says. 'You take care of Jeffrey tonight, and I'll calm Woody down. We can rely on Adil in the morning to get us into the van, and once we are out past those gates the entire picture changes. Small steps, yes?'

They all agree. Keep calm and carry on, just like it says on the poster hung in Dawn's kitchen back at home.

Chapter Twenty-Five

The sun has yet to rise on what was to have been Geraldine and Jeffrey's last day on earth, but such thoughts have been put aside for the moment. A countdown of a different nature has commenced and, all being well, they will soon be free of Charon House. Geraldine is pensive as they reach the sanctuary of her room. She makes up a bed of sorts on the sofa for Jeffrey, but neither feels like sleep.

Geraldine wonders what thoughts would be going through her head at this moment if her plans hadn't changed – how oppressively would every minute be bearing down on her? She recalls a quote from her schooldays – *O lente, lente, currite, noctis equi.* Doctor Faustus wishing time would stop as he awaits midnight and the arrival of the devil to collect his soul. 'O run slowly, slowly, horses of the night' – it made a lot more sense to her now than it ever did back in college. Faustus couldn't really complain as he'd had his end of the bargain fulfilled, but it pains her to realise how she'd been ready to wield the jockey's whip to reach the finishing line more quickly. The thought sends a shiver down her spine and she reaches for the kettle for something to do. 'Tea?'

'I never say no to a cuppa,' comes back the enthusiastic response.

'Sugar?'

He pauses momentarily, before declining. 'Had to think about that for a second,' he laughs. 'Must be going senile.'

They settle, and she decides she needs to get this out of the way. 'Do you remember having a blackout tonight, Jeffrey, over in the theatre?'

He looks surprised. 'Me? No. I was fine.'

She tries again. 'This sodium deficiency problem, you understand how it can cause you to feel?'

He's quiet. 'I think so. I know it's the reason I'm in here and if it wasn't for you, I wouldn't be seeing out the day. But since you've been giving me that stuff I'm back to my old self. Really.'

'I'm no expert, Jeffrey, I just had a lucky guess and knew enough to scratch at the surface. But you're not out of the woods yet – you need proper medical treatment to get you fully back on your feet. Adil says you zoned out in there and, to be honest, you blanked out with me earlier in the evening as well. Do you recall that?'

Jeffrey reacts with astonishment. 'Get away. Truthfully?' He sighs. 'I don't *feel* I've been absent, not since you've been helping me.'

Geraldine smiles. 'Well, I'll not let you out of my sight now until we get to Dawn's. Then we'll contact Simon and Vicki, explain this horrible mistake, and you can put it all behind you.' She brandishes a bottle of saline. 'Just need to keep you going with this. We know it works; only we must keep an eye on how much to give you, and when.'

He shakes his head in sorrow. 'I can't believe how I ended up in here with something as daft as that. It's outrageous when you think about it. Where were all the checks?'

'I think you fell through the cracks,' Geraldine says. 'They're not really interested in medical backgrounds in this place – most people are here of their own volition.'

Like Geraldine, he realises, and feels guilty for not having once asked her why. 'You must have had your reasons. Do you want to talk about them?'

It the first time anyone has directly asked her that question (excluding Go Gently, who were more interested in selling her add-ons). She's touched. She thinks of the letter she wrote to herself, sitting in the drawer opposite, in which she tried to justify throwing away the most precious gift in the universe: life itself. 'I will, Jeffrey, I really will, but not now. We'll have time for all that tomorrow. The important thing is I realised my mistake, and you were a big part of that.'

Not a man to waste a compliment, Jeffrey accepts her admission with good grace and a wide smile. 'It was the least I could do.'

She calculates this might be a good moment to raise a further concern. 'Do you mind not driving tomorrow, Jeffrey? I know you want to but, with these blackouts being so unpredictable, we think it would be safer if Woody drove. Safer and better for you as well.'

His face falls, unable to hide his disappointment. 'I was only trying to help. Stepping up to the plate and all that.'

'I know. But I think it's for the best. You're OK with that, aren't you, under the circumstances?'

He nods meekly. 'I know I can be a bit of a bull in a china shop at times. Action man, get things done. I sometimes forget other people have a say too. Rosemary said I could be a right bossy boots.'

'Only "could be"?'

He acknowledges a direct hit. 'Well, not with her I wasn't. She ruled the roost, not me. Maybe that's why I tried so hard at work, to make her proud of me.'

'You talked about Rosemary a lot when you weren't well. You must miss her a lot.'

Jeffrey's eyes moisten as he considers how much he misses his wife. 'It's like losing an arm or a leg. I can still feel her presence, like a phantom limb. I know I was in a fog when I was ill, but the truth is I've been lost for six years, pretending I was all right, trying to keep busy.'

'You were lucky to have had a relationship like that, Jeffrey. And Rosemary was lucky to have had you too, don't forget that.'

He brightens. 'We did everything together, especially after Simon left home. Holidays, walking every weekend, meals out, the cinema – like a couple of teenagers we were. We had our own Saturday night specials at home too – no TV, just a candlelit supper and music for two. She loved our old records.'

Geraldine can picture the scene as if they were brushing off their napkins in front of her. 'It sounds lovely, especially the music. Who did you and Rosemary listen to most?'

Jeffrey guffaws. 'That's an easy one, that is. There was only one man for us.' He imitates a club show host: 'Ladies and gentlemen …the Memphis Flash, The Tupelo Tornado, The King of Rock and Roll himself, the one and only Elvis… Aaron... Presley.' He unselfconsciously throws in a lip curl as he drawls the name.

With those three magic words Geraldine's heart lifts and an image of Jeffrey dressed in a studded Aloha Eagle white jumpsuit and cape, complete with shades, pops into her mind. She lets out a shriek of delight. 'I don't believe it. I'm the world's biggest Elvis fan. Who'd have thought?'

Jeffrey shakes his head. 'On that, we'll have to disagree. I think you'll find *I'm* the world's biggest Elvis fan if we put it to the test.'

'Oh, we will,' she says, 'we definitely will.' But no sooner have the words left her mouth than she is brought back down to earth with a bump as she remembers the Love Me Tender package she'd signed up for later today. What on earth was she thinking? She decides she won't be mentioning that to Jeffrey any time soon.

Not that's he's listening now. Buoyed with the memory of his former Saturday nights, his shoulders sway and jerk as he hums the tune to one of his old faves. He doesn't want to be a tiger, he doesn't want to be a lion, he just wants to be a teddy bear.

Eventually the excitement of the night catches up and they subside into a deep, natural sleep, heads touching, side by side on the sofa. In another hour, the birds will begin to greet the morning and the new day will begin.

The adrenalin rush of the night subsiding, Dawn can feel her cancer reasserting itself, reminding her who's boss. She's keen Woody doesn't notice the full extent of her discomfort so surreptitiously slips a couple of painkillers into her mouth and tries to wash them down with a glass of water. But to no avail – she ends up spluttering and choking out loud.

Woody gently pats her on the back to help ease her coughing, and spots the pill bottle in her hand. Of course. 'The cancer?' he gently asks.

Regaining her composure, she nods and tries to laugh it off as she has so many times before. 'Spoiler alert: we all die in the end.'

Woody doesn't find her quip amusing or diverting in the slightest. 'I know you try to make light of it, Dawn, but when we get out of here you have to get proper treatment.'

She smiles. 'I will. Promise.'

Woody hesitates. He's not really spoken to Dawn about her cancer in the whirlwind of the past few hours and suddenly feels enormous guilt over his lack of consideration. All they've talked about is him. His past, his descent into the abyss, and the grisly appointment booked in his name for Saturday. Dawn was open with him over her cancer and how it had brought her to Charon House, but he's not really probed into the detail of her situation. What sort of cancer, was it inoperable, if it was operable why wasn't she doing anything about it? What did her family think? Why, since arriving, had Dawn changed her mind about going through with an assisted death? He could pretend it wasn't his place to ask, or tell himself his interest – nosiness? – wouldn't be welcome, but Dawn hadn't exercised the same self-absorption in her dealings with him. Sharing had reduced his burden; he should try to lighten hers. 'What have they said about, you know, your condition?'

It's the early hours of the morning, she's tired and in pain, but she's glad he's asked. It's an opportunity to help make sense of it all with an up-to-date account of her journey here, of her change of heart. Woody sits in silence alongside her on the sofa as she takes him through the chapters of her tale – losing Mark, the day she found out she had ovarian cancer, her inability to fund treatment and how, in the final analysis, she had decided she'd be better off dead than alive.

He's so absorbed in her story he doesn't realise he's holding her hand, urging her on when she falters. When she gets to her last conversation with her daughter – the point where Kimberley finally convinced her she was loved and cared for, that she wasn't a burden, that life is too precious to be thrown away no matter the circumstances – Woody almost punches the air in jubilation. *Yes*! 'She sounds quite a girl, does your Kimberley. A chip off the old block. I'd love to meet her.'

'Well, you will in the morning,' says Dawn. 'In a lay-by on the A635, probably.' Then she remembers – Kimberley still doesn't know she's not going through with it. She's probably wide awake at this precise moment, tossing and turning and dreading what the day will bring. Praying her mother will see sense at last, and be waiting with her fake Louis Vuitton packed and ready to come home when she arrives but, in reality, fearing the worst: a brief and sterile parting of the ways, never to see her Mum again. 'I should have got word to her,' says Dawn ruefully. 'I've put her through enough without making her play guessing games with me.'

'I know,' says Woody, 'but Adil is right. We can't afford for anybody to get wind of our plan. As soon as we're out of here you can call her. Just think how pleased she's going to be when she hears from you – hold on to that for now.'

Dawn's face lights up at the thought of making such a call. 'Oh, she'll be well made-up, although I expect I'll get a huge bollocking for being such a silly bugger in the first place.'

'I wouldn't worry too much,' says Woody, deadpan. 'You'll probably get cut off after thirty seconds – just long enough to tell her the good news and no time for any earache back.'

Dawn has a sudden panic. 'Do we need coins? For the phone box?'

Woody wonders where she's been for the past few years. 'I was only joking, Dawn. You use a card these days. Honestly, stop fretting.'

She punches him playfully on the shoulder. 'Well, whatever we use, all being well, we'll be out of here in a few hours and they won't be able to touch us. You, me, Geraldine and Jeffrey.' She lets the thought sink in before letting out a relieved sigh. 'This has been a very close shave.'

Woody has learned the hard way not to take anything for granted, but refrains from pointing out they have quite a way to go yet. He turns the subject back to Dawn. 'Can I ask you, weren't you scared about facing the end? I mean, it must have taken an enormous amount of courage to decide to, you know, call it quits on your own life.'

She doesn't answer straightaway, as she mulls the question over. Finally, 'Was it courage, or was it cowardice? I couldn't really say. But what about you – you made the same choice.'

'Oh, no, I didn't. I was dead either way, and I just took the easiest way out. Nothing brave about my reasons for volunteering – I was as terrified at the thought of living as I was of dying. You seem to be much more composed about it.'

'You think so, Woody?' she muses. 'I don't know who I was fooling – myself probably. I convinced myself it would be like turning the light off and drifting into a lovely long sleep. Because you have to find ways to justify it to yourself, don't you?'

He nods – he knows it only too well.

She continues. 'But it wasn't just the cancer. My life was pretty shit to be honest. Then it got shittier still. I was lonely, broke, felt a nuisance to my daughter and had nothing to look forward to except more shit. "Tired of life" they call it, but to me it was more a case of being "sick and tired of life". The cancer basically gave me a prod to do something about it, so I decided to call it a day. And they sure as hell make it easy for you. They should call this place Go Like a Lemming instead of Go Gently.'

'You know that's a myth, don't you? That lemmings commit suicide?'

'I'm going to learn something new here, aren't I?' she laughs. 'Go on then.'

'Well, they don't. When a concentration of lemmings becomes too big, due to breeding, a group will break off and migrate to a new home. But they can swim, so crossing water isn't a problem. Yes, they lose a few along the way because of the sheer volume of bodies, but it's not suicide – it's survival.'

'But I've seen them on TV, charging off the edge of a cliff.'

'So have I,' he laughs. 'That clip is from Disney's *White Wilderness* where they pushed the poor things over a high precipice for a bit of dramatic footage. See, that's how big lies start. Never believe what they tell you.'

Dawn is full of admiration at Woody's grasp of both the natural and disinformation worlds. 'Like here, you mean?'

'Something like that,' he snorts, but then immediately becomes solemn again. 'But the key question is, you don't feel like a lemming now? You're not still looking for a cliff edge to chuck yourself off?'

She shakes her head firmly. 'Not with this lot I'm not,' she laughs. 'My eyes have been opened. Kimberley for a start, and meeting Geraldine, has made me see this so-called assisted dying for what it is.' She squeezes his hand. 'And you too, Woody. What they were planning to do to you is scandalous; we're better than that. Yes, I've still got cancer, and I've still got physical pain but, whatever happens after today, I'll die happy. And I wouldn't have truly been able to say that if I'd popped my clogs in here.'

Woody can't help but smile at this remarkable, brave, vibrant, funny woman. 'You put me to shame, I lost it tonight when I saw that bloody death machine. My whole life flashed before me and I knew I didn't want that to be my end.'

She nods. She knows.

Propped up on cushions at each end of the sofa they fall into silent reflection, happy and content that they have made peace with themselves and with each other. Just as they are about to drop off, Dawn stretches to pull the duvet from the bed and drapes it across their legs.

She has only one question left: 'Can we sleep with the light on?'

Chapter Twenty-Six

'I detest these breakfast briefings,' moans Lady Margaret as she picks at a stale brioche of indeterminate shape. 'It was hardly worth going to bed.'

Isabella Pestel, on the other hand, is a woman who is used to getting up early. 'It's to fit in with the news cycle, you see.'

Lady Margaret eyes her with unconcealed scorn. Tell her something she doesn't know. 'To fit in with Lawrence's news cycle, you mean?'

Isabella's face reddens – already on the back foot with Lady M after thirty seconds. She ignores the slight, and remembers the key thing here is the commencement of the Lawrence Pestel media offensive that has barely an hour unaccounted for over the course of the next week. Her husband's crowning glory, his final ascent – and she will be beside him every step of the way. 'And a big day for Go Gently and Callan, of course,' she purrs.

Lady Margaret remains unimpressed. 'Every day is a big day for Callan.'

Isabella is determined not to be cowed. 'Lawrence has ensured a good media turnout this morning.'

Lady Margaret sips her coffee thoughtfully before replying. 'Yes, news of the pod has certainly piqued media interest. Journalists just adore Callan's innovation and his mastery of the soundbite.'

Isabella cannot fail to catch the dig at her husband's tendency to use strangulated political jargon when he's talking. 'I think the main emphasis is on how the pod will speed the nation's wellbeing agenda, Lady Margaret. The end, as much as the means.'

'Well, we'll see, won't we?'

Isabella presses on. 'Of course, the big hook is the photo-opportunity. Do you know what they're planning? It was Lawrence's idea.'

Lady Margaret knows full well what's in the pipeline as Callan hasn't stopped complaining to her about his parade being rained on by the pushy Parliamentarian. 'Two peas in their pods – I had heard.' She allows herself a brief pause before adding, 'Although politicians have to be so careful these days over photos. People are so mischievous – you aim for iconic and end up as a meme.'

Isabella blanches as she recalls the launch of Lawrence's 'STREET WATCH' local vigilante initiative, following which some wag cropped his photo so the word 'TWAT' hovered above his head. She refuses to rise to the bait. 'Will you be here tomorrow as well, Lady Margaret?'

Lady M almost forgets herself as she enthusiastically replies. 'Oh, I will. It's almost biblical, isn't it? An eye for an eye, and a tooth for a tooth. We've been soft on crime in this country for far too long – there's nothing as effective as a strong deterrent. Yes, I'm looking forward to seeing that.'

Isabella is confused. Her husband's early release scheme is supposed to be a humane solution to prison overcrowding, an advance in prisoner welfare and a means of reducing cost for the taxpayer – it's not a draconian punishment scheme. Or is it? Lady M seems to think so. She looks for an off-ramp. 'I have a

Lawrence appears to be harbouring lingering doubts. 'And we won't suffocate when the cockpit is closed? There will be plenty of air in there?'

Callan is bemused at the minister's caution. 'Yes, Lawrence, there will be plenty of air in there.' To demonstrate there is nothing to worry about, he adds the ultimate reassurance: 'Remember I'm in the other one, so that should set your mind at rest.'

But Lawrence isn't finished yet – he hasn't got to where he is today without paying attention to the optics. 'And the media can see into the capsules, and we can see out?'

Callan confirms this is the case. 'Yes, totally transparent for our purposes; the two-way screen won't be engaged as the pods won't actually be turned on. Plus, we've done a promo film to highlight the operational features of the pod, the personalised image settings, the music choices available and so on. We're totally good to go.'

Lawrence finally sniffs his assent, and checks his wristwatch. 'Right. Time for my make-up, I think.'

Callan crosses over to where Lady Margaret is helping herself to her third espresso of the morning. Isabella has withdrawn, tail between her legs, to 'powder her nose', leaving Lady M with a triumphant smirk on her face.

'Pestel is up to his usual tricks of changing all the arrangements at the last minute,' he moans.

'Ignore him, darling,' she breezes. 'Just rejoice you're not married to that awful woman, and he is.'

Callan cheers up slightly at the thought of having escaped such a fate. 'And I've just had twenty questions from him over how safe the pod is. What a wuss.'

'Well, it will be anything but safe tomorrow, so maybe he's just checking he hasn't got his days mixed up.' She expects her little joke will lighten her husband's demeanour, but instead his face darkens.

Checking that Pestel is out of earshot, he whispers, 'The prisoner has apparently gone AWOL. Not in his room this morning.'

Her reaction to this potentially unsettling news takes him by surprise as she lets out an amused shriek, not unlike a horse whinnying. 'Oh, I must say, that's too much.'

Callan shushes her before continuing. 'I can't see what's so funny about it. Lawrence will crucify us if tomorrow's launch goes tits-up.'

Lady Margaret is made of sterner stuff in the face of potential calamity. She composes herself before explaining. 'Look at it this way, Callan. It's his launch tomorrow, not yours. *Ergo*, the prisoner is *his* responsibility. You told him not to let convicted felons randomly wander around Charon House, so now he'll have to put a stop to that. In any case, this chap is probably enjoying a hearty breakfast somewhere on site – it is his last chance, after all. Honestly, darling, relax.'

He recognises there is a lot of sense in what she is saying, but what if she's wrong? 'What if he *has* hauled ass and somehow left the premises? What then?'

Lady Margaret idly flaps her hand in front of her face as if shooing a fly away. 'Do you seriously think Lawrence Pestel won't have a back-up? All he has to do is snap his fingers and the governor at Strangeways will send over an oven-ready replacement. *Hey presto!*'

Callan considers this for a moment. 'Yes. You're right. The guy's probably not missing anyway, and even if he is, the whole premise of Lawrence's initiative is there's no shortage of prisoners keen and ready to sign up.'

'Exactly. Lambs forming an orderly queue for slaughter.' Her metaphor reminds her of something she said earlier. 'You know, I was just telling Lady Macbeth how biblical the day is going to be. I confess, the thought of seeing it for real is quite turning me on.'

Callan, taken aback at his wife's less-than-conventional erotic ruminations, simply says, 'Let's just get this morning out of the way first, shall we?'

'Spoilsport,' she giggles. She draws the matter to a close. 'Just don't tell him anything until afterwards. What he doesn't know needn't concern him. Strictly *entre-nous* for now, yes?'

Callan nods.

She reaches for his necktie and adjusts the knot with a sharp tug. 'Come on, now. Can't have you looking like the stable boy in there. Standards, dear boy, standards.'

Chapter Twenty-Seven

Adil reverses the Wash 'n' Go Laundry (*We Clean up After You!*) van into the corner of the Harmony Wing car park and scurries to the rear doors to check the cargo area. Devoid of a load, the interior is considerably larger than he'd remembered and it occurs to him it will be none too comfortable for those rattling around in the back. But there's little he can do about that now. He's chosen this spot so the fugitives can cross the grounds and emerge next to the van via a gap in the hedge. Lifting the keys to the van was a doddle but as he surveys the car park he can't help wonder if, standing all by itself, the vehicle sticks out like a sore thumb (as if the signage on the side has been amended overnight to 'Escape 'n' Go (*We're on the Run)* by some prankster). He looks at his watch – time to get the gang together and set them on their way.

The four musketeers have already convened in Dawn's room when Adil enters. He is unsure as to what demeanour he will find them in ahead of their impending flight – will they be nervous, tense and fearful, or resolute, calm and focused? None of these, as it turns out, but there is a problem: Jeffrey is unhappy they're not having breakfast before their escape. 'But I'm starving,' he protests.

'We need to lie low,' Geraldine explains, 'do nothing to attract attention.' She can see by his face what the next question is going to be and cuts him off at the pass. 'No, Jeffrey, we can't order room service, either. Breakfast for four would blow our cover even more.' Jeffrey, his stomach rumbling, resorts to rummaging through Dawn's tea tray for any stray biscuits.

An exasperated Adil notices two carry cases and a wheelie stood next to the door. 'You can't take those with you,' he remonstrates. 'It will give the game away if you're seen with luggage.' *Couldn't they have worked that out for themselves?* No.

'I've some very expensive items in there,' Dawn declares as if she's been hauled in by Customs. 'Personal effects too. I can't possibly leave them.' Geraldine and Jeffrey also look pleadingly to Adil in the hope of avoiding confiscation.

The luggage stirs a memory in Adil of the small suitcase his father carried all the way from Syria, across eight countries and three thousand miles, only to have it brusquely dumped in the Channel by the people smuggler as they boarded their overcrowded dingy in Calais. He, too, claimed it was essential baggage (but not so essential that he needed to follow it himself one hour later). 'Think of all the times you've flown,' says Adil. 'You wouldn't try to collect your bags from the overhead locker in an emergency evacuation, would you? Well, this is similar.' (Jeffrey is on the verge of positing some legitimate exceptions to that rule until a sharp glance from Geraldine stays his hand.) 'Go Gently will have to return your bags to you once this is all over. Let's stay light on our feet for now.'

Adil waves the keys to the van, giving them a merry little jingle. 'The good news is we're all set. The van is ready and waiting and I've checked there's enough fuel to get you to Yorkshire. Unfortunately, the three in the back might rattle around a bit, so you're going to have to hold on as best you can, at least until you're well clear of here.'

'We could take some pillows with us to make us more comfortable,' suggests Dawn. 'Or some towels, or….'

She's cut off by Adil. 'I think crossing the lawn carrying your bedding would raise more attention than the suitcases. No. You'll just have to drive especially carefully, Jeffrey.'

The self-designated driver, perhaps not wishing to admit he's been demoted, stands on his dignity and leaves it to Geraldine to explain the change of plan.

Masking his relief at this welcome turn, Adil instead hands the keys to the stand-in driver. The jittery yardbird, who's hardly uttered a word all morning, proceeds to fumble and drop them on the floor as they're passed over. 'Sorry,' he stammers, and scrabbles to retrieve them. The air in the room appears to shrink.

It's left to Dawn to break the silence with a cheery, 'You've got this, Woody.' Adil and Geraldine offer the driver similar encouragements and pats on the back, while all Jeffrey can do is eye him with steely resentment.

Adil checks his watch again – ten minutes to nine. This is it, as he wants them driving off just as the conference is due to commence. 'It's time to be making a move.'

The starting gun has the secondary effect of sparking Jeffrey's bladder into life and he raises his hand. 'Have I got time to go to the toilet first?' he asks. 'Just in case.'

Geraldine immediately declares she needs to go too. 'You've set me off now,' she says weakly.

Adil knows from long experience that the best way of hurrying things along is not to argue with an elderly patient over the real or imagined state of their pelvic floor. 'Not a problem,' he says without a hint of sarcasm. 'Make yourselves as comfortable as you can.'

Nine o'clock. They're behind time, but at least they are ready. They inch their way out of the door and around the back of Dawn's chalet. Adil points across the green expanse to the hole in the hedge that gives out on to the rear service car park and the van. 'One at a time,' he instructs them. 'Geraldine, Dawn, Jeffrey and Woody in that order. Walk slowly, casually, and the next one only goes when the one in front reaches the gap. Wait there and I'll follow up last.'

This is it. Geraldine takes a deep breath and plants her foot on the green sward as if she's entering a minefield (which in a way, she is). She's simultaneously conscious of not wanting to draw attention to herself and the four pairs of eyes drilling a hole in her back. The strain causes her legs to function independently of her brain, making each step a struggle. She's nine years old again, her mother dragging her off the stage at the Irish Dancing competition after the planned jigs, reels, polkas and hornpipes failed to materialise. Reminded of this embarrassing childhood humiliation and determined not to freeze again, she forces herself forward, each pace an almighty effort, until she reaches the hedge.

Her companions can see she's struggling, her slow progress acting as a prompt to plan their own traverses. Dawn, up next, decides she will keep her eyes directly ahead as she closes in on the target. She glides across the space like Blondin crossing Niagara on a tightrope, all without the aid of a balancing pole.

Not to be upstaged, Jeffrey draws himself up and sets off on a stiff-looking march, whistling under his breath the tune to *The Great Escape*, one of his favourite childhood films. He's Steve

McQueen, James Garner and Richard Attenborough rolled into one as he defies the Bosch in a bid to reach the frontier.

Next, Woody sets off after him, with several edgy backward glances towards Charon House. It's like he is being stalked by a pack of zombies and is reluctant to break into a run, in case they do too. While his passage is less than elegant, he at least covers the ground briskly enough.

Finally, when all four have made it to the protective cover of the hedge, Adil, having satisfied himself they remain undetected, saunters across to join them. It's now ten minutes past nine. Assuming the launch started on time, they should still have plenty of time in hand to exit the grounds before it finishes. He ushers them towards the van and opens the rear doors, beckoning first to Jeffrey to clamber aboard. The loading height is only two feet above the ground but Jeffrey's creaking knees baulk at the prospect: 'You couldn't give me a lift up, could you?' he says to Adil.

An exasperated Dawn pushes past him, and proceeds to sit on the lip of the van floor. 'All you do is park your bum and swing your legs round. Like this,' she says, demonstrating with a neat pivot. Geraldine follows her example without fuss while Jeffrey harrumphs he would have worked that out for himself. 'Except you didn't,' retorts Dawn testily from inside the van.

Jeffrey ignores her, and stiffly manoeuvres himself inside. The next problem: 'Do you think it would be better if I sat there?' he says to Geraldine who's taken up a position with her back to the partition separating them from the cabin.

'Does it really matter where we sit?' Dawn cries. 'Just plonk yourself down anywhere.'

'I was only thinking ahead,' Jeffrey says defensively. 'In case I need to speak to Woody.'

Dawn is on the verge of explaining that she and Geraldine are equally capable of communicating with the driver if the need arises, when Adil claps his hands sharply to shush them. All this bickering – he can't believe the simple act of organising four people to cross a field and get into a van could be so problematical. It's like herding cats. But at least his moggies are now aboard. 'Listen,' he says. 'We're all set. Make yourselves as comfortable as you can, and not a word until you're clear. Woody will have you out of here before you know it.'

'Thanks for everything, Adil, we won't forget you,' says Geraldine.

There's no time for speeches, so he simply gives them the thumbs-up before pulling the doors shut. He walks around to the front where Woody is gripping the steering wheel so tightly, he's in danger of instant carpal tunnel syndrome. Adil nods to indicate it's all systems go, but Woody, uncomprehending, remains rooted to the spot. Adil mimes turning the ignition key and turning the steering wheel instead. This time there's a flicker of recognition, and Woody reaches down to insert the key. The next second the engine cranks into life, its thunderous roar bisecting the morning air.

Adil audibly sighs with relief and steps back to wave them off. At last. Take it away, Woody!

Inside Charon House, the launch has finally started. It's busy. Not only is there a very good media turnout (Callan grudgingly concedes that the secretary of state for wellbeing has his uses sometimes), both Go Gently and Lawrence have their own photographers, videographers and PRs on hand to record and package every detail in the race to own the moment for their respective masters. Unsurprisingly, as their boss takes the floor, it's Lawrence's team who are a hive of activity, making sure not a word or a gesture is missed. Callan's crew sit picking their noses until he's on.

Lawrence, thinking ahead to tomorrow's penal policy announcement and next week's conference speech, is keen to build his narrative across the next few days to the point where it all knits together. He calls it joining up the dots (behind the scenes his aides will brief the media on this very phrase and the genius behind it). Consequently, he's straight into the meat.

'This government never shirks from expanding choice and confronting wastage in all its forms. Where previous administrations dillied and dallied, we get things done. Five years ago, we were responsible for bringing in the assisted dying bill, at a stroke removing the fears and anxieties of citizens previously denied their inalienable right to die. In giving nature a helping hand, we democratised death, and the people of this country have not been slow to avail themselves of the empathetic services provided by our good friend here today, Doctor Callan Clay of Go Gently.'

Callan twitches on hearing his 'democratise death' line being hijacked, but remembers to smile modestly at the early plug for his business.

'But a strong government, a resolute government, never stops caring. The job is never done; there's always another paradigm to be shifted.'

Isabella suppresses a squeak of excitement at the teasing reference to the conference theme her husband will unpack next week. (*He could have expressed it less clumsily, perhaps, but so, so clever.*) Callan, on the other hand, starts to wonder how long it will be before Lawrence attempts to steal the shirt from his back.

226

'The assisted dying bill I pioneered proved the doubters wrong. Now, wherever I go, I have grateful families telling me I made a difference to their parents', their spouses', their loved ones' lives. No longer are the terminally ill forced to suffer unnecessarily; no longer are those who have enjoyed a completed life pressurised to extend their stay on earth against their wishes.'

Callan notes with admiration how quickly Lawrence has jumped from 'we' to 'I'.

'I am proud of the fact that this country is leading the world when it comes to assisted dying, but I have never been one to rest on my laurels. That is why, today, I am announcing how I intend to take the next step – the next leap – forward in our wellbeing agenda.'

For the purpose of the cutaway shots, Callan's head pumps away like a nodding donkey in search of an oil strike, as if bowled over at the oratory and sheer force of what he's hearing. (Inside, he's cursing Lawrence for his repetitive use of the term 'assisted dying', which he has airbrushed from the Go Gently stylebook in favour of 'final journey'. Why can't the minister at least switch from one to the other?)

'My mission is to bring healthcare and health resolution within the reach of every citizen. If there was one criticism of the assisted dying bill to date it was that the options available were cost prohibitive for lower earners. Of course, Clean Bill solves that problem for many, but today I want to go further still. Today, I intend to make it possible for everyone, even those of the most modest means, to "Choose Death" as and when it suits them.'

Isabella swoons with devotion as Lawrence builds to his climax. Conversely, Callan curses under his breath at

Lawrence's cavalier introduction of a tagline, one Go Gently most definitely won't be adopting. "Choose Death"? Is he serious? Why can't he stick to the bloody script?

'I am a firm believer in "the market will provide", which is why I invited the leaders in the field, Go Gently, to help make this dream of mine a reality.'

Callan smiles in a manner meant to convey humility and gratitude as his invention is further appropriated by the sticky-fingered politician.

'My brief was this: build a better mousetrap and the world will beat a path to your door. The challenge: to devise a means of providing a quick, painless and peaceful end of days for one and all, irrespective of an individual's economic means.'

Isabella almost jumps up to applaud but manages to restrain herself.

Lawrence, in an attempt to appear visionary, is now gazing over the heads of the audience as if seeking out some unseen deity in the clouds. (It puts Callan in mind of Saint Sebastian, tied to a tree. If only there were a couple of archers handy.)

'The perfect example of state and industry working hand in hand, I now call upon Doctor Callan Clay, of our hosts Go Gently, to demonstrate exactly how we plan to bring the final choice, without fear or favour, within the reach of all.'

Chapter Twenty-Eight

The van in the rear car park (despite the promise implied by the name emblazoned on its side) remains rooted to the spot. Woody is just engaging first gear when loud knocking and frenzied shouts from the back stay his hand. The long-suffering Adil groans in disbelief and hurries back to investigate.

The reason for the hold-up soon becomes apparent as a red-faced Geraldine climbs out to explain. 'We've left the notes behind,' she gasps.

Adil is stunned. Jeffrey has shown him his carefully annotated account of what they saw in the theatre last night, the evidence this rickety runaway believes will help prove to the world that Go Gently is a sinister organisation. *They've left them behind.* How is that even possible?

'It's not my fault,' says Geraldine before anybody can accuse her. 'There was a mix-up.'

Woody shuts the engine off and joins the conference at the rear. 'Where are they now?' asks Adil, focusing on the practicality of the situation. Impressively, he remains totally calm, determined not to spook his charges in any way.

'Er, in Dawn's room,' says the chief witness.

'I didn't leave them there,' Dawn interjects, before anybody can level such an accusation.

'OK,' says Adil. 'Where exactly in Dawn's room?'

Geraldine doesn't answer straightaway, instead looking to Jeffrey for support. None is forthcoming. May as well come out with it: 'In my wheelie,' she admits.

Adil, Dawn and Woody are stunned. By any stretch of the imagination, Geraldine is the most together of the group, the safest pair of hands. And she's somehow left their precious collateral behind? It's hard to credit.

It's left to Dawn to ask the obvious. 'But how? I thought Woody and Jeffrey had the notes.'

'I didn't have them,' Woody splutters, fed-up of always being in the dock.

All eyes turn to Jeffrey. 'The thing is…' he stutters. 'It's all rather complicated. You see…'

Conscious of the time constraints, Geraldine cuts to the chase for the benefit of all: 'Jeffrey placed the notes in my case for safe keeping. I didn't know he'd done it until he remembered and told me just then. An innocent mistake, compounded by the decision to leave our baggage behind. But the question is, what do we do about it now?'

They're all thinking the same thing: *Why on earth did Jeffrey do that? Why didn't he tell Geraldine? How could he forget he'd put them there?*

But there is no time for an inquest. 'If Go Gently find them, the cat will be straight out of the bag,' Adil concludes.

They all groan.

'I'll go back for them,' volunteers Jeffrey. 'I feel I should.'

They all shake their heads in alarm.

'No, I'll go,' says Adil firmly. He checks his watch – coming up to twenty minutes past nine. He can be there and back in five minutes. He feels as much to blame given he should have checked Jeffrey had the notes before leaving Dawn's room. Actually, best to make sure now: 'So they're in the wheelie, and there's only one wheelie, correct?'

Geraldine nods. 'It's bright red.'

Adil checks the gap in the hedge preparatory to a controlled, fast-but-not-too fast sprint relay. 'Wait,' comes a voice. It's Geraldine again. 'You need the combination. For the lock.' *She's locked it?* 'Well, I didn't know, did I?' she cries. 'But it's easy to remember. One-Seven-Zero-Three. St Patrick's Day, you see. I bet everyone in Ireland has the same numbers.'

One-Seven-Zero-Three. Got it. Adil turns to go. 'Hang on,' comes a second voice. It's Dawn, dangling a key with a large Forget-Me-Not fob hanging from it. 'You'll need this to get back in.'

When Callan rises to his feet, there is a bustle of activity as Lawrence's lensmen sit down and Go Gently's team spring into action. The entrepreneur is making quick mental edits to his speech given how Lawrence filched his best lines for his own address. (If the minister was a bird, he'd be a magpie or a jackdaw, and Callan would spend every night dreaming of blasting him from the sky with a twelve-bore.)

'Go Gently has guided many final journeys over the years with unstinting care and compassion, resolving life's final challenge for a multitude of grateful clients. Where there is physical pain, we bring relief; where there is existential angst, we bring peace.'

Lady Margaret allows herself a covert smile. She wrote those opening lines and if she says so herself (she does), she absolutely nailed it there.

'When the secretary of state outlined his vision to me, to bring this most personal of personal choices within the scope of millions rather than thousands, I must confess I was excited, because I too had been seeking that holy grail for some time. In fact, we were already well down the path.'

Lawrence stiffens slightly. Is Callan trying to steal his thunder here? He distinctly remembers it being his own idea.

'A number of factors were uppermost in our thinking.'

One in particular, thinks Lawrence – price gouging the cost of barbiturates by big pharma. However, he's had to brief Callan not to cite this today, given the sector's special relationship with government extends to zero tax status and subsidised grants – *best not to draw attention to it, capiche?* (Nevertheless, as a precaution, the secretary of state has instructed his broker to dump certain pharma shares from his extensive portfolio.)

'Here at Go Gently, we facilitate the biggest decision a client will ever make in their life. As a result, we never lose sight of what is important to each-and-every one of them: lack of fear; absence of pain; peace with their own decision – decorum in other words. Every one a life lived, every one a life fulfilled, in the best possible way. A release, also, for those left behind.'

Lawrence sneaks a surreptitious look at his watch. *Enough of the corporate shite. Just get on to the pod, will you? We haven't got all day.*

'So, to the big question: how to make this freedom available to all? How, as the secretary of state has just said, can we bring health resolution within the reach of every citizen, irrespective of income? Ladies and gentlemen, today we can reveal the solution.'

On cue, the lights dim and a spotlight picks out the two covered shapes to the side of the lectern. A dramatic and soaring musical score emanates from the theatre's sound system as the drapes rise slowly to reveal the gleaming glass and steel cylinders beneath. The overall effect is topped off with a cloud of dry ice – all part of the 'interstellar, celestial vibe' Callan was after. He waits until the pods are fully exposed before continuing.

'Behold, the Peregrine Pod. A bespoke, individual, one-trip conveyance designed to take the traveller on the longest journey for the price of a local train ride.' (Callan had been unsure of that line in the run-through. For one thing, he hadn't realised how expensive a short train journey was in these parts, and he also wondered if the comparison might be rather trite. Lawrence, on the other hand, said the tabloids would lap it up.)

'You may well ask what is the significance of the name "Peregrine?" Well, for those familiar with Latin – and I'm sure that's most of us here today – you will know that the noun "*peregrinus*" denotes a pilgrim, a wanderer, somebody able to roam without borders. It is exactly this level of unfettered release our pod delivers; the name couldn't be more apt.'

(Lady Margaret, who happens to hold a First in *Literae Humaniores* from Oxford University, has resisted explaining to her husband that the term *peregrinus* only applied to non-Roman citizens, as opposed to *cives Romani,* on the grounds of not wanting to bestow second-class status on the pod.)

Next, Callan tees up an explanatory film clip detailing how the pod works – no point in doing all the leg work himself – and spends the next three minutes studying the faces of the assembled hacks as they are led through the 'science'. The noun and verb 'gas' are notably absent from the accompanying commentary, while 'hypoxiation' gets only a single mention. Instead, the video concentrates, with the zeal of a pusher selling Ecstasy at an illegal rave, on the spaced-out and euphoric 'experience' that awaits the lucky user. (Lawrence, embracing fond memories of such outings, reckons Go Gently are on to a winner with this 'in-tune' approach – 'Think of the target demographic, Callan. Over sixties, old, knackered, nothing to live for, looking back fondly. "Sorted for E's and Wizz" and all that.')

The film clip concludes and the two presenters reunite to take questions from the media. As usual, the journalists are pre-selected, and their enquiries merely offer the opportunity for the main soundbites from earlier to be repeated irrespective of what's being asked. In any case, in Lawrence's words, today is all about the 'headline froth'. The serious stuff – economic impacts and the way in which the minister has spearheaded, and continues to lead, the improvement of healthcare in the country – has all been taken care of by his press team who have written and placed several in-depth exclusives and interviews across the course of the weekend.

To finish off, both Callan and Lawrence will do a couple of one-to-one camera interviews immediately following the conference, but the main item on the agenda now is the photo opportunity. Receiving the nod from their respective PRs, they wrap the questions and prepare for boarding.

There is a palpable buzz in the air as the lights come up and the technicians start to busy themselves. At the request of the photographers, Lawrence and Callan first pose in front of the pods. Both bear fixed, stoic smiles – true pioneers, as if they can hear destiny calling. They can almost picture tomorrow's headline: *To infinity and beyond.*

Then the moment comes when they slowly shuffle backwards into the erect pods and are swallowed up inside the contoured velvet interiors. Callan possesses a far more imposing physique than the weedy Lawrence but, in a triumph of ergonomics, both men fit comfortably inside the chambers. At a given signal, the pods are slowly swivelled backwards until they reach a forty-five-degree angle facing the press pack. The final check is made – thumbs-up from the two occupants – and a red-suited operative secures the cockpit windows with a barely audible click. Peering out through the clear apertures, Callan and Lawrence resemble a couple of gift-wrapped action figures on the toyshop shelf waiting for the Christmas rush to begin.

Three rows back, Isabella experiences a sudden pang of anxiety. She turns to Lady Margaret and nervously whispers, 'They are safe in there, aren't they?'

Her companion can hardly mask her condescension as she replies: 'Of course they are. What do you take my husband for?'

Chapter Twenty-Nine

Adil makes it across the great divide and back to the van with the notes intact. Beads of sweat dot his forehead, he's out of breath and long past talking. He thrusts the papers into Jeffrey's hands, shoos them back into the van, and briskly jabs his finger in the direction of the road: *Go, go, go.* Woody leaps into the cabin and fires her up. First gear, then second gear, as the van lumbers forward, leaving a relieved Adil to offer a faint *bon voyage* as they head for the service road.

The three passengers in the rear cling to each other as the van picks up speed. As they turn the first corner, the remaining bottles of Geraldine's homemade saline slide across the floor, slapping into the rear doors. She manages to stop Jeffrey trying to retrieve them, and they hold on even tighter.

Up front, Woody is willing himself into a positive frame of mind by reciting a mantra he learned in jail: *Don't overthink. Just let it go* (advice he wished he'd received earlier in life). Charon House is now on his left, and in a few seconds he'll be on the main drive. He's doing under thirty miles per hour, all is under control.

Dawn can tell from the steady motion of the van that Woody is maintaining his composure under pressure. She can't risk calling out encouragement to him from behind the partition so instead offers up a silent imprecation to any deity who happens to be passing: *Come on, Woody; you can do this.* In contrast, Geraldine and Jeffrey appear to be transfixed by the three bottles of solution now rolling from one side of the van to the other like a Newton's cradle.

The van clears the building, and is now only five hundred metres from the sanctuary of the main road. Woody can see the barrier is down as he nears the gatehouse, and prepares to decelerate. The manifest Adil promised is sitting on the passenger seat but, all being well, fortune will favour them today and they'll be waved through.

Behind him, his fellow escapees calibrate the distance travelled, time in motion, trajectory and speed, and deduce they are approaching the critical point of the extraction operation. They brace themselves. This is it.

As Woody drops into second gear, a number of things happen simultaneously, seemingly triggered by the windscreen being struck, directly in Woody's eyeline, by the biggest dump of birdshit ever excreted from an avian undercarriage. (Many consider being shat on by a bird a portent of good luck, but that doesn't prove to be the case today.) Woody automatically reaches for the windscreen wipers to clear the mess, instead spreading the poop evenly across his line of vision. At that precise moment the security guard, nonchalantly chomping on a bacon roll, strolls out of his gatehouse. He is followed, at speed, by a black cat (Styx, the estate's adopted stray) who shoots across the road in pursuit of the feathered precision bomber. His vision blurred, and panicked by the motion, Woody instinctively hits the brakes, swerves violently, and slams into the newly-vacated kiosk where the van comes to a shuddering halt. Styx, who has proved about as lucky as the birdshit deposit, keeps running and disappears into the bushes. The guard gawps in amazement, sandwich still in hand, as the flimsy booth totters and creaks, before, as if in slow motion, collapsing on to its side. Woody turns to the gateman in horror as if about to explain, but is unable to summon a single utterance. In the same instant the security guard realises he's seen that dumb face before. Yes, there, taped to the back of the kiosk door, now staring up at the clouds, is a mugshot of the driver with the accompanying message: *Dangerous. Do not approach. Code Red.*

Sacrosanct's commander in chief has thought long and hard about her pledge to *not let these bastards get away with it,* finally determining that direct action is the only way. Dr Andy, on the other hand, has been less then convinced, given that he 'doesn't want to get into any trouble'. Despite this threat of a schism, the duo have nevertheless resolved (at Ruth's insistence) on their course of action – they will take the fight to Go Gently. They don't know it yet, but as they approach the headquarters of Go Gently, they are about to have a different impact on the day's proceedings to the one they'd envisaged.

Ruth and Andy have selected mountain bikes as their mode of transport in order to escape across country once their 'hit' is accomplished. Following the seven-mile ride from Manchester to Stalybridge they are blowing and glowing in equal measure. No matter: the plan is to reconnoitre the walls and pick their spot. Their equipment is neatly stowed on Ruth's rear pannier rack (while Andy's front basket carries a picnic for the return journey victory celebration).

Stealth is the watchword as they approach the estate, rather undermined by their decision, on a fine sunny day, to wear balaclavas as a precaution against identification. Thankfully, it's not too busy on the road, although their headgear does make it harder to see exactly where they're going.

All is quiet as they prepare to strike their blow for humanity. Ruth's eyes lock on to Andy's through the woollen slits and she raises a clenched fist to signal the start of their action. But no sooner can they move, there is an almighty crash from around the corner, the sound of crunching metal and breaking glass rending the still morning air.

Andy pulls off his balaclava. 'That's a car crash,' he says concernedly. 'We're going to have to help.'

Ruth keeps her mask in place and instead hisses back. 'We're on a bloody mission here, not on bloody duty.'

Andy shakes his head slowly from side to side. 'Our primary duty as doctors: "Make the care of the patient your first concern",' he recites.

'You're serious, aren't you?' comes the withering reply. At which she too rips off her mask, and pushes down hard on the pedals towards the source of the commotion.

It takes a few seconds to register what has just taken place. A white laundry van has ploughed into the gatehouse of Charon House, toppled it over, and appears to be firmly stuck in the wreckage. A uniformed figure is running towards the van, and the two doctors instinctively dismount to assist him in freeing the stricken driver from the cab. Except, it soon becomes clear the intentions of the would-be rescuer are anything but benign as he rips the driver's door open, and starts to pummel the poor unfortunate behind the wheel with his fists.

'Stop, stop,' shouts Ruth as she runs towards the vehicle.

The security guard grabs the driver in a headlock and, both surprised and relieved to have received such speedy back-up, squeals breathlessly, 'Escapee, escapee. Secure, secure,' as if he's barking into a walkie-talkie, not talking to the figurehead of a leading protest group.

Ruth realises they have stumbled directly into a war zone, and immediately flips into fight mode, hurling herself at the unsuspecting uniform and pulling him from the cab where he hits the tarmac with an almighty crunch. He curls into a ball to protect himself as she aims a succession of kicks (surprisingly heavy for such a small woman) at his torso, each blow accompanied by one of a string of indictments: 'Murderer'. 'Pig'. 'Fascist'.

Shocked, humiliated and confused, the guard rolls desperately away from his assailant, springs to his feet and, without a backward glance, bolts towards the main building.

Andy can only stare in disbelief as Ruth, the heat of battle coursing through her veins, turns next to the driver of the van. 'Are you alright?' she demands. She is met with a stunned, not altogether convincing nod. 'Well, don't just sit there,' she urges. 'Try the ignition. Get out of here.' He hesitates. 'What are you waiting for?' she shouts. She gestures with both hands for him to back up: 'Reverse.'

Inside the van, oblivious to what's unfolding, Dawn, Geraldine and Jeffrey extract themselves from a crumpled heap as the reality of their situation hits them: things are not proceeding to plan. They climb unsteadily to their feet and Dawn calls for hush as she strains to listen for any clues as to what's happening outside. They can make out muffled thumps and shouts following which the engine suddenly restarts, the van jolts back sharply, and they're deposited on to their backsides once more. A sudden screech of brakes catapults them forward, before the whine of the accelerator being floored thrusts them backwards once more. The next second they are being tossed into the air as if they've run over a sleeping policeman (or even a wideawake one). Or, as is the case, they've just crashed through the heavy boom blocking the van's way.

Out on the main road, Woody checks his remaining wing mirror as the smashed gatehouse and barrier recede into the distance. The first thing (after *Shit*) that pops into his mind is: *Don't overthink. Just let it go.* And that's exactly what he proceeds to do as he nudges the speedo up to sixty miles per hour.

'Wanker!' Kimberley shouts at the vehicle as it disappears around the corner. Going far too fast, on her side of the road as it approached, no sign of slowing down as it almost forced her off the road: everything they say about white van drivers validated in a second. She pulls into the lay-by to calm her nerves. She can't afford to let anything distract her from today's single objective – to bring her mother home.

When Kimberley last left Charon House, she felt she'd managed to create a sliver of doubt in Mum's mind over going through with this mad plan. It had given her hope. Since then, however, she's also been mulling over her final words to Dawn that afternoon: *You pack that bag and come on home with me or we say goodbye properly. Am I clear?'*

But had she been clear enough? It wasn't supposed to be an 'either/or' choice. Kimberley desperately wants her mother to come home so she can care for her but, in raising the alternative, had she inadvertently bestowed equal validity on saying goodbye properly?

She has also been gripped with a deep sense of shame and guilt that she is only now coming to terms with the gravity of the situation. Her mother could be nailed down in a coffin by tonight, and all she's done about it to date is twiddle her thumbs. She can't even answer, truthfully, the question of why her mother has opted for an assisted death. Yes, she has cancer and she is in pain, but is that really enough to voluntarily end it all? Deep down, Kimberley fears the real reason for her mother's decision is her. Ben, her pillock of a husband, hasn't helped, of course. He resented her mother from the off, and made it clear he didn't want her around. Later, when he realised they'd be in for an inheritance, he had positively relished the idea of cashing in on her demise. Selfish bastard, but what about her? Hadn't she bowed to his meanness too readily, been pathetically weak in prioritising his needs over her mother's? The truth of it was, she'd abandoned her mother to the point where Mum didn't see the sense of sticking around anymore. There had even been times – it fills her with self-disgust to acknowledge it – where she'd convinced herself her mother's decision 'might be for the best'. *For the best* – to lose her mother and never see her again? *For the best* – to idly stand by as she was injected with life-cancelling drugs? What had she been thinking? How could she have got it so wrong? How could she have blinded herself to the grim reality of what assisted dying actually meant?

It *was* her fault. She had driven her mother to this. She had let her down and been a poor daughter under the circumstances. Well, enough of that, she'd woken up at last. She'd set off early this morning and was going to march in there, tell the Gently folk where to go, collect her mother, and have her back home for lunch – Welsh Rarebit followed by *The Chase*. After that, she was going to make sure Mum had the best healthcare they could afford, and all the love and care in the world until her final, natural, breath. It was time for her to be a proper daughter; it was time for this madness to stop.

She pulls herself together and drives the final half mile to Charon House, two speeding cyclists whizzing by uncomfortably close to her car as she turns in. There she is met with a scene of complete devastation, bent metal spiralling skywards in crazy contortion, broken glass strewn upon the ground. Tied across the gates is a large hand-painted banner: ASSISTED DEATH IS MURDER. SACROSANCT IS LIFE.

Adil slips back inside Charon House, worried his absence will have been noticed, but that thought is soon overtaken as he hears the announcement over the internal sound system. *'Could Doctor Sands please make his way to Consulting Room One.'* The message, delivered in a soothing female voice and repeated three or four times, is of little interest to a casual listener, whereas the staff at Go Gently immediately recognise it as an emergency code. Code Red no less. Code Red is a security warning, not a fire warning – either a patient has gone missing or there is some form of external threat to the establishment. His heart sinks – the escapees have been spotted, or even worse, caught. On hearing a Doctor Sands announcement he is supposed to head to the staff assembly point at the loading bay to await further instructions. The sensible thing to do would be to keep his head down, go along with it – after all he could be jumping to conclusions. But he knows he's right and it's all gone awry. And what of the consequences? Woody is an escaped convict – is Adil now an accomplice to a crime? He knows the answer to that already. What if the oldsters implicate him when they're interrogated? Is deportation preferable to prison? Worse, what if, as is likely, they're dragged back here and summarily despatched before any family members get to speak to them? Fall victim to the very thing they're trying to expose?

He has grown fond of Jeffrey, Geraldine, Dawn and Woody over the past few days. They realised this week that they didn't want to die, not here at least, on the SS Euthanasia, the good ship lollipop of self-destruction. He doesn't want them to die either. He makes up his mind, and heads towards the theatre in Zone Z. Surely, he has a better chance of finding out what's happening there than by mustering at the assembly point.

Chapter Thirty

S nuggled securely inside their respective pods, Callan and Lawrence are unable to hear Doctor Sands being called to the consulting room. They're taken by surprise then as, through the restricted view their narrow window on the world offers them, they realise the photoshoot is being disrupted by a member of the Go Gently security staff. He's called a halt and is pushing the cameras back in a firm, but calm, 'not messing about' manner. One of Callan's men informs Lawrence's security detail, *sotto voce*, that it's a Code Red. He doesn't get to add the reassurance 'there's nothing to worry about' because that's when, to coin a phrase, the balloon goes up as the special agents put their training to good use and scramble into action. Within seconds the fire alarm is blaring and an immediate enforced evacuation of the theatre is underway. Why the urgency? It turns out that while 'Code Red' in the Go Gently handbook signifies an offsite 'walker', in the protection squad's lexicon it means an assassination attempt is being made on the minister. (Now there's one for the debrief – if only they'd liaised more closely.)

It's fair to say, from their vantage point, Callan and Lawrence have a grandstand view of what unfolds next, albeit, without the benefit of sound (better described in that case as a dumbshow). Lawrence looks first to his wife, Isabella, for any clues. He's disturbed to see her running towards his pod with a look of sheer horror etched on her face, but just as she's about to reach him a burly dark-suited colossus intercepts and throws her to the floor with a flying rugby tackle. *What the...???* She disappears, and he can't see what's happening beneath the pod, but then the prop-forward reappears in his line of vision with Isabella draped over his shoulder. (Curiously, the image puts him in mind of The Rape of the Sabine Women by Giambologna in the Piazza della Signoria in Florence, an exquisite, twisting sculpture carved from a single piece of marble. How he and Isabella had admired it on their recent trip there.) Lawrence shouts at the gorilla to stop, but to no avail, as no one can hear him through the cockpit hatch. Then Lawrence recognises the man who is bearing his wife away – it's one of his own security detail. His heart freezes as he realises they must be under attack. But wait a minute, there are strict protocols laid down for this sort of thing: any sign of trouble, the minister is to be protected at all costs and removed from harm's way before anybody else. So what are they doing extracting Isabella first? Where's *his* human shield? He'll be having bloody words about this as soon as they get him out of here. (Could someone add that to the debrief agenda too?) Meanwhile, Isabella is borne aloft through a scrum of frantic figures and out of his eyeline. *Bollocks to this,* he thinks, and starts to push at the Perspex bubble above his head. It doesn't budge. *FFS!* He starts to pound at the canopy but soon stops after grazing his knuckles. This is so undignified, so demeaning, heads are going to roll (especially the one belonging to that jumped-up, moonshine-distilling mountebank who put him in here in the first place). He twists to his right – they can only see the side of each other's faces from their semi-supine positions – to check if Callan is out of his pod

246

SHAKING HANDS WITH ELVIS

yet. No, he's trying to communicate through the impenetrable screen with one of the techs.

Callan is pointing at his ear as he mouths, *I can't hear.* The red-clad assistant nods and slowly articulates two syllables back to him. *Co-ed.* Callan doesn't understand. What's co-education got to do with what's going on? He shakes his head. *What?* Back comes tech man, this time with a goldfish impression: *Code Red.* Oh, shit. The whole point of Code Red is that nobody panics, but it's mayhem out there. Could it be that Pestel is under attack somehow? Let's face it, it wouldn't be that big a surprise – nobody likes the oily little shit. And everybody admires and looks up to Callan, so it can't be him. As he takes in the frenzied scene in front of him, people scrambling, tumbling, being hurled aside like marionettes, his heart plummets. Everything is falling apart in front of him. Surely, the crowning glory of Callan's career (strike that, his whole life) isn't to be ruined by some low-grade dissident incapable of spelling antiestablishmentarianism even if they tried? The bastards. He gestures to the assistant to raise the canopy and let him out. He needs to take control, to restore calm. Maybe, after that, even carry on as if nothing has happened. Red fiddles with the catch for a few seconds and then shakes his head forlornly as if he's been asked to untangle the Gordian Knot while wearing boxing gloves. He shapes his lips: *It's stuck.* Callan punches the Perspex in frustration. *Stuck? No, it's not, you fucking jackass.* The Tennessee trouble-shooter doesn't do shoddy equipment, *no siree.* The fastenings are quick-release and failproof. *Try again,* he mouths, but to no avail, because his would-be rescuer has disappeared into the maelstrom. Callan's cry of *Fuck!* reverberates around the confined interior – it's the only thing he can hear clearly. He rotates his upper body to his left to check if Pestel is out yet. No, and he's giving Callan daggers. It's an absolute certainty that, if looks could kill, Lawrence would be despatching people far more efficiently than the Peregrine Pod ever could.

Woody drives like a madman for a good two miles before yielding to the shouts and loud bangs emanating from the back of the van. Finally, he pulls in and apprehensively opens the rear doors to be met with a scene of biblical proportions. Geraldine cradles Jeffrey's head in her lap, Pieta-style, while a vengeful Dawn looks as if she is about to rain fire and brimstone down on some miscreant's head. Or, to be more specific, on the driver's head.

'We could have all been killed,' she screams. 'What the hell were you doing?'

'It all went wrong,' says Woody sheepishly. 'It wasn't my fault. I…'

Fortunately for him, he doesn't get much further. 'We haven't time for that now,' Geraldine thunders. 'Jeffrey is injured. We have to take him to hospital.'

They look to their incapacitated colleague more in alarm than concern. 'We can't take him to a hospital, Geraldine,' says Dawn. 'We're trying to escape, remember.' Woody can only agree.

'He's out cold. He could have had a heart attack.' Geraldine addresses this comment directly at the disgraced driver.

'He might just be stunned,' says Dawn hopefully. 'Sit him up. Give him some air.'

They get him into an upright position, and almost at once his eyes begin to flicker and he lets out a lengthy moan.

'What did he say?' Dawn asks.

Geraldine leans in closer to listen. 'It's hard to make out,' she says. She presses her ear closer to his mouth, before shooting up ramrod straight. 'I don't bloody believe it,' she laments. 'He's calling for Rosemary. He's gone again.'

'So, my driving wasn't to blame,' Woody protests, with an equal measure of relief and indignation in his voice. They ignore him.

Geraldine takes charge. She directs Woody to retrieve the scattered electrolyte bottles, and lays out Plan B. 'Jeffrey is going to be fine, apart from his bruises. We can't go back because, if we do, we'll be dead before teatime, and we can now assume they'll be out looking for us.' It's a blunt summary of their present plight and difficult to contradict. 'We need to dump this van and get back to Yorkshire some other way.'

'Kimberley,' exclaims Dawn. 'Kimberley can fetch us. She'll be setting off around now – we can hide the van, call her, and tell her where to pick us up.' She beams in triumph. A simple plan is always the best plan, and as nobody comes up with anything better it's nodded through.

'Jeffrey needs to sit up front while he recovers,' says Geraldine firmly. 'In fact, we all do because I'm black and blue and I'm not going through that again.'

'Won't that draw attention to us?' says Woody. 'We'll be seen.'

His concern is met with a loud snigger from Dawn. 'Have you seen the state of the bloody van, Woody? You think nobody will notice the damage first? I'm amazed it's still driveable.' Sure enough, the van is looking in a sorry state with the front bumper, windscreen wipers and a wing mirror hanging off, and a massive indent across the bonnet. 'So, let's get in, and get

SHAKING HANDS WITH ELVIS

moving. Somewhere offroad, and close by, where we can keep out of sight. Anybody any ideas?'

Nobody is local, of course, but it's Woody who comes up with a winning suggestion. 'I know,' he says. 'A garden centre. They'll never find us in one of those. We'll blend right in, there will be plenty of car parking, and there's sure to be a phone to call Kimberley.' It's a genius idea and they enthusiastically give it the thumbs-up.

'But will there be one nearby?' asks Dawn. 'We can't keep driving around willy-nilly.'

Woody breaks into a broad smile. 'We just passed one, a mile back. It's got an over-sixties 2-4-1 breakfast offer on. We can spend all day in the restaurant if we need to – nobody will say a word.'

There's little time to lose. Dawn squeezes into the cabin alongside Woody, with Geraldine to her left and Jeffrey wedged up against the passenger window, still being drip-fed despite the cramped conditions.

Woody turns the ignition key. 'Drive carefully,' coaxes Dawn, patting his knee. He nods and, without looking, pulls away sharply from the kerb to perform a U-turn in the narrow road. He takes the van into the hedgerow opposite, before crunching the gears to reverse into the shrubs behind him on the other side of the road. Finally, he straightens and sets off, a huge clump of foliage now lodged underneath the rear bumper. Dawn rolls her eyes. 'A mile, you reckon? At least we've got some camouflage now.'

Simon and Vicki are making their final visit to Charon House, and the mood in the car is sombre. Vicki is driving as her husband is too emotionally overwrought to take the wheel, woebegone at the enormity of his decision (or should that be his father's decision?) and the approaching final hours.

In a twist on the question the father asks the bride on the way to church, Vicki has been finding various ways of putting the same petition to Simon: *Are you sure you want to go through with it?*

'It's not too late,' she urges. 'I know you think it's what he wants but there are other options.'

They've been through this a thousand times, but still Simon responds with: 'Like what?'

'We could put him in a home, couldn't we? Where they know how to look after dementia patients. Proper, professional, trained care.'

'He'd hate the thought of that.'

'Yes,' Vicki counters, 'but then he wouldn't know, would he, so where's the harm?'

Simon lapses into silence – how many more times must he have this discussion?

Vicki isn't giving up though. 'All we have to do is go in there, tell them we've changed our minds, get your dad discharged, and we can be back in Peterborough for teatime. Put him in a home next week. See, it really is that simple.'

'And visit every week for an hour, to fulfil our duty and salve our consciences?' is his sarcastic retort. She shakes her head wearily and drives on.

Simon stares out of the window. Could he? Should he? If he did place Jeffrey in a home, was it merely kicking the can down the road? (Not that he's calling his dad a tinplate container, you understand.) Other people put their ageing parents in homes, after all. But surely, a son was bound to honour his father's wishes, solemn undertakings had to be met. It was Jeffrey himself who had taught him that. Here's a question though: was 'Dad' really Dad these days, as that man had disappeared into the ether and been replaced by a phantom. In carrying out 'real' Dad's express instruction, was he in fact condemning an altogether different person, without the right of reply, to oblivion? He didn't know much about metaphysics or linguistics, but that sounded to him like a double negative. Except that would make it right. Lost in thought, he bemoans yet again how this dreadful burden, this decision over life and death, has befallen him. Why him?

He's shaken from his reverie as Vicki suddenly beeps her horn. Looking up in alarm he sees a white van, on their side of the road, heading straight towards them. He braces as Vicki resists the impulse to brake and instead swerves adroitly to the oncoming lane to avoid a collision. 'Wanker' she screams, as she swings the car back to the correct side of the road, grateful for the advanced motoring course she and her friends had booked as 'a different day out' last year (which, incidentally, her husband had called a waste of money at the time).

Simon is ashen, visibly shaken, but it's not the near miss that's draining the blood from his face. 'Dad,' he exclaims. 'It was Dad in that van.'

Vicki is about to tell him not to be so ridiculous when he shrieks, 'Get after them. Quick. Go, go, go.'

Vicki has rarely seen him so animated. Humouring him, she jams on the brakes before executing a perfect two-point turn. 'You can't have seen your father,' she yells over the roar of the engine as she accelerates to seventy miles per hour. 'It's impossible.' Despite the ludicrous implausibility of the situation, Vicki is finding the excuse to thrash the car in a hot

SHAKING HANDS WITH ELVIS

pursuit a real buzz. She's channelling her inner-Thelma (or was it Louise that did the driving?)

'It was him,' Simon cries. 'No doubt about it. He was less than a foot away as we passed.'

Taking the next bend in the road, they spot the rear of the van up ahead, a tell-tale garland of greenery leaving no doubt. 'There,' he wails. 'Don't let them get away. Stop them.'

Vicki smiles and presses the accelerator through the floor.

Up ahead, yielding to protestations from his shell-shocked companions, Woody has slowed so they don't miss the garden centre. He's just about to indicate a left turn when he spots, in his one remaining wing mirror, a black Range Rover closing rapidly on them, its lights flashing urgently as if relaying a message in morse code: Y-O-U-R-E-N-I-C-K-E-D. Spooked, he has but little choice. He pushes the pedal to the metal. All thoughts of 2-4-1 breakfasts are forgotten as A Day in The Leaf nursery flashes by.

Chapter Thirty-One

The theatre empties rapidly in the ensuing panic. Lawrence is mystified as to why his security detail has neglected him thus far, not realising the officer in command has deemed the pod the safest place for him to remain until the situation is brought under control. The evacuation has been underway for less than a minute, although each second feels like a parliamentary session to the entombed minister whose stress levels are now bouncing into the red. The more he wriggles and bangs against the sides of the capsule, the more breathless he becomes. His perspiration, now pumping from every pore, is causing the cockpit canopy to mist up, adding further to his anguish. Glancing down, he espies the blank tablet screen – he recalls seeing it lit up when Callan first demonstrated the Peregrine to him. He'd asked why there needed to be a control panel inside the pod and it had been explained to him it was a hangover from the pre-assisted dying days when it was necessary for patients to self-administer the means of despatch to avoid any helpers being prosecuted. Callan claimed it as a positive design feature for the pod as they would charge extra for a DIY demise. Lawrence had been impressed at the effrontery of the salesmanship and had laughed at the time. Now it might be able to get him out of here if only he could activate the screen. There must be a self-release button somewhere – the pod would never pass health and safety if there wasn't one. He fumbles around the perimeter of the tablet feeling for a switch or a button and lets out an almighty sigh of relief as the display leaps into life. Within a flash – Go Gently only uses the best microprocessors – he's staring at an array of icons.

In the pod alongside, Callan is horrified when he sees Lawrence's face suddenly illuminated by his screen. The pods were to be inert for the purposes of the photocall – God knows what will happen if he starts messing around with the computer. He shakes his head violently in Lawrence's direction, but the minister's attention is now firmly fixed on the display. 'Turn it off,' Callan shouts, to no avail. Thankfully, the bloody thing isn't armed. 'Don't touch anything,' is his next entreaty, although that message also fails to land. Despite the commotion still unfolding in the theatre, the captain of industry's full focus is now firmly fixed on the occupant of the pod opposite.

Lawrence is confused by the multitude of symbols confronting him. He thought these things were supposed to be intuitive – goodness knows how a client would cope. In the case of a DIY customer, there would be one pictogram only – the one that mattered – to select from on the screen. Here, because it's not been set up for use, every icon loaded in the applications folder is visible. In the rising heat and hysteria of his situation, Lawrence reverts to every man's solution when faced with a multiple choice – he starts to punch away indiscriminately at the icons in the expectation it will somehow work. The first thing that happens is the silence of the pod is abruptly filled with music. He recognises it immediately – the swelling melody of "Nimrod" from *Enigma Variations* by Elgar. It's poignant, plaintive and majestic in its sweep, and was one of the songs his

SPAD had suggested for his *Desert Island Discs* selection when they were trying to get him on the programme. *Well*, he thought, *bugger that*, now it would remind him of being stuck in this tin can. He jabs randomly at the icons again, and is deafened as the pastoral perfection of "Nimrod" gives way to a succession of rasping electric guitar power chords. He doesn't recognise the classic rock anthem "Highway to Hell" and has little time to wonder at the type of person who'd kick the bucket to such a cacophony, so he hits the screen again. This time the cockpit canopy, which he'd previously been able to see out of, transforms into a personal video screen and he has the sensation of travelling through an endless corridor of flashing colours, closing, closing, closing on who knows what. The accompanying rhythmic, pulsing soundtrack provides a strangely hypnotic and reassuring effect, as if the destination ahead holds no fear. (Not being a movie buff, Lawrence fails to recognise Go Gently's 'tribute' to the Stargate sequence in *2001: A Space Odyssey*. Kubrick's estate had given them a firm 'no' over using the original, so Callan had one of the lads in the studio knock up 'something close' on the Apple Mac.) Lawrence tries again, almost bashing the screen off its mounting. Now the pulsing colours give way to a time-lapse film of a rose bursting into bud, then blooming majestically before slowly withering in decay, the beautiful Renaissance choral *Spem in Alium nunquam habui* by Thomas Tallis providing a mournful musical accompaniment.

Callan is making further desperate efforts to extricate himself from his pod, not least to stop the bungling minister setting back the Peregrine programme and the fortunes of Go Gently for eternity, but he, too, remains firmly sealed in place. He can feel it all slipping away – his dream project, his business, his wealth, his reputation – all because he got into bed with this dickhead of a government minister. Why didn't he just go it alone? He scrabbles at the smooth, unyielding interior of the pod and prays for deliverance. Where is everyone? Why have they abandoned him? Where's Margaret and why hasn't she instructed someone to get him out? Also, is it his imagination, or is it getting stuffy in here?

Although Lawrence is unfamiliar with combinatorial mathematics and a stranger to the theory of discrete probability, his frenzied sequence of punching and stabbing suddenly yields gold as the screen unexpectedly clears of all its icons and starts to re-load. It's as if he's bought a random lottery ticket and the first five balls have fallen in his favour. And here come the lucky stars as a single pictogram pops up in the centre of the display. It's of a large padlock with a single word written across it: *Release*. Does Lawrence stop to consider the meaning of these seven letters? To wonder, even, if it's a verb – to free, to unlock, to liberate – or a noun – a permission, a grant, a surrender? No. It's exactly what's he looking for – a means of getting out of here. He stabs furiously at the icon and waits for some form of click, for the cockpit to open. Nothing. The padlock disappears to be replaced by two boxes, a green one reading 'Proceed', and a red one labelled 'Abort'. Beneath, a message: *This is your last opportunity to change your mind*. Bloody stupid question, thinks the secretary of state for wellbeing as he punches the green button. Nothing happens immediately, leading Lawrence to curse the pod's inventor over poor functionality and design – why the man's nothing short of a charlatan. Then he hears it, a faint hiss, like a radiator being bled or the air slowly seeping from a balloon. Simultaneously, a new music track fills the small space, a melody he instantly recognises. Frank Sinatra. He likes this one. No wonder, as Lawrence has always been certain of any case he's stating, a man proud of doing it his way.

It's strange, because barely a few seconds ago he was lying in here trembling with anger and fear, in a cold sweat over how to extricate himself from this infernal machine, and now he doesn't have a care in the world. Why does he find it all so deliriously distracting? It must be Big Frank with his words of wisdom. A wave of elation washes over him and he pictures his dear darling Isabella, his rock. Was there ever a happier union? What a perfect pair they make. With her, he will achieve his life's dream: the black door, with the cast iron lion's head knocker and its brass letter plate inscribed 'First Lord of the Treasury', announcing he'd arrived at Number Ten. There was nothing he couldn't achieve if he set his mind to it. Lawrence Pestel, Prime Minister. He'd show them, he'd show them all. It feels good, so good, he doesn't want this feeling to subside. It's as if he's already walking through that doorway, from one world to another, on a cloud of joy. Maybe, if he just rests his eyes for a short while, it will help him to preserve this state of euphoria a little longer, prolong the best dream he's ever had. No regrets.

Callan, like a Peeping Tom spying through a hole in the nudist colony fence, has witnessed this unscheduled sideshow with mounting horror as he realises what's unfolding. The silly bastard has only gone and topped himself. How on earth is that possible? Even allowing for the unlikely odds of Lawrence unwittingly arming the deadly discharge, the pods contain dummy cylinders, not actual liquid nitrogen. Yet he'd witnessed (unofficially, of course) death by hypoxiation before and didn't need telling twice what he'd just seen. But how? His heart sinks. It doesn't really matter how, because he is ruined. Utterly and totally ruined. There would be no coming back from this, not with a dead secretary of state to explain away. Everything was resting on the success of the Peregrine – he'd overreached and he had fallen. He could hardly argue Lawrence had signed up to put his own bill to the test – Callan would be sued, he'd be hounded out of the country, he'd be bankrupt. Worse, he might even go to jail for corporate manslaughter. Lady Margaret would divorce him on the spot and his life wouldn't be worth a fig. But still, the mystery remains. It's inexplicable. Might it really have been an assassination attempt, more sophisticated and ingenious than a gun or a car bomb? But how did whoever set Lawrence's death trap switch the dummy canister, tamper with the settings, and hack the panel to trigger the gas release from the outside?

The theatre is empty now – they've all run away. And he's stuck, and for how long? How is he going to explain everything? He's not, that's how. He'd be better off staying in this cocoon, because once he is stripped of this protection that's when the real shit will begin. Another thought strikes him. How did the assassins know which pod Pestel would be in? He could just as easily have been in the one Callan now occupied. Unless, of course, they've armed both? If that's the case, he could be next. How are they controlling all of this? He looks up at the red light of the security camera in the far corner. Of course. They've hacked into that as well. They were watching him now. *Well, go on then, you bastards.* He has nothing left worth living for now. *Do your worst. Blast me into eternity. I don't care.* But nothing happens.

Adil swims against the tide of the dispersing throng before slipping inside the theatre in the hope of discovering what's happening. It takes him a few seconds to adjust to the scene of devastation that greets him – an empty room, overturned chairs, smashed cups and papers strewn across the floor. The fire alarm is deafening and it's hard to collect one's thoughts. His eye is automatically drawn to the flashing red light of the security camera in the corner – has it been fixed yet? He's just about to turn and exit when he sees that the two pods at the front contain figures, like recumbent effigies on a catafalque. He is momentarily torn – he should scarper, but there's something not quite right here. Why has everybody evacuated? Why leave these two behind inside the pods? Do these people need help?

Warily, he approaches the front of the theatre, and peers first inside Lawrence's Peregrine. Adil has seen plenty of dead people in his time and doesn't need telling twice that the occupant won't be attending the post-launch buffet. What a strange smile the poor fellow is wearing, as if he died happy (is that even possible?). Despite the blissful visage, Adil recognises that the stricken figure inside the pod is the secretary of state for wellbeing, clearly not living up to his brief today. But what has happened here? It's impossible the pod could have been armed for a photocall. It's with mounting dread and realisation he recalls his visit the previous night and replacing the canisters Jeffrey and Woody had removed from the pods. Trembling, he flicks the lever beneath the fuselage to reveal a black gas canister, with a yellow warning triangle stencilled across its surface: *Danger. Risk of asphyxiation.* Oh shit. He looks towards the two steel cages they encountered last night: in one corner, a pile of black cylinders like the one inside the Peregrine; in the other, a stack of dark blue canisters with the word 'Dummy' clearly visible on the side. Simple to distinguish in the bright overhead light, but not so easy when it's murky and you're under pressure. He's only gone and killed a high-ranking government official.

It's with considerable trepidation that he inspects the second pod. Has he killed this fellow too? He immediately recognises his boss, Doctor Callan Clay, and is mightily relieved to see he's moving still. Adil doesn't want two deaths on his record of employment so immediately makes to unlock the cockpit before there's a similar gas release to the one that saw off the luckless Lawrence. It's stuck. Adil can't afford to risk the gas going off and making the American the second goner of the day. He needs something heavy to crack the cockpit open with, and runs to snatch a fire extinguisher off the wall.

Inside the pod, Callan is aware of the arrival of the cavalry – or of one of his olive tunic-clad menials at least. Is this his moment of salvation? He weighs up his situation: once he's out of this pod, only hell awaits. He's washed-up, finished, hoist by his own petard. He's nothing to live for and it's clear the assassins aren't going to oblige. *Hoist by his own petard.* Yes. That's it. He calmly reaches for the button on the edge of his screen and watches the display spark into life. It will be painless and quick (although in his case it has cost him everything). He doesn't have time for music or movies – never mind that – and with a few deft swipes of his finger finds the self-same padlock that did for Pestel a few short minutes ago.

As the mogul is attending to his computer settings, Adil rushes back to the pod with a heavy extinguisher in his hand, gesturing to Callan to cover his face while he breaks the canopy open. To Adil's great surprise, the entrepreneur slowly shakes his head and signals a clear 'no' to his would-be rescuer. Adil can only stare in disbelief as Doctor Clay smiles, shrugs his shoulders, and taps twice at the centre of his screen. He knows exactly what Callan is doing, if not why, and must act quickly if he is to save him. He raises the extinguisher high above his head but leaves it hovering there. What if he opens the canister compartment and simply removes the noxious nitrogen instead? That would do it. Then a third thought forms as he takes in the sight of his employer. He looks at peace with himself; content with his decision. This, after all, is the man who has shepherded so many to their deaths, not all of them willing or even party to the decision. This is the businessman who would, all in a day's work, have seen off Geraldine, Dawn, Jeffrey and Woody without a second thought, other than how much he'd be paid for services rendered. This is, no less, the ghoulish creator of the Peregrine Pod, the architect of a 'pile it high, sell it cheap' sales pitch to popularise premature passing, the grim reaper himself. Adil lowers the extinguisher and waits.

Inside the pod, Callan needs no amplified music as he drifts. He can hear, like he did that day so long ago on the hog farm, the words of Pastor Prentis Pfeiffer ringing in his ears as he goes to meet his maker: *Revelation 21.4: He will wipe every tear from their eyes. There will be no more death or mourning or crying or pain, for the old order of things has passed away.*

Chapter Thirty-Two

Cries go up inside the van as Woody misses the turn-off to the garden centre. 'They're on to us,' Woody proclaims in a high-pitched voice. Nobody can see behind even if they wanted to, and have to take the driver's word for it.

'Police?' Dawn gasps.

'Black Rover. Bearing down on us, flashing its lights. Go Gently security?' Woody ventures.

A council estate appears on the right. Without warning, he throws a sharp right, followed by a quick left, another right and two more for good luck. The resulting G-Force compresses his passengers' features into all manner of contortions, like contestants in a gurning competition.

'Don't let it catch us,' Geraldine implores as gravity reasserts itself. She makes the sign of the cross and offers her eyes up to heaven: 'Please God.'

Woody's pallor matches the paintwork of the van as he steers into a cul-de-sac. He's just about to engage reverse gear when Dawn stops him. 'Did they see you turn into the estate?'

Woody thinks about this for a second. 'No,' he finally decides. That's why I took it, because there was a bend in the road.'

'In that case, I say we sit tight for a while,' she proposes. 'Out of sight. Off the main road. Get Kimberley to pick us up from here.'

'But we don't have a phone,' reasons Geraldine.

'That's the least of our problems if we haven't shaken them off,' says Dawn. 'We're sure to be nabbed if we drive back to the main road. But if we don't see anybody in the next five minutes, we know we've lost them.'

Jeffrey, fully restored after #J8, pipes up with a further idea. 'Unless we ditch this ride and knock off another set of wheels?' They're so surprised at Jeffrey's sudden appropriation of gangster lingo, nobody addresses the actual suggestion.

Silence descends, as if any further conversation at this stage will undo them. *Keep calm and say nowt.* Woody's eyes remain fixed on the one remaining wing mirror but the estate is as quiet as a grave and there's not a single vehicle in sight, never mind a black Rover. Geraldine, determined to avoid Jeffrey blanking out again at this delicate stage of their operation, slips #J9 into his hand. The minutes pass and they begin to visibly relax, praying they have slipped the net. And they're not wrong, either, because Vicki and Simon are by now in Longendale, miles down the road.

That's when they hear it. The chimes. A tinny, tinkly tattoo of notes, conjuring up childhood, innocence and summer days. *Ding dong,* as an ice cream van enters the cul-de-sac, turns around at the bottom, and pulls up on the pavement diagonally opposite.

Jeffrey is beside himself with excitement. 'Do you hear that?' he gushes to Geraldine, winding the window down. 'Listen.'

Dawn and Woody exchange baffled glances at Jeffrey's priorities in their present plight, while Geraldine instead concentrates on the melody emanating from the pink and white gelateria on wheels. 'Elvis,' she triumphantly proclaims. 'It's Elvis.'

Jeffrey beams as if Geraldine has just laid an egg.

Dawn can't help being drawn into their exchange. 'That's not Elvis – it's from an old ad. Oh, what was it called?' It comes to her and she starts to sing: "Just one cornetto, give it to me, delicious ice cream, of Italy".'

'Now, that's where you're wrong,' says Jeffrey. 'They stole that tune from an old Neapolitan song, "O Sole Mio".'

'Yes,' Geraldine chips in, 'When Elvis Presley heard the original song, he asked for new English lyrics to be written, so he could sing it.'

'"It's Now or Never",' affirms Jeffrey, as if expecting a prize. 'I mean, that's the name of the Elvis version.'

'Number one for eight weeks, and his biggest-selling single ever,' Geraldine adds for the benefit of the uninitiated. 'Not many people know that.'

The ice cream van reloads and refires its twenty-five second, eight-bar refrain. 'I could just eat a 99,' Jeffrey giggles.

'Is he open?' asks Geraldine. 'It's a bit early, isn't it?'

Dawn, despite her reluctance to encourage the current direction of discourse, is a mine of information. 'They start from sparrowsfart around here. Stop me and buy one.'

Woody is becoming exasperated at all this lazy sundae talk – they need to get a move on. 'Can we concentrate on how we're going to get out of here?' he pleads.

Jeffrey, fortified with two bottles of Geraldine's homemade electrolyte, decides it's time he took control again. 'Good point, Woody. Now listen. I have a plan.'

Five minutes later, Dawn crosses the road to the serving hatch side of the ice cream van to make the first purchase of the day. She taps on the window, which is opened by a dozy-looking youth listening to music on his headphones. He grudgingly removes them to take her order: 'Two small cones, please. Vanilla. Hundreds and thousands, no juice.'

'Juice? What's juice?'

Dawn points at the syrup pourer on the counter. 'That. But as I don't want any, it doesn't make much difference, does it?' She looks down casually and feigns surprise. Nodding towards the rear of the van: 'You've parked on top of a bottle there. You're going to end up with a flat tyre.' The youth groans and hangs his head out of the hatch to inspect. 'You're not going to move it from there, are you?' says Dawn sarcastically. A shake of the head later he clambers out of the passenger door to deal with it, oblivious to Dawn's three companions who have outflanked him to reach the front of the vehicle. As soon as he disappears around the back, they make their move. In the time it takes to dispense a Mr Whippy they are all aboard, including Dawn, who Woody pulls in via the hatch. Within seconds they are heading out of the cul-de-sac, leaving the vendor defrosting in their wake, peals of laughter ringing out at their own derring-do.

'Told you the keys would be in,' Jeffrey crows as he finds third gear. 'To keep the fridge working.'

Now, perhaps a little late in proceedings, the passengers contemplate the potential shortcomings of Jeffrey's bold stratagem. Is it wise for him to be driving? How quickly will the theft of the ice cream van be reported? Isn't a pink and white ice cream van (with a sign reading 'I'm A Bit Nutty' mounted above the cab window) a tad conspicuous? No matter – they're on their way and heading back to the main road.

Dawn and Woody are rooting around in the back. 'Look,' she says, holding up the day's cash float. 'We can call Kimberley when we find a phone box.'

As they reach the junction, Jeffrey hesitates. Right or left?

'Head to the garden centre again,' Geraldine decides. 'It's not far, they won't think we've doubled back and there's bound to be a phone box there. Plus, we can mingle until Kimberley arrives.' It makes sense, so left it is.

'Shall I put the chime back on?' asks Jeffrey hopefully, messing around with various knobs and levers on the dashboard. 'For authenticity?'

'Just keep your eyes on the road,' Geraldine chides. 'Don't miss the turning.'

'Who wants a choc ice?' comes the call from the back. Dawn has discovered the freezer compartment. Three hands shoot up.

'I'll unwrap yours,' the safety-conscious Geraldine informs the driver.

They're nearly there. Jeffrey is just about to turn right into A Day in The Leaf when, to their dismay, they spot a police car on the verge of pulling out. Inside are two well-fed coppers (courtesy of the garden centre's belly buster breakfast: 'half-price to our friends in the force') listening to an urgent all points alert regarding a stolen ice cream van. Jeffrey doesn't flinch and drives straight on, leaving the police to their double take.

'Shit, shit, shit, shit,' wails a hyperventilating Woody, once again anticipating the kiss of cold steel on his wrists. As the van picks up pace, he and Dawn shuffle to their knees behind Jeffrey and Geraldine's seats for an urgent powwow.

'We're buggered,' Woody laments.

'Nonsense,' Jeffrey snaps as he selects top gear. 'We're not giving up now.'

'Exactly,' says a defiant Geraldine. 'If we get caught, we're as good as dead.'

Dawn nods in agreement. 'I'm with Geraldine. Shake them off.'

They're out in open country at this point. Woody cranes his neck to check the road behind. 'I can't see them,' he shouts. 'Cut off before they catch up?' Needing no further invitation, Jeffrey slams on the brakes and almost topples the flimsy vehicle as he takes a ninety-degree turn down a narrow, unmade lane. He adds the warning to 'hold on' only after he has completed the manoeuvre. Within seconds they are out of sight of the road. Geraldine squeezes the driver's arm. 'Keep going,' she enjoins. 'As far as you can go.'

Chapter Thirty-Three

The sun breaks through the overhanging canopy of trees to cast a dappled light on the gang of four's progress. It's been some minutes since they left the main road, and they dare to believe they've given the police the slip. A sense of giddy relief breaks out all round as the ice cream van dips and bumps across the fields; it doesn't feel premature, it feels like fate is smiling down on them.

'What now?' Woody asks.

'Home,' Dawn replies. 'But I've a feeling we're not in Kansas anymore.'

Her comment doesn't even make sense, but they all laugh heartily for the sheer release of it.

Not wanting to miss out on the end of term high jinks, Jeffrey is inspired to break into a spontaneous song of exultation:

> *Ma n'atu sole*
> *Cchiu' bello, oi ne'*
> *'O sole mio*
> *Sta 'nfronte a te*
> *'O sole, 'o sole mio*

Sta 'nfronte a te
Sta 'nfronte a te

It's an expertly delivered rendition and Geraldine melts in admiration at his rich baritone. 'You dark horse, Jeffrey. And in Italian too.'

Jeffrey is modesty itself in reply. 'Yes, well, I've not got a bad set of pipes.'

'What do the words mean?' Dawn wants to know, moved by the stirring, impromptu performance.

Jeffrey is in his element. As the lane narrows to a dirt track and the van bounces over exposed roots and stones, he proudly instructs his pupils. 'The first verse says what a beautiful thing a sunny day is, but then we get: "But another sun, even more beauteous, oh my sweetheart, my own sun, shines from your face! This sun, my own sun, shines from your face; it shines from your face!"'

'That's beautiful,' Dawn sighs, wiping a tear from her cheek. As the adrenalin of the past hour subsides, she feels a sharp and familiar wave of pain reminding her she's not really free, and never will be, from her cancer's merciless grip.

Woody relaxes enough to join in. 'Elvis should have stuck with those words for his version.'

Nobody disagrees; they simply smile their assent.

As the van trundles on, they each settle into a deep reverie, united in the warm glow of comradeship and at peace with the world. At peace with themselves.

Only for that peace to be shattered, seconds later, as the van shudders to an abrupt halt. On a level crossing. Directly on top of the Leeds to Manchester railway line.

Does the theft of an ice cream van really call for the entire constabulary of a county to turn out? Maybe not, especially as the hijackers don't appear to have any direct link with the serious security breaches that have just been reported at Charon House. Still, best not take any chances, and important to look busy, which is why the roads around Stalybridge are now abuzz with blue flashing lights.

Simon and Vicki, having lost their quarry earlier, return to Charon House just as the blue and white POLICE LINE DO NOT CROSS tape is being stretched across the entrance. Amid the confusion they learn, from a distressed fellow relative already on the scene, that some form of breakout has occurred. Her mother is missing too. Matters become murkier still when they overhear the police radios crackling with the news that the fugitives have now transferred to an ice cream van. Without missing a beat, Simon and Vicki head for the Range Rover to renew their pursuit; Kimberley, uninvited, clambers into the back seat before they can turn the car around.

'Do you think they've been kidnapped?' Simon ventures as they speed off in the opposite direction to before.

'By who, though?' counters Vicki. 'And why?'

'Well, it's not like they've come up with this themselves, is it?' he reasons.

Kimberley takes in their conversation in silence. Could her mother possibly have something to do with this? A wry smile crosses her lips.

'How bloody hard can it be to find an ice cream van?' Simon grumbles. 'I mean, they only go at five miles an hour.'

Vicki immediately slows down. 'Exactly. That's it. They're not on the road – they must have turned off.'

'But where though?' he asks.

'Farm tracks. A quarry road, a disused barn or something like that. It makes sense,' she says. 'Keep your eyes peeled.'

Half a mile down the road, she triumphantly exclaims, 'Something like that!' and pulls the car over in front of a sign reading 'Strictly No Trespassing'.

Simon protests. 'We can't go down there, Vicki. We don't know where it goes. And you'll be breaking the law.'

'Do you have any better ideas?' she counters, and rolls the car slowly forward to flatten the flimsy chicken wire barrier blocking their way.

Three minutes later, they hit a dead end. Vicki screams in frustration and prepares to do a twenty-point turn as Simon bites back on his 'I told you so' homily. Suddenly, through the trees, they see two individuals wearing high-viz bibs running towards them, arms gesticulating wildly. Wardens, workers, or walkers? Kimberley sits up – it's the two mountain bikers who nearly hit her car at Charon House.

'Come quickly. Help,' they shout. There's no time for explanations as they turn on their heels and charge back in the direction they've just appeared from. Vicki, Simon and Kimberley scramble out of the car and race after them. It's only after they clear the undergrowth and reach a narrow bridge spanning a sunken railway line they spot an ice cream van, bearing a sign reading 'I'm a Bit Nutty', lodged firmly on the track below. No sooner do they register the sight than they hear a distant low frequency rumbling sound, not unlike a waterfall in full flow: a distant train, coming down the line.

Try as he might, Jeffrey cannot get the van to move. 'Bugger won't shift,' he grumbles as the ignition wails like an impaled vampire.

Geraldine spots the empty fuel gauge and grimaces. 'We need to get out, it's not safe,' she urges her companions. 'We're sitting ducks here.'

That's when they hear it – the mournful air horn with its two-tone dirge, presaging doom and disaster.

How long is a second? A year? A lifetime? They have no way of knowing how far away the train is or how much time they have before impact – their first reaction is to stare in stupefaction at each other. Geraldine is the first to come to her senses: 'Jesus, Mary and Joseph, come on. Quick.' She reaches for the door handle.

Jeffrey snaps to, and begins to paw blindly at his door as Woody scrambles to slide the serving hatch open at the back.

'No,' comes a faint voice from the back, barely audible amid the mounting panic. It's Dawn, body bent, lips pursed, the blood drained from her face. She slowly shakes her head and repeats the single word: 'No.'

Her three companions are stunned, unable to immediately grasp the significance of this simple negative.

'You'll get us all killed if you don't shift,' cries Geraldine in shock. 'We've got to get out. Now.'

Dawn takes a small step back to the corner of the van and grips the side of the counter for support. 'You go. Please. I'm staying.'

Jeffrey and Woody remain open-mouthed, unable to speak or move given the extremity of this new situation. It's left to Geraldine to plead, 'For the love of God, Dawn, what do you think you're doing?'

With some effort, Dawn draws herself up to her full height to deliver her sombre pronouncement. 'This is where I get off. Here and now,' she rasps.

'You can't be serious. You'll die if you stay here.'

Dawn nods. *Exactly.* 'I'm dead if I leave, too, the cancer will see to that. So, who am I kidding?'

'But we've been through all of this,' Geraldine protests. 'We've just escaped Charon House and certain death. I don't get it.'

Dawn remains stoic. 'Yes, but there we didn't really have a choice, did we? We were lambs to the slaughter. Here, now, I can end it on my own terms. I'm ready.'

Jeffrey, straining to look down the track, joins the fray. 'This is madness, Dawn. Life is too precious to simply throw away, I should know that more than anybody.'

Dawn smiles ruefully. 'I know, Jeffrey. Life *is* precious, I understand that. Precious enough for *me* to choose when and where to part with it, not leave it to *them* or anybody else.'

Geraldine regards her brave, defiant friend in desperation. Only a few days ago, she had been willing to shuffle offstage to the strains of "Are You Lonesome Tonight". She had rejected life, thinking life had rejected her. But this week had taught her she didn't want to give up or let go; she wanted to cherish every single breath still left in her body. In opting for death, she had once again found life.

A further high-low blast of the approaching train rends the air, louder and closer now, like a dog howling in the night.

Jeffrey looks at Geraldine and shakes his head – further remonstration is futile. She nods, touches her fingers to her lips and blows a soft, sorrowful kiss towards Dawn, her beautiful friend. Seconds later, the two front seat passengers heave the doors open and tumble on to the stone ballast below. Geraldine is first to her feet, rushes to help Jeffrey up, and they start to back away from the track as quickly as their tottery old legs will carry them.

Above them on the bridge, the anxious spectators spot the wiry old woman and Jeffrey nose-diving from the van, and shriek at them wildly to *run, run,* scarcely believing they will make it. As the pair slip over the bank edge and dodge certain death, Vicki and Simon cling to each other in relief, grateful for this last-minute reprieve. Kimberley, on the other hand, looks in vain for her mother. Her heart sinks. A single word escapes her throat like a last breath: *Mum.* In a blind panic, she charges wildly from one end of the short bridge to the other, desperately looking for a way down to the track but to no avail. In a flash, all hope is lost – from their vantage point they see the train appear around the bend and realise it's too late. All they can do is watch in horror as the inevitable collision looms.

Down below, Woody hovers at the open serving hatch. *What is she doing? Why?* This is madness, Dawn. I'm not going to let you do this.'

She turns to him and shakes her head. 'Get out while you can, Woody,' she beseeches. 'Just bloody go.'

He registers the resolution and determination in her face and realises she's in no mood to listen. He swings one faltering leg out of the window, never taking his eyes off Dawn's. She gives him a gentle nod, relieved to see him finally move; but he goes no further. He perches on the counter, suspended between her and safety, between oblivion and life itself.

As he teeters on the edge, it strikes him that at the start of the week he had less reason to live than any of them, only to discover, with the help of this remarkable woman, the cruel deception being played on him. He'd cursed his own timidity while admiring Dawn's unflinching fortitude. Now she is making the bravest choice of all. He understands. Death isn't taking her; she is taking death.

The resigned, baleful trumpet call of the onrushing train almost drowns out Dawn's last, urgent entreaty: 'Jump, Woody, jump.'

'No,' he says, and hauls himself back inside the van. Moving swiftly towards her, he enfolds her in a tight, protective embrace.

Acknowledgements

Without the encouragement and enthusiasm of a lovely bunch of people, Shaking Hands with Elvis would never have left the desktop, never mind the building.

New aviator shades all round for my attentive beta readers Nathalie Bagnall, Catherine Barrett, Patrick Carroll, Liam Ferguson, Neil Fox, Brendan Gore, David Hargreaves, John Kelly, David Lomax, Gerry McLaughlin and Sue Townsend (no, not that one). Your invaluable feedback and comments did not go unheeded.

Take a bow, Mark Beaumont of Dinosaur for another stunning cover design (with creative, liaison and illustrations from Ellie Bate, Alice Carruthers, Jess Mosoph, Dan Pitchford and Joe Wellens).

And not forgetting a well-earned nod in the direction of Glenn Jones, Suzanne Darke and Lucy King for the design and build of the www.paulcarrollink.co.uk website.

Especial thanks to my brother, Patrick Carroll, for his editing skills and eagle-eyed assistance at MS and proof stages. We got there in the end.

I'd also like to single out David Baboulene for his laser like insight, clarity and killer notes in helping Shaking Hands with

Elvis aim higher than the local dance hall for an audience. Story theory works!

And lastly, a massive shout out to Edward J Marsh of my publishers, DreamEngine, for taking care of business and unleashing Shaking Hands with Elvis on the world. Or on Stalybridge, at least.

About The Author

Paul Carroll

Writing that puts the 'stab' into establishment

Paul's novels consistently let fly at the latest social trends in an entertaining mix of cutting observation, human drama, dark humour and compassion.

Born and brought up in Leeds, Paul has a degree in English Language and English Literature from the University of Manchester, and worked in PR for many years before becoming a full-time author. Paul lives in Altrincham, Greater Manchester.

A marketing gamekeeper-turned-poacher, Paul is to be found peering behind the curtains of 'the next big thing' when he's not writing.

Previous novels
by Paul Carroll

Don't Ask (2021)

A DNA ancestry test opens up a Pandora's Box of secrets. Two families become reluctantly entwined as inconvenient truths and long suppressed memories resurface.

Trouble Brewing (2017)

A celebrity chef whose star is on the wane is enlisted to help save a small Yorkshire brewery and its 'miracle' ale from closure.

Written Off (2016)

Don't be fooled into thinking that writing a book never killed anyone as four wannabe authors dream of getting their work into print.

A Matter of Life and Death (2012)

In the new zeitgeist of conspicuous public mourning the government's 'bereavement czar' single-handedly puts the 'fun' into funerals.

Website:	www.paulcarrollink.co.uk
Twitter:	@paulcarrollink
Instagram:	@paulcarrollink
Facebook:	@paulcarrollwrites

Published by DreamEngine

Printed in Great Britain
by Amazon

43116970R00165